P9-CLR-545

TARNISHED

kate jarvik birch

Also by Kate Jarvik Birch

PERFECTED
DELIVER ME

TARNISHED

kate jarvik birch

This book is a work of fiction. Names, characters, places, and incidents are the product of the author's imagination or are used fictitiously. Any resemblance to actual events, locales, or persons, living or dead, is coincidental.

Entangled Publishing, LLC
2614 South Timberline Road
Suite 109
Fort Collins, CO 80525

Visit our website at www.entangledpublishing.com.

Edited by Heather Howland
Cover design by Kelley York and Heather Howland
Interior design by Heather Howland

Hardcover ISBN
Paperback ISBN
Ebook ISBN

Manufactured in the United States of America

First Edition December 2015

10 9 8 7 6 5 4 3 2 1

To my Bry.

Chapter One

Remember. This wasn't freedom. This room, with its dingy walls and small, square window, was just another cell. Another cage. Only this time Penn wasn't here to love me. Or to help me get away.

This time, I'd have to escape on my own.

I cracked the door and peered down the hallway toward the desk at the end of the corridor. I hadn't even taken a step yet and already my heart thundered against my chest like it, too, longed to escape. There was still one more item I needed to find before I could leave this place.

There were nine other girls—*pets*—in the refugee center, and I knew they were in the common room watching television the way they did every night. I waited until the main light down the hall switched off, signaling all but one of the workers had checked out for the night. Only the small glow from the lamp that sat on the desk in the reception area lit the room, casting the hall in shadow.

The people who ran this place were nice enough, with their order and their routine. They probably thought it was kind of them to make one of their personnel available at all times, just a few steps down the hallway if we got scared or had a question. But to me, it felt like they'd positioned a prison guard to watch over me.

I closed the door behind me. All I needed to do was stroll past the reception desk the way I'd practiced for the past six days. To the woman sitting there, I would look like all the other girls: small, unsure, lost in this big world. She would only see the things I chose to show her.

Not that there was much left of me to show.

When my world split in two, after the U.S. police dragged Penn in one direction, while the Canadian officers pulled me in another, a part of me felt like I stayed tethered somewhere across the border, waiting for Penn to come walking across that bridge, no handcuffs weighing down his wrists, no bright red gash across his forehead. Just him, whole and well and complete. But with that half of me gone, I couldn't think straight anymore. There was only space for one thing: getting back to Penn.

I crept forward. On my left, the door to the common room was open. The other girls sat side by side on the small couches. The television's blue light flickered across their faces. It had been almost a week, but I still couldn't remember their names. There was no room in my mind for formalities.

"Good evening, Ella," the woman at the reception desk said, setting down her magazine as I approached. "Everyone else is watching the season finale of Pro Chef in the common room. Don't you want to join them?"

"I'm planning on it." I smiled, praying she couldn't see the way my pulse pounded in my neck. "But I was hoping

I could convince you to make us some popcorn again. I've been craving it since you served it the other day."

She grinned and clasped her hands together. All you had to do to make one of the workers happy was to ask about food. It was the easiest way to distract them. They were excited by any sign that we were starting to fit in, but nothing thrilled them more than showing interest in their favorite foods.

"Let me see if we have any." She pushed back her chair and practically bounced toward the small kitchen down the hall.

Her excitement stabbed me with guilt. I'd already taken three things, but it wasn't getting any easier. The staff here had shown me nothing but compassion. In return, I'd stolen from them.

You need to find Penn. You need to make sure he's safe. The mantra I'd repeated to myself for the past week washed away my doubt.

I could still see Penn and the fear in his dark eyes as they pulled him away from me. I always saw the same thing, whether my eyes were opened or closed, whether I was alone or someone was speaking directly to me. I couldn't *not* see his face, the worry, the fear, the sadness. Sometimes I wanted to rub my fists into my eyes to make it go away.

But in this moment, I clung to it.

I held still, waiting for the woman to round the corner before I stepped behind the desk. On the top shelf was a row of books. They weren't the kind Penn's little sister, Ruby, had on her bookshelf, ones filled with stories of cursed kings and clever heroes. Most of these were marked along the spine with a common word. My reading skills were still almost nonexistent, but I remembered the letters that Ruby had taught me. I could still feel the sound of them inside my mouth as if they'd left a residue there, and I knew that if I stared at these words long enough they would start to turn into something, even if that thing was only the leftover taste of hope.

It had taken me a day or so to figure out what it spelled. At night I traced the letters on my palm, trying to sound it out. C-A-N-A-D-A. Canada, my newest cage, but if I was lucky, it might also spell my passage back.

I plucked the smallest book off the shelf and quickly flipped through it. Yes, some of the pages were packed dense with words, but the first few were covered with the thin, colored lines of a map. They weren't the same as the one Penn had looked at when we drove from Connecticut to the border, but they had to be similar.

Down the hall, a door slammed. I quickly slipped the little book into the back pocket of my jeans, pulling my T-shirt down over the top of it, and hurried toward the common room.

It wasn't the television show that I noticed when I walked in—it was the girls. The blue light still flickered across their faces but instead of sitting side by side on the couch with a dazed expression, they now kneeled in front of the television, so close that they could reach their fingers out and touch it. None of them turned to face me when I walked in.

I stared at the screen, trying to figure out what could possibly hold their attention this way. The camera showed a crowd of reporters standing in front of a small stage. Atop it, a podium was filled with microphones.

"What are you—" I began to say, but then the camera panned over to the side of the stage where the crowd was parting and through the sea of people, Congressman John

Kimble stepped forward, looking as confident and impressive as I'd ever seen him.

A cold jolt shot through my body and instinctually my hand flew to my pocket. In it, the collar the congressman had given to me burned like a lit beacon. The delicate gold pendant was the only material remnant left over from my life at his house. A reminder of where I'd been and why I'd left.

I stepped away from the television, but before I turned, something caught my eye and the terrible sickness in my stomach lifted, replaced with the electric rush of adrenaline. Standing just behind the congressman's left shoulder, in a crisp navy suit, was the congressman's son.

Penn.

My heart leaped and I stumbled forward. I needed to be closer to him. It didn't matter that it was only an image on the screen. Reality smudged around the edges, leaving only the two of us. I closed my eyes and I was next to him, lying on the cool, mossy flagstones inside our garden. His fingers traced the shape of my arm as a breeze stirred the top of the pond, sending a ripple across the surface. I rolled against him, feeling the heat of his skin soak into mine…

The television screeched, startling me. I blinked at the screen, at the sight of the sound crew adjusting the microphones. Once they finished, the congressman took his place behind the podium. Penn, stony faced, stayed glued to his side.

"Thank you for coming out," the congressman said, addressing the crowd of reporters in front of him. "This has been a difficult week for our family."

Our family. My owners.

He sighed and glanced to the side of the stage where the rest of his family stood. My attention had been so consumed with Penn that I hadn't even noticed the congressman's wife, Elise, or his daughter, Ruby. My heart swelled, seeing her sweet little face surrounded by crazy brown curls that her mother had obviously tried to tame. But the sadness in her big brown eyes couldn't be tamped down the way her hair could. I swallowed back a lump in my throat, knowing how much she must be missing me.

"As I'm sure you've heard, our family has had someone very dear taken from us. Our Ella was a part of our family, and having her stolen has left a big hole in our hearts."

The sound of my name on his lips made my legs weak and I took a small step away from the TV. Lowered myself back down onto one of the sofas.

His cold, dark eyes pierced through the television screen. Was he talking to me? None of it made sense. The congressman knew that Penn and I had run away together, yet there they were standing shoulder to shoulder, as if they were one big happy family.

"It's no secret that I've been a strong backer of Bill 467 since its inception," the congressman went on, "and in doing so, I've put myself, and my family, under attack from a diverse group of extremists. They call themselves the Liberationists, an insulting knockoff of our great country's tragic history, but they're nothing but zealots. They have no regard for the law. No regard for life. This is a frighteningly dangerous group that hides behind vitriol and false rhetoric. They're nothing short of homegrown terrorists, and I compel anyone listening to be on the lookout. If you suspect that someone close to you might be involved in one of these organizations, I urge you to reach out to the authorities."

"What does he mean by 'terrorists'?" one of the girls asked. "They're trying to save us, not hurt us."

Behind the congressman, Penn stood, eyes glazed. He gave no impression that he was even hearing what his father was saying.

I glanced between the girls' faces. Did they understand? Did they know that it had been Penn who had helped me escape? Did anyone know, or had I dreamed it all?

As if he'd read my mind, the congressman turned to Penn, placing his hand on his shoulder. "Our family isn't exempt from blame," he said. "My son's actions played a part in the loss of our dear Ella, and he's here with me today to ask for your help in returning her to us."

The congressman moved aside as Penn stepped up to the podium. For a moment he simply stared down at the microphones, unblinking. The camera zoomed in on his face. From the outside he looked like a perfect example of a congressman's son. His tousled dark hair had been tamed, and his clothes had been pressed. But even though someone had obviously styled him to look this way, something about him looked…wrong.

There were dark circles underneath his amber eyes that someone had tried to mask with makeup, and even though his hair had been combed down to cover the cut above his eyebrow, the skin beside his eye was still tinged with the sunset hues of an old bruise.

I wanted to reach out and stroke the hair back from his forehead, to press my lips to his injuries as if my kiss could heal him, could make him whole.

Finally, Penn gave his head a small shake and looked down at the notecards that he'd been clutching. He spread them out on the podium. "Thank you all for coming here today," he said. "My family hopes that by speaking out we might not only help inform some of you about the misconceptions of Bill 467, but also find a way to bring home our pet."

He sounded different. Flat. His voice normally sounded like laughter was about to push its way out at any moment. But it only sounded tired as he began detailing the ways that people had been misinterpreting the law.

"Even though these pets *seem* human in every way, they were scientifically engineered to be companions," he read from the cards.

I cringed at his words. *Seem human*. What was that supposed to mean? I *was* a human. Penn, of all people, knew that.

My hands quivered in my lap, thinking of the way his fingers had felt interlocked with my own. No one could tell me we were that different.

"It's easy to forget that they're pets," he went on. "I know it was for me. They look like us and they've been trained to interact with us. Those of you who've had a chance to meet one know that they're capable of intelligent conversation, but the same is true for robots or chimpanzees for that matter."

We all cringed and one of the girls sucked in a shuddering breath, covering her eyes with her hands.

"I don't know if I can watch any more of this," one said, reaching to turn off the TV.

"No, stop." I scooted forward, pushing her hand away. I didn't want to hear another hateful word from Penn's mouth, but somehow it seemed even worse not to hear it.

"He's not…" She looked from the TV to me, the realization that I was the one they were talking about spreading across her face.

"This isn't like him," I said. "Those cards… Someone

told him to say this!"

"I had a chance to talk to the scientists at NuPet," Penn continued. "They told me that, because of the extensive genetic modification they undergo, pets can't be classified as humans. They use test tube insemination and incubation. They're raised in kennels and training centers, not loving homes. They've taken away the human element, not just from their genes, but from the process. They're…bred. Grown. And pets grown in labs aren't capable of being fully human." He lowered the cards. "NuPet has made all the data publically available. You can see for yourself."

My eyes stung and I shook my head, trying to tune him out. These couldn't be Penn's words. They couldn't.

"…help us bring home our pet, Ella."

My ears perked at my name. Penn's voice changed ever so slightly. I'm sure no one else noticed it, but I did. I *did*. The dullness that had weighed down his speech slipped away, if only just for a moment. I stared at the screen, willing him to say my name again. To say anything that sounded like himself.

"My family won't rest until she's returned to us and that's why we'd like to announce a hundred thousand dollar reward for her safe return."

The girls stared disgustedly at the screen, even though any one of their owners would probably pay exorbitant sums to have them returned. They just hadn't announced it on television.

Penn's hands shook and the notecards he held fell to the ground. He lifted his eyes, staring into the camera for the first time.

"My father will do *anything* to get her back. He'll find her and he'll bring her home," he said. "I promise."

The intensity in Penn's eyes pushed me back in my seat and before I knew it, the woman from the desk was beside the television, switching off the screen. The happy look on her face was gone.

Her jaw clenched. "It's going to have to be a 'no' on the popcorn. Television isn't a good idea, either," she said. "Please return to your rooms for the evening."

The girls nodded, obedient as always, and headed for the hallway. I didn't take my eyes off of the black TV screen. In it, my own reflection stared back at me, but I would never forget the look in Penn's eyes. The other girls might not have seen it. The world might not have seen it. But I did. And I knew it was meant for me.

"Are you okay?" the woman from the counter asked, placing her hand on my shoulder.

I pushed back the urge to brush her hand away. "I'm fine."

"Do you want me to call your counselor? I'm sure she'll come in. That's what they're for, to help you through tough times like this." She sounded like the video they'd shown me at orientation.

"No. I'll be fine. I think I just need to lie down for a minute."

I stood. The small rectangle of my stolen book still burned in my pocket. I didn't need sympathy. I didn't need to talk to one of their counselors. I didn't need a life skills class or a lecture on self-sufficiency. I just needed to get out of there.

Get the book. Get back to my room while everyone was busy watching TV. Gather up the handful of items I'd stolen to get me back to Penn, and *leave*. That had been the plan. Not this.

In my room, I shut the door and latched it. It was only a small privacy lock. It wouldn't keep someone out for long if they really wanted to get in.

I slipped the case off of my pillow and shoved the book inside. Then, lifting the corner of the mattress, I fished out the other items I'd collected. A thin, black wallet was the first thing I'd taken. I slipped it, far too easily, out of the back pocket of the man who had come in to speak to us about becoming Canadian citizens.

I opened it, the way I'd done every night since I'd taken it. I knew all its contents by heart: the bent picture of two small boys, the worn business cards, twenty-seven dollars in bills, a few laminated cards with the man's sad, unsmiling face staring back at me. I plucked out the cash, shoving it into the front pocket of my jeans. Everything else, I left inside.

Besides the wallet and the book, I'd managed to steal a small folding knife that I found in one of the drawers in the kitchen, and a needle and thread that someone had left sitting on the counter in our life skills class.

It wasn't much, a few little items knocking around at the bottom of the pillowcase, but I refused to believe they were useless. They were all I had.

From the small drawer beside the bed, I pulled out another pair of stiff blue jeans and a T-shirt, and added them to my bag. This was what I wore now. I should have been excited, after only wearing ball gowns for so long, to finally have clothes that didn't scream to be looked at, but these clothes didn't feel right either. They weren't mine. Nothing was.

Outside, the night was already dark. Maybe it would be smarter to wait a few more hours, until I was sure that the others had gone to bed, but I couldn't bear the thought of spending another minute trapped inside these walls.

I heaved up on the old window that looked out onto the fire escape, and past that into the deserted alleyway. The window was heavy, trimmed with flaking paint. And it was stuck. Tight. Obviously, no one had tried to open it for years.

I strained, pushing up on the window, and finally it let out a large *crack*, as the old paint that had sealed it shut finally broke free. I held still, my heart pounding in my chest, as I waited for someone to come running, but the room stayed silent. Outside a heavy truck rumbled down the narrow streets, and the wail of a crying child drifted in the breeze.

I shimmied out, pulling my small bag with me onto the narrow metal landing that surrounded the second story. Below me, the building faded into darkness. I didn't know where all the volunteers went at night, but the place seemed deserted.

One good thing about my new clothes was how much easier they were to move in. Without yards of billowing fabric flowing behind me, it was easy to swing my legs over the side of the landing. The ladder that led down to the ground floor was old and rusted, but my arms felt strong enough to hold my weight. I held on fiercely, moving slowly from rung to rung until I dangled only a few yards above the street below.

A single bulb lit the street at the end of the alleyway, but between the valley created by the buildings, it was too dark to see.

I hardly cared.

I was almost out.

Finally, after a week, I was on my way to Penn.

I didn't know what direction I was headed, but I was confident I could find my way once I made it to the street. The memory of my ride here was seared into my mind. I could recall every detail of that drive, every tree we passed, every turn the van made as it took me further and further away from Penn. I could still feel the tires humming beneath me and the rough fabric of the blanket wrapped around my shoulders. We'd driven over an hour to get to the refugee center, which meant that it could take me days to make it back to the border on foot. Once I was there, I'd have to find a way back across.

I couldn't worry about that yet.

A bit of broken glass crunched under my feet as I dropped to the ground and took off down the alley. A second later, the whine of a siren cut through the cool air. I rounded the corner, bursting out of the alleyway. My feet hit the street's pavement and a bright light flashed on in front of me, blinding me. I skidded to a stop, raising my hands to shield my eyes.

"Stop."

Next to me, a hand tightened around my arm.

My heart sank. I was caught.

Chapter Two

The glare from the floodlights swam in front of my eyes, a ball of light that hung in the center of my vision, blinding me.

I struggled against the hand that clamped my arm, jerking my whole body, but it only tightened.

"Let me go," I hissed, striking out with my other arm. My fingers met flesh and I dug in, feeling the tear of skin beneath my nails.

"Damn it! Stop fighting! I'm just trying to help you."

In my periphery I could just make out the dark brick walls of the building next to me as I was pulled back into the alley, back toward the fire escape and my dingy little room.

They couldn't lock me inside there again. They couldn't keep me.

From the street came the squeal of the front door as it was thrown open on its hinges.

"We've got a runner," a worker called.

Muffled voices grumbled in response. I could imagine them assembling, an army of volunteers ready to retrieve me, all of them imagining that they knew what was best for me.

"You can't keep me here," I said. "I'm not your prisoner."

Feet thudded down the front steps of the building as the volunteers from the refugee center poured out onto the street. They called over their shoulders to one another, fanning out to find me as if I was some dog that had escaped the pound. They wanted to help me, but only as long as I submitted to their rules. Only as long as I stayed obediently inside their walls.

I dug my feet in, my heels grinding against the loose gravel.

"Will you stop fighting and let me help you?"

That voice! Where had I heard that voice?

The world shuddered with splotches of light, but I turned, letting this person drag me back down the dark alley. Behind the Dumpster, the rear of one building backed up against the apartments from the next block, creating an opening a couple feet wide. We ducked inside, our pace quickening as the sound of voices drew closer.

The darkness between the buildings engulfed us. We raced forward toward the strip of light that rose like a column in front of us. My shoulders scraped the brick on either side as I ran, but I didn't slow.

Behind us, a volunteer called out, but my own ragged breathing muffled the sound. Had they seen where we'd gone? Were they close behind?

The staccato of our footsteps echoed off the walls. For a second, it sounded like percussion, like music, the beating of drums urging us on. A moment later we burst into the next alley, swiftly dodging past a large truck and down another small opening between the buildings.

We moved quickly. My legs strained to keep pace. Even as the blurry halo of light finally disappeared from my eyes, I couldn't get a good view of the hooded person who pulled me after them. I trailed behind, concentrating instead on the ground beneath my feet as we zigzagged past Dumpsters and through viaducts until I was completely disoriented from all the twists and turns.

My lungs burned and my feet throbbed from slapping against the pavement. It was impossible to tell if the beating that thumped in my ears was the sound of footsteps trailing behind me, or the mad pounding of my own heart.

Finally we skidded into a small alcove behind a construction site. Next to us, the hulking body of a giant tractor shielded us from view.

I collapsed against the monstrous tire. My heart threatened to burst through my throat and I rested my hands on my knees, hanging my head between my legs as I fought to catch my breath.

"Did we lose them?" I gasped, finally looking up.

The face that greeted me stole the rest of my breath and I reared back, the hard rubber of the tire digging into my back.

"You," I whispered.

It was a ghost, that face, pale in the small bit of light cast from a lone streetlamp near the sidewalk.

But there was no mistaking her.

Missy.

Her smooth, white skin glowed like a moon.

She threw back the hood of her jacket. "What's wrong with you?" she panted, rubbing the red gash my fingernails had left along her forearm. "This is how you treat people who try to help you?"

My mouth hung open as she wiggled a small backpack off her shoulders and dropped it on the ground beside her feet, slumping back against the tire beside me.

Staring at her was like staring at a ghost, at a dead part of myself. I hadn't seen her since the night I'd snuck in through her window, asking her to escape with me. The way she'd betrayed me had hit like a brick to the stomach then, and the pain of it still reverberated through me now. I never dreamed that I would see her again.

I never *wanted* to.

And yet, despite everything she'd said to me, everything she'd done…she'd come to Canada. To me.

I took her in, *all* of her. Even though Missy and I were identical in stature, she'd always seemed like a giant, as if her age and personality tripled her size. And even though she looked quite a bit worse for wear compared to the last time I'd seen her, she still startled me with her beauty. It didn't seem to matter that her gowns had been replaced by dirty black tights, which were ripped and torn, holes running up the legs until they got to an equally ripped pair of denim shorts. Her shirt was whole, but it was dirty and mostly covered by an olive green jacket that must have originally belonged to someone twice her size because it hung limply on her small frame.

Her hair, which was normally silky smooth and curled with just the right amount of wave down her back, was knotted and crazy. I'm sure her owners would have been appalled to see her like this, but she didn't seem to mind one bit. In fact, the look suited her.

She turned to appraise me, the arrogant smirk I was familiar with twisting her pouty lips. "You don't look so great."

I rested a hand on my chest, trying to calm the crazed beating of my heart. "*I* don't?" I choked out. "Have you looked in the mirror lately?"

Missy snorted, running a hand over her wild hair, and I glanced past her toward the street, worried that any moment one of the volunteers from the center would come charging around the corner.

"Don't worry," Missy said. "We lost them."

"How do you know?"

"I know how to lose someone," she said. "Besides, those people don't have a clue what they're doing. Their security was primitive at best."

My cheeks flamed. Already belittling my attempted escape. So very like Missy. "What are you doing here?"

She sat with her head leaning against the tire, almost relaxed, but my question made her bristle and she sat up, arranging herself more stiffly beside me.

"That's it?" she asked, narrowing her eyes at me. "No *thank you, Missy, for saving my ass*? No *I wouldn't have made it without you, Missy*? God! You obviously haven't been taught any new manners since you arrived."

I shook my head, wishing I had it in me to roll my eyes at her the way she would have rolled them at me. Her appearance might have changed, but she was the same old Missy. "How did you get here?" It seemed impossible that she could just show up out of the blue like this.

"I'm glad you're happy to see me," she said, rising up from the ground to stare out into the dark pit of the construction site. She didn't speak for a minute and I was about to repeat my question when she swung around to face me. Her face changed. She wasn't wearing the painted on version of herself that she normally showed to the world. Her expression was rubbed raw. "I traveled the black market," she said. "But I don't want to talk about it."

The ache in her voice made me regret being so sharp with her. She'd obviously been through a lot to get here.

"Why are you here?" I asked.

"I had to come," she said. "*You* made it impossible for me to stay where I was."

Her words came out like a hiss and I scooted away from her. "I did?"

She crowded closer. "You think I could have stayed after what you did?"

"What are you talking about? I didn't do anything to you!"

I hadn't. Sure, I'd asked her to run away with me, but she'd refused. She was the one who'd rung that bell so her master came running. She was the one who turned me in, who made *my* life unbearable. If anyone was to blame, it was her.

"You think your actions don't have consequences?" Missy asked. "You think your little stunt with your lover boy only affected you?" She threw her hands in the air.

My back stiffened. "At least I tried," I snapped. "All you did was sit there. You hated your life, but you were too big of a coward to do anything about it."

"Don't you *dare* call me a coward," Missy snapped. "I had to weigh all my options. I had to be smart. I couldn't afford to make stupid choices just because my heart told me to." She emphasized the word *heart*, spitting it out as if it was the ugliest word she'd ever heard.

I opened my mouth but she narrowed her eyes and the look on her face stopped me from speaking.

"You don't have any idea what you've done," she said. "You made my life *unbearable*. It didn't make any difference to my master whether I turned you in or not. He wasn't going to look at things logically. Men like that never do." She shook her head. "No, from the moment I rang that stupid bell, my world has been tipped on its head. And don't think it's just my life you ruined."

"You can't blame me for—"

"Shut up! Just shut. Up," she interrupted. "It's a full-blown disaster to every single pet in the whole state." She stared off over my shoulder as if she could see something there. Her face was almost red with rage and her fists clenched and unclenched at her sides. "It might have been bearable if I only had to deal with my master," Missy said, clearly getting some sort of pleasure from not answering my question. "He was suspicious, which was annoying, having to stay close to him all the time, like I was going to run away any second." She wrinkled her nose, the distaste of his memory so clear on her face. "And after I'd worked so hard to make myself invisible to him. But I could wait that out. Or I could have waited that out if…"

"If what? Will you please just tell me what's going on?"

She glared at me.

"You can't just come here and treat me like this," I said, stomping my foot so hard a spray of loose gravel and dirt skittered past Missy, bouncing noisily into the deep hole of the construction site. "I'm sorry that your master was cruel to you and blamed you for my actions, but it's not my fault."

"Oh…you have no idea."

I clenched my fists. "Not if you don't tell me."

She narrowed her eyes.

"Why did you come here if you hate me so much?" I asked.

"I don't hate you," she said, turning her nose up at me. "I don't care about you enough to hate you."

I didn't have to stay. I was free to make my own decisions and I didn't have to listen to Missy if I didn't want to.

"Fine." I snatched my pillowcase off the ground. "I'm sorry coming all this way was such an inconvenience to you, but I'm getting out of here."

Her eyes grew wide. "You can't just *leave*."

"Yes, I can."

"But you wouldn't," she said.

I put my hand on my hip. The position felt natural after seeing Ruby do it so many times. "If you need a refuge, I'm sure they'll house you back at the center. All you have to do is ask."

Missy's face was wild with fury. She crossed the few feet that separated us in a flash.

"You fool. They're killing us, okay?" Missy spat in my face. "The pets! They're murdering pets! And here you are, clueless and free when other people are dying because of you."

"What are you talking about?"

"Do you understand English? I said *they're killing the pets*," Missy said. "A dozen pets have turned up dead in the last week."

"But…" It felt like I'd been struck in the gut. I tried to get a breath, but I couldn't.

She folded her arms and her face settled into a look of satisfaction. She hadn't just come to rub it in. She actually thought I'd want to know, didn't she?

But what could I do about it?

"I need you to help me," I said.

She brushed at her legs as if she was wearing a long satin ball gown. Maybe our gestures were so ingrained in us they would never disappear. "Why would I help you?"

I swallowed, thinking of the refugee center. The dinginess was a glaring difference from the opulence that we were used to, but that wasn't why I needed to leave. None of that stuff really mattered. There were more important things, things that no amount of money could buy, like the slant of light through a window, or a slice of crisp blue sky, the feeling of strong arms pulling you in tight.

"I need to get back," I said.

"Back?"

"Home." Maybe the word seemed peculiar to her. I didn't mean home, as in staying at the congressman's house. But it was the only word to explain where I needed to be. Home. With Penn. Next to him. Together, we'd figure out what to do.

She shook her head, turning away from me. "No," she said matter-of-factly.

"No?"

She glanced back over her shoulder. "No," she repeated. She bent down and grabbed her backpack.

I lunged at her, grabbing her arm. It felt surprisingly small beneath my fingers. "I have to get back to Penn and you're going to help me. You made it here. You can make it back."

I expected Missy to tear her arm away from me, but I didn't expect her to throw her head back and laugh. It rang clear into the night air, three loud barks, deep from her belly.

"You really are that stupid, aren't you?" she said, wiping at her eyes. "I'm never going back there and neither are you. You couldn't even make it away from your friends at the refugee center without getting caught. If it weren't for me, you'd be back inside right now, locked away in your little room. If you go back to the United States, you'll get caught by someone worse."

My face burned red in the dark. "You don't know that."

She snatched the pillowcase out of my hand. "You were going to get there with this?" she asked, peering inside. "That master of yours has started a war over you, and what? You're going to fight him with a pocketknife? It's not safe for anyone, not the black market dealers, not the Liberationists. Certainly not the pets. Not any of them."

She moved closer, like maybe she wasn't done with me. "You can't just go marching back. It's not that simple. If you aren't caught outright by your master, you'd get picked up in less than a minute by someone wanting the reward money he's offered to get you back. You're better off here. Stay for a little bit. Get on your feet. I bet you might even start feeling happy in a month or two."

"Happy?" The word felt like a slap. The thought of being happy without Penn was almost more painful than being separated from him to begin with. "I could never be happy if I stayed."

Missy snorted and slung her bag over her shoulder. "Fine, don't be happy. What do I care? At this point I'll just be satisfied with making my own choices. Heck, I'd be fine just staying alive."

"I don't believe you," I said, throwing up my hands. "You are the most selfish, inconsiderate person I've ever met. You came all this way just to make me feel terrible, and now you're just going to leave me."

"I never said I was going to leave you. You're welcome to come with me. I'm just not going to be a part of your stupid plan to get back to your one true love, or whatever he is."

"Don't mock me."

Missy shrugged. Unfazed. She looked out toward the street and I could feel that she was about to leave, this time for good.

"Please, Missy," I begged. "I have to try. I can't stay here knowing that Penn's father is still controlling him. That he's out there somewhere without me and I didn't even *try* to get back to him." I heaved in a breath. "I know it's dangerous. If all those pets are dying because of me, how can I stay here and do nothing? If I do, they're still controlling me. They're controlling me just as much as if I had a chain around my wrist. More than that because I wouldn't just let them be controlling my body, I'd be letting them control my mind, too."

Missy didn't move. She stared at me long and hard. "I'm sorry," she said finally, tightening her grip on her bag. "But this isn't my fight."

"Then you might as well leave," I said.

Missy stared at me a moment longer. Her eyes narrowed. Did she expect me to feel bad? She was the one who was deserting me. A moment later she tossed my pillowcase at me. It flopped to the ground at my feet and she spun on her heel, heading out into the night.

A lump rose up in my throat but I fought it back. I wouldn't let her hear me cry. I snatched my things up off of the ground. I had everything I needed: a little money, a knife, a map. What help would she be anyway? If Missy could make her way across the border, I could, too.

I made my way past the construction equipment and out onto the street. I hadn't really paid attention to the direction that Missy had pulled me in as we left the refugee center and now I was all turned around. I just needed to get my bearings. I leaned up against the cold glass window of a dress shop and closed my eyes, trying to visualize the path that I was supposed to take. But it wasn't just that I felt disoriented. Seeing Missy had shaken me up on the inside.

The cold from the window pressed into my back, making me shiver. I dug into my bag and pulled out the stolen book. My hands shook as I flipped to the map in the front, wishing that I'd had more time to study it. The volunteers from the refugee center hadn't found me yet, but that didn't mean that they'd stopped looking.

"What's this?"

When I looked up, Missy was standing over me. She plucked the book out of my cold hands.

"What are you doing?" I asked warily.

"I asked you first," she said, tapping the book against her palm.

"It's a book."

"I know it's a book, stupid," she said, cocking her head. "What are you doing with it? You can suddenly read?"

"Why did you come back?" I asked, ignoring her question.

She studied me. "You know," she finally said. "I liked you better when you didn't ask questions and just did what you were told."

I swallowed. "No you didn't."

She shrugged. "Maybe."

"Maybe?"

She flipped through the book. "I'm not carrying this with me," she said, tossing it on the ground. She kicked it a bit with her foot, shoving it further into the corner before she emptied the rest of my belongings into her own backpack.

"You can't just throw that out," I said, reaching for the book.

"I'm not carrying around a stupid book. We can't afford to have stuff like that weighing us down."

"We?"

She stared me down. There was so much power in that stare. I had no idea how she'd learned to do that. "I got down the street and I felt like crap, okay?" she said, hitting her hands against her sides like a child throwing a temper tantrum. "Why did you have to do this to me? It's not fair."

"Then leave."

"I can't," she huffed. "You won't make it ten minutes without me."

"I already did."

She rolled her eyes. "Yeah, and you're pretty much in the same spot that I left you. If you want *any* chance of making it back, you need me. It's not something I'm proud of. It's just a fact."

"I'm not helpless," I said. "I can figure it out." Which was worse, trying to find my way back to Penn all by myself, or doing it with Missy? I snatched my book back. "I'll carry this. I can carry all my stuff."

"Do you want my help or not?"

I took a deep breath. *No, I don't want your help*, I wanted to yell. I bit the inside of my cheek to keep myself from screaming it. "Yes," I finally muttered.

"Well then listen to me." She snatched the book from my hand. "This thing is heavy. The first rule: don't lug stupid stuff around."

"It's not stupid. It's a map," I said, snatching it back. I tore out the small clump of pages from the front.

"Fine, keep them," she said. "But you can't carry your own things. What? You're just going to walk down the street carrying this?" She held up the pillowcase. "You realize we're trying *not* to draw attention to ourselves, right?" She shook her head, dumping the rest of the contents of my bag into her own before she zipped it with a huff and marched off.

I chased after her, cramming the torn pages into my pocket. Maybe she was right, but I wasn't about to admit it.

"If you want me to help you, then you've got to listen to me," she said. "First things first." She stopped mid-stride and spun around to face me. "We can't go walking down the streets with you looking like this. You're practically a neon sign with a huge arrow pointing at the two of us. Look at the two runaway pets!"

She snatched up a piece of my hair. "We'll start with this."

Chapter Three

"Wait out here," Missy said, pushing me up against the brick wall of a convenience store.

The bright overhead lights from inside bled out onto the street. I stared through the window, watching the way the crisp jingle of the door's bell made the cashier turn his eyes away from the TV just long enough to glance at Missy. My stomach clenched for just a moment, afraid that he would recognize her for what she was. It didn't matter that we were in Canada now; he could still turn us in.

I wasn't sure how she'd done it. How had she stopped looking like a pet? Maybe it was the dark makeup around her eyes that I could see more clearly now that she was cast in bright light. Maybe it was the torn up clothes and the wild hair, or maybe it was something subtler. She carried herself differently, even than she had when we were together a few moments ago.

I studied her as she moved up the aisles, snatching a few

things off of the shelves before she made her way back to the counter. It was hard to tell what the difference was. Something had changed in the slope of her shoulders, the swing in her hips.

We'd spent so many years learning how to glide when we walked, learning how to hold our bodies so that they looked fragile and elegant like a flower balanced on its stem. Carriage was just as important as any of the other skills, but it seemed that when Missy walked through the door she forgot all that.

It wasn't a glaring difference. Not to someone who hadn't studied this sort of thing. But it was apparent to me. It was as if she'd shed the skin of her old body and had climbed inside a normal girl, one who had gone to high school and rode in cars with boys. I didn't understand it, but I wanted to. I wanted her to teach me how she'd done it, this metamorphosis.

Missy's face was tense when she finally pushed the door open and rounded the corner to find me. Maybe the easy and confident way she had carried herself inside the store wasn't so natural after all.

She shoved a few dollar bills and some change into her pocket. "That's almost all the money I had left," she said, scowling as she pulled me around to the other side of the building where two metal doors stood slightly ajar. She opened one up and peered inside.

"Oh, this place is gross," she moaned, glancing back out to the street. "Damn. It's going to have to do."

She opened the door wider and shoved me in, following close behind. It was a bathroom, but even though it was a big box of a room there was only a metal toilet and a shallow sink inside. The long fluorescent lightbulbs flickered up above, giving off just enough light so that the corners of the room stayed hidden in shadow. It was probably for the best. At least the darkness hid some of the dirt. The places where the light hit were grimy and unwashed. Next to the sink, a small trash can overflowed with paper towels, a few of which had fallen onto the ground, now wet and stomped with dark footprints.

Missy thumped her bag down on the back of the toilet and riffled through the plastic bag full of things she'd just gotten from the convenience store.

"Have a seat," she said, gesturing to the toilet.

I stared at the dirty metal bowl.

"Get used to it. You're going to see a lot worse on the road."

I lowered myself down onto the edge. "What are you…" My voice trailed off as Missy pulled a pair of scissors and a box of hair dye from the bag and set them on the edge of the sink.

"Do we really need to?" My voice came out a small squeak.

Missy nodded. "I'm sorry." It probably wasn't a phrase she was used to saying, but at least she sounded sincere.

Before I had a chance to prepare myself, she grabbed a chunk of hair from off my shoulder and snipped. A long lock of hair fell to the ground and I stifled a cry.

"I'll be quick," Missy said. "Let's just get this done. I promise, you'll survive."

She kept snipping, moving around me and turning my head from side to side until the floor was littered with piles of hair.

She grabbed the box of hair color. On the front a beautiful older woman stared out at me with dark hair almost the same color as the congressman's wife. "Almost done."

The liquid was cold on my head. A tiny bit dribbled down my back and Missy wiped it off with a bit of toilet paper.

"Give me your face," she said, tilting my chin up. In her hand she held a dark pencil, probably the same one she'd used on her own eyes. Her hand was steady as she traced along my lids. She took her time, turning my head this way and that. When she was satisfied, she finished off by brushing a bit of black onto my lashes.

"You're going to have to rinse in the sink."

The water felt like ice no matter how much I twisted the faucet and by the time the dye was rinsed, my neck was frozen and numb.

I stood up, shivering. "Can I look?"

"Not quite," Missy said, dabbing at a bit of the makeup that had smeared below my eyes. She stood back, taking me in as I blotted my hair dry with a clump of stiff brown paper towels.

"Okay." She nodded.

I stared at myself in the mirror. The lighting was terrible and the surface was blanketed with a thin film covered with scratches, but I could see my reflection well enough to know that I looked nothing like the girl I'd been half an hour ago.

My damp hair was cut in a blunt line ending just below my ears. Never in my life had I had short hair across my forehead, but Missy had trimmed it so that it lay straight across my brow, cutting a crisp dark line above my eyebrows. The dark brown color set my eyes off in stark contrast.

"It's not perfect, but it's a whole lot better than before," Missy said defensively, reacting to my stunned silence.

But I wasn't angry. I didn't hate this new look. If anything, it strengthened me. Maybe now this new girl, the one that stared back at me from the mirror, would have a fighting chance to make it back to Penn. She looked tough, and strong, and fearless.

And I wanted to be her.

I turned away from the mirror and caught Missy's eye. "Thank you."

The compliment caught her off guard. "It's fine," she said, brushing my words away. "We should get going. If we spend too much time in here they'll probably report us and that's the last thing we need."

Hastily, we scooped the chunks of hair that littered the floor into the garbage, and in a couple minutes the place looked slightly better than when we'd found it.

Outside, the air was crisp and goose bumps spread up my arms and along my exposed neck. I wrapped my arms across my chest.

Missy watched me out of the corner of her eye. "We'll see if we can find you a jacket," she said. "But I'm practically out of money."

I pulled the small wad of cash out of my pocket. "I've got some."

"Where'd you get this?" she asked, counting the bills I held out.

I swallowed. "I found it."

She raised her eyebrows. "Sure," she said, smiling like maybe I wasn't such a disappointment after all. "This helps. It'll give us a little bit of breathing room before we have to get creative."

"Creative?"

"Don't worry about it," she said. "Right now we have other things to think about." She glanced down at my feet. "How good are those shoes?"

I shrugged. They'd gotten me this far.

"Well, you're about to find out," she said, sighing as she tucked her arm through mine. "Actually, the middle of the night is the best time for walking. There's no traffic, no eyes to stare at you. Mostly the world is quiet, which is great for thinking, if you like that sort of thing. Or singing." She hummed a few soft notes, accompanied by the beat of our feet along the sidewalk.

I'd never asked Missy what her talents had been, but now I guessed that one of them must have been singing. She would have been trained classically, of course, and wouldn't know the songs that Penn had sung to me, but for a moment I wished that she did.

We moved along in silence. Every once in a while Missy would begin to hum again, but it never lasted long, certainly not long enough for me to piece out what the tune was.

"Tell me about the pets," I said.

"What pets?"

"The ones that died."

She shoved her hands in her pockets and frowned. "I shouldn't even know about it."

"Then how do you?"

The smallest smile pricked the sides of her mouth. "You know how they are. Forgetting we're in the room. Forgetting we have ears. Forgetting that we actually understand things. If my master knew how many conversations I'd listened in on…"

Her eyes sparkled, but only for a moment.

"My master bought me from a black market dealer," she went on. "They're getting scared. I don't know if NuPet is sending anyone out to talk to its clients, but four days ago, a man from one of the markets came to see my master," she said. "It was almost midnight when he showed up. I was sitting in the chaise lounge like always—I never want to lay eyes on that stupid chair again."

She crinkled her forehead, concentrating, trying to

remember. Off in the distance, a siren wailed. The sound made me shiver, like it was a warning, a harbinger of things to come.

"I recognized this dealer right away," Missy went on. "Some of them aren't too bad, but this one…" She swallowed, composing herself. "He must not have seen me sitting there because I'm sure he would have had something foul to say to me. Instead, he launched right in. He was so worried that people would find out about the deaths. He kept saying that. *They can't find out. They can't find out.* I'm assuming that he meant NuPet, although he never really said. He just kept wiping his hands on his pants and looking toward the door like he expected someone to come bursting in at any second. It was just…weird…to see those men act that way, you know? They're used to the world behaving exactly the way they want it to."

"How many pets have died?" I asked

"I don't really know," Missy said. "He said he knew about four. And those were just the ones they found near their market! The last one was dumped outside the doors of his office, like a mouse that some cat dropped on the doorstep. But the rest were spread out a bit more. I think that's the reason he came by, to ask my master to help pay off the cops."

"But don't they need to find out who's doing it?"

She shook her head. "Probably. But they don't want the feds involved. I think that's what's scaring them. It's not like they really care about the girls. They're just upset about people finding out."

"Why?"

"They each have different reasons. The black market dealers don't want any attention drawn to them. So far,

NuPet has been fine with them reselling pets after their masters are done with them, but I'm sure it's not really legal. And then there are people like my master. They're just afraid their friends will find out that they bought their pets secondhand. My master told everyone that he got me from a breeder in California, which is technically true. I was bred there. But he'd never tell anyone that he actually bought me from a black market. He'd be appalled if any of his friends found out. He doesn't want them to know I was just another one of his cheap finds."

"It doesn't seem like that should matter," I said.

"Well, it does," Missy snapped. "Anyway, my master kept asking who the dead girls belonged to. *Whose pets are they?* he kept yelling. Like he could just go track down the owners and solve everything."

Her face was white. Her eyes wide.

"Whose pets were they?" I asked.

Missy shook her head. "They don't know. The microchips were removed from all of them and I guess they didn't do a very delicate job cutting them out either."

Both Missy and I lifted our hands to our necks at the same time, feeling the place where the microchips had been. The cut on my neck was healing nicely. It was difficult to tell in the dark whether Missy's hand hovered above a new wound and I wondered whether she'd had to cut out her microchip the way I had when she ran away or whether it had been removed a long time ago, after she'd been sold by her first owner.

"But it doesn't make sense," I said. "How could my leaving make any difference? It's not like I'm the first to leave. There are other girls here. They've had plenty of others here before that. For years. Why would girls start showing up dead after I left?"

"I don't know," she sighed. "Maybe you didn't cause it all to happen, but you must have been the tipping point. Maybe it's because your master made such a big deal of you leaving. Before that, people were probably too embarrassed to admit when their pets ran away. I mean, it's pretty humiliating, and these are not people who want to be made into fools."

"But it doesn't explain things. You think all those people would kill their own pets? After they spent all that money on them?"

Missy shrugged. "Someone like that might rather kill their pet than have it run away."

She was right. I knew it. My fingers flittered to my pocket, to the collar. I couldn't imagine what the congressman would do to me if someone turned me in. Death seemed like the best option.

"Maybe the other girls heard that you were free and it put ideas in their heads," she went on. "All I know is that I don't want to end up dead along with them." She glanced around. "It's going to be getting light soon. Can you walk any faster?"

My feet already ached, terribly. My heels felt raw and chafed, and the pinky toe on my left foot felt like it might have already fallen all the way off from the amount of pain that radiated up my leg.

"I can try." I groaned, hardly picking up the pace. "What happens when it gets light?"

Already there was more traffic on the street than when we'd left. In front of us, a car turned the corner and its headlights flashed over us like a spotlight, making me freeze in my tracks, but the car buzzed past us, the driver a young woman bleary eyed and yawning.

"If it gets light, it blows our cover and we'll have to waste one whole day before we can get back across the border."

"Our cover for what?"

Missy sighed, clearly annoyed by my questions as well as my pace, and hitched her backpack up on her shoulders. "For sneaking into one of the cars."

"Whose car?"

She rolled her eyes. "The railroad company, I guess, or the manufacturer."

"You mean, like a train. Is that safe?"

"Safe?" She laughed. "None of this is safe. If you want safe, you should let me take you back now."

I clenched my jaw, but I didn't respond.

"It's how I got here…if that makes you feel any better," she said after a minute.

"Not really," I mumbled.

"Do you have a better idea?" She picked up the pace and I winced, trotting to catch up with her. "It's not like we can just hop in someone's car and ask them to take us back over the border."

She glanced back at me, as if she was looking for signs on my face that would tell her that yes, that was exactly how I'd assumed we would get back.

"We don't have papers," she huffed. "I shouldn't even be here in the first place. And I'm pretty sure if you go waltzing across the border like a normal person, someone's going to stop you in less than a minute and turn you back in to your old master. There are plenty of people watching out for you who would be perfectly happy to take his reward money."

She trudged ahead of me, only glancing back every now

and then. Maybe she was hoping I would be gone, vanished, and she wouldn't have to deal with me anymore. She could go back to whatever her plan had been before she came to find me.

After a while, the sky started to lighten ever so softly. What had been black faded into a beautiful shade of teal. The buildings on either side of us gave way to homes and after a while we came to a long stretch of empty road. It was wide enough for six cars to drive across at the same time, but even though a car passed us every once in a while, it stayed mostly empty. In the distance, the boxy shape of a dozen huge white buildings came into view.

Missy pointed. "That's it. They make the cars there."

"And we have to sneak into one of those buildings?" I asked.

She shook her head. "No, the train tracks are behind." She looked up at the sky. "If we run, we might be able to make it before the workers get there."

"Run?" The word was almost painful to say.

"You don't want to find a place to hide all day around here," Missy said. "Believe me."

I gave her a small nod. I'd save my energy for running. I'd need every last bit of it.

Missy took off at a trot and I followed behind, with the pounding of each step I repeated Penn's name over and over in my mind. My eyes began to blur. My breath came in gasps and a sharp pain wiggled its way between my ribs like a blade aiming for my heart. Finally, I looked up from the ground in front of me. The buildings loomed large in front of us. We rounded the corner of the nearest one and Missy slowed.

"There," she panted, coming to a stop.

I looked up from the pavement. In front of us a long train cut a line across the blacktop, through the gaps in between its cars, a sea of vehicles stretched out in the dark. There had to be thousands of them. Maybe more.

"Most of the train cars will be locked, but hopefully we'll be able to find one that's open," she said, taking off again at a run.

I followed. My legs shook. They felt like dead weight, like they hardly belonged to my body anymore.

"Look for one with an eagle on the side," Missy called back to me as she ran along the side of the train.

It was huge. So much bigger than I would have imagined. Each compartment must have been big enough to fit two-dozen cars stacked on top of each other. Each of the train cars looked almost identical, huge metal containers painted a rusty orange. Along the bottoms of some of the cars, someone had spray painted big, bubbly shapes. On the car nearest to me, there was an image of a skull, but nothing that looked like an eagle.

"None of these have eagles," I panted, coming to a stop next to Missy.

"It's still dark," she said. "Maybe we just didn't see it."

"What's wrong with these other ones?" I asked. There must have been hundreds of cars. Surely *one* of them would work.

"No." She shook her head. "They'll be locked. Someone told me to look for the one with the eagle. It's the only one that will be unlocked."

"Who told you that?"

"I don't have time to answer all your questions right now, Ella," she snapped. "I'm going to look on this side again. Maybe I missed it. You go check the other side."

I climbed over the metal posts that connected the cars and stared down the seemingly endless length of the train. It seemed impossible that humans could have built something so huge, yet here it was. And somehow Missy had known about it. How? How did she know that there would be an eagle?

I stopped, staring up at the huge doors on the back of one of the cars. Near the bottom, a metal padlock held them closed. I pulled on it, testing it, but Missy was right. It was locked tight.

I trudged more slowly now that Missy couldn't see me. The sky was definitely changing color now. The deep turquoise was shifting into purple and the edges of the horizon were tinged with gold. I didn't know what would happen if we didn't find the right train car before the sun came up, but I didn't want to find out.

Behind me, a pair of headlights cut across the gigantic parking lot and a moment later, the beams of light bounced across the train, slicing a golden path almost directly in front of me.

"Missy," I squeaked. Her name stuck in my throat. Should I duck underneath the train? Go back to the other side?

I ran faster, scanning the sides of the cars. She must have been wrong. There wasn't anything that looked like a bird. These marks were just wild scribblings. Maybe Missy and I were better off finding a hiding place. But if we were going to, we needed to go now, while there was still a bit of darkness to hide us.

I slowed down, ready to make my way between the train cars to the other side, when I saw it.

The eagle.

Chapter Four

Maybe I'd just been looking for the wrong thing. I'd imagined that it would be a bird with its wings outspread, but the image was more abstract, just the head of a bird, its regal beak and fierce stare were so simple, just a few quick strokes of white paint, so stark that it almost got lost amid the tangle of shapes painted around it. It was possible there had been others just like this and I'd walked right past.

I scrambled back over the huge metal latch to the other side. Missy had traveled much farther than I had—almost four train cars farther down. I called her name, hoping desperately the person in the car was still far enough away that they wouldn't hear me.

"Did you find it?" Missy panted, running up to me.

I nodded and brought my finger to my lips. "I think I found it," I whispered, "but there was a car that pulled up a minute ago. Maybe we should forget about this for now and just find some place to hide until tonight."

Missy peered between the cars. "I don't see a car," she said. "Maybe you just imagined it."

"I didn't—" I started to say before I cut myself off. We didn't have time to argue. "Never mind."

I headed back toward the car with the eagle on it, Missy trailing behind.

"It's this one," I whispered.

The two of us rounded the corner, coming to a stop at the base of the gigantic doors that bisected the entire back panel. Here too, there was a solid metal lock, latched to hold the doors securely closed, but where I'd seen a padlock on the other door, this one was empty.

Missy smiled, relieved. With two hands, she pulled on the metal latch and the large door to the right cracked open ever so slightly.

"Help me open this," Missy said.

Together, we pulled and the metal door groaned. Somewhere behind us, a car door slammed and the two of us froze. Missy's eyes widened.

"Hurry, get inside."

The door wasn't open wide, but there was enough room for someone small, like me or Missy, to fit through. The large metal post connecting the train cars was only a few feet off the ground, but to my tired muscles, it felt like ten feet. I heaved myself up, and collapsed through the doors with a thud, landing far too loudly against the metal floor. It was almost pitch black inside and I tried to scramble out of the way, but a second later Missy followed, landing on top of me.

"Quick, help me close this door," she hissed near my ear.

There wasn't a latch on the inside and our fingers scrambled to find something to hold onto to pull the door closed. Outside, the sound of voices drew near. The noisy sound of my own breathing and the scratch of my fingernails against the metal blurred out their words.

"Pull," Missy growled in my ear and the two of us tugged.

The door groaned shut again, blocking out all the light. Missy and I froze together in the darkness, listening for the sound of the voices to draw nearer. Her knee jabbed into my thigh, but I didn't move.

"…all but the last few containers are loaded." The voice sounded close. It couldn't be more than a few yards away.

"Steve's guys are supposed to finish loading in a couple hours," another voice said, moving in our direction.

"Just so long as they give me enough time to get 'em cleaned out first."

The two men kept talking and after a few minutes their voices faded away.

"Do you think they're coming back?" I asked.

"No," Missy said. It was too dark to see her face, but her voice sounded strong. Confident.

I scooted backward, crashing into something metal. A… car?

"Come on," Missy said. "We should go find a better place to hide. Just in case anybody decides to check on that door."

I heard Missy scuffle across the hard metal ground and I scrambled forward on my knees, trying to follow behind her. I got to my feet and stretched out my arms in front of me. My fingertips brushed the smooth metal of a car and I kept my hand there, dragging it along the surface as I stepped forward, one small step after another until I bumped into Missy.

I waited for her to scold me, but she didn't. "We'll just move back a little," she said. "Two or three cars in should be plenty."

I kept one hand on the side of the car and raised the

other to hold lightly onto Missy's shoulder. Together we inched our way forward. Underneath our feet, the metal floor rose and fell, shaped to cradle each of the cars. My fingers traced the outline of a window, a door handle, the sharp, jutted angle of a mirror. We stayed close to the car, tracing the line of the hood until its shape ended in darkness. Here the floor slanted up ever so slightly, the tiniest ramp that must have kept the car from crashing into the one in front of it.

Missy paused for just a moment before she stepped forward into the blind darkness. "Just a few steps until the next one," she reassured me.

A moment later my hand touched metal again. We scooted slowly forward, finally coming to a stop at the next car.

"Hopefully it's open," Missy said. "I don't want to spend ten hours sitting on the floor."

There was a small click and she sighed, relieved. "Come on," she said, pulling me inside the dark interior of the car.

Paper crinkled noisily underneath our feet, but the seat was soft and I let myself relax into it, resting my tired head against the back. I closed my eyes, the lids suddenly more heavy than they'd ever felt before.

A small tapping sounded at the car window and I sat up, turning toward the dark rectangle. But in the space where I thought there would only be darkness, every star in the whole sky suddenly shone down on me. My galaxy. My universe. My Penn. His beautiful smile illuminating the train. How could it be?

"Ella." He said my name and the next moment he was beside me. His strong arms encircled me, pulling me close to his heart. That heart, pounding so hard it felt as if it were beating in my own chest.

"I want to be with you," I said, pulling on his shirt. "I need to be closer. I can't bear for there to be any more space between us."

"I can't either," he said. "It's killing me, Ella."

I stared up into his face, into his dark eyes, their own mini galaxies. How had I never noticed before? His long hair fell in front of one of his eyes and I pushed it back. I wanted to stare into those eyes, lakes so deep I could swim in them forever.

I touched a strand of his hair, rubbing it between my fingers. That hair…why did it make me feel like I was supposed to remember something? Something important. But before I could think about it, his mouth was on mine and everything else slipped away. We were one breath. One heartbeat. One body. I moaned and the sound came from somewhere so deep inside me that it must have traveled miles to reach my ears. An eternity.

Penn.

I opened my mouth to say his name, but no sound fell from my lips.

Penn.

A screech of the train startled me and I gasped awake, clutching at the air in front of me as I sat up. Alone.

My arms empty.

I hadn't realized that I'd fallen asleep, but when my eyes blinked open quite a bit of time must have passed because the small holes that lined the walls now filtered in enough pale light to see by. It was still dim inside the train cars, but at least I could tell that Missy and I were sitting in the backseat of a medium-sized car. She was turned slightly away from me, with her head tipped back, in what I thought was sleep, but when I shifted in the seat, she raised her head.

My stomach let out a long growl and I covered it with my hand, embarrassed. I hadn't even thought about food. It would have been so easy to save a bit of each meal from the refugee center instead of leaving it all sitting on my plate like a sullen and ungrateful child. It didn't matter that I didn't like the food, at least it would have given me energy. Even the overly sweet breakfast cereals that they gave us each morning sounded appealing now.

Missy reached down and dug through her bag. "Here," she said, handing me a small bag of nuts. "It's going to have to last all day, so you might want to save some."

I tore open the corner of the bag and dumped a few salty peanuts into my palm. My stomach growled again, even louder this time, and Missy suppressed a laugh.

"Thank you," I said.

"It's nothing great." She shrugged. "But at least it has some protein."

I looked down at the bag in my hand. "I didn't mean these," I said. "I mean, I *do*, they're great and I was starving, but I meant…thank you for this. For coming."

It was probably naive to trust her. For all I knew, she could be leading me back to a trap. What if the congressman had hired her to find me and lead me back to him? There was nothing in this for her. No real reason to help me get back to Penn. She wasn't doing it out of the kindness of her heart, that was for sure. It wasn't her style. And it was pretty difficult to believe that she was helping me for a bigger cause. This was Missy—selfish, demanding, egotistical Missy.

But what other choice did I have?

Missy closed her eyes for a moment, unsmiling. "You're welcome," she finally said. "But for the record, I think it's stupid. I think *we're* stupid. Both of us. Obviously you are, for wanting to go back. And for a boy, no less. That's not a good reason. It's a dumb reason. You don't even know if he wants you back. And me…" She paused. "I'm stupid for taking you. There can't be a good outcome to this. I have this terrible feeling of impending doom, like I'm walking straight into a fire. I can practically feel it licking at my feet, but am I turning around? No. I just keep walking, even though it's probably going to get me killed."

The hairs on my arms prickled. It didn't seem like a good idea to be talking about death that way. If we were in one of Ruby's stories, saying something like that would be the surest way to end up dead. A curse.

"So, now what?" I asked, looking out the car window at the sides of the train car. The tiny holes that dotted the sides were only big enough to let in a coin-sized bit of light, beyond that, it was impossible to see anything that was going on outside.

Missy shrugged. "We wait," she said. "At some point the train will start moving and then we'll know that we're on our way."

"And then we just wait until it stops?"

Missy nodded.

"And then what?"

She sighed and stared up at the ceiling. "We backtrack."

"What does that mean?"

"It means we go back to the place I just barely got away from." Her face looked pained.

"But you said you got here through the black market."

"Yeah."

It was only one word, but it spoke volumes, telling me that I was the dumbest person she'd ever met.

"Isn't it dangerous?"

"What other choice do we have?" Missy asked. "You want to try calling your boyfriend and ask him to come pick us up? Because something tells me that's not such a good idea."

"I didn't—"

"Look, the black market isn't ideal. Yes, it's dangerous, but at least I've been there before. I know every greasy, dirty, dingy corner of it. It isn't fun and it isn't pretty, but we'll have a place to stay. We'll have some food to eat and a way to make a little money of our own. And best of all, we'll have a way to hide you."

"Hide? I thought people bought pets on the black market. How are we supposed to hide when people go there looking specifically for pets?"

Missy's grin widened. "That's it exactly," she said. "We'll hide you in plain sight. No one's going to think to look for you there. They'll expect you to be safe inside Canada, or hidden away with a group of Liberationists."

Somewhere behind us, there was the loud clang of metal hitting metal and Missy and I ducked, cowering down in our seats. My heart clamored, like those same huge chunks of metal were being struck together inside me, reverberating through the rest of my body.

"Is someone coming?" I whispered.

Missy poked her head up above the seat, glancing back toward the big doors we'd snuck in through. "The doors are still closed," she said.

From the front of the train, a whistle blew. The sound

was enormous, blaring, filling the space around us. If sound had been a color, it would have been a shock of red, lighting me from the inside. It still rang in my ears. But before I could prepare myself, the train lurched beneath us, jerking us back in our seats as we began to move. The wheels squealed and the metal frame of the train car groaned as we picked up speed.

Missy's face looked almost as alarmed as mine, but after a moment she relaxed. "Get comfortable," she said. "We've still got a few hours until we get there."

"And where is there, exactly?"

"Buffalo," Missy said.

The name didn't sound familiar. "That's in the United States?"

She nodded. "Say good-bye to freedom. A couple more hours and you'll be the property of Congressman Kimble again."

The train swayed underneath me. Maybe this was how I was going to feel from now on, as if steady ground was forever rushing past my feet, nothing solid to stand on.

The train moved forward, pulling us along. The wheels continued churning beneath us and after a while the steady and subtle rocking lulled me a bit. Missy was silent next to me, but the car was filled with noises, the *clicks* and *whirs* and *clangs* of movement, and every once in a while the whistle cut through it all, as if to remind us it was in charge of all this.

Time hung suspended, rocking on its hinges. We could have been inside the train for an hour, or a week, or a year, I couldn't tell. Without conversation, there was nothing to punctuate the time except for the occasional wail of the horn and the sense of moving forward toward some scary future that I both dreaded and longed for.

"Missy," I finally said, breaking the silence within our tiny vehicle. "Tell me about the black market."

She sighed and stayed quiet, shifting slightly in her seat, but I couldn't tell if she was getting ready to speak, or if she was actively ignoring me.

"What do you want to know?" she finally asked.

"It's just a big scary blob in my mind. I don't even know what questions *to* ask."

"Yeah, well, it's kind of a big scary blob in real life, too," she said. "Not really. I'm making it sound worse than it is." She fiddled with her fingernails, pulling at the small hangnails on her thumb. "It's hard to explain, because each one is a little bit different. At least that's what I've seen. The market in Buffalo is small, but there are quite a few free agents there."

"Free agents?"

"It means they don't have owners, but they still choose to stay on the black market. Some people just can't get used to the idea of being in charge of their own life. They need someone else in charge."

"I don't understand."

"It's a way for them to make money. It gives them a place to stay and a network of people. It sounds screwed up, but I guess it's the closest thing to a family that they'll ever get, you know?"

I nodded, even though I didn't really understand.

"But free agents aren't the norm. Most markets are there to sell pets to families. Or at least that's what they claim. The buyer's credentials aren't as high as they had to be with the kennels. There aren't any background checks. It's all about the money. The highest bidder gets the girl."

"But you were in the black market and you ended up in a decent home the second time." I'd met her previous family. They were pretentious and vain, but they had treated her well.

She lifted her chin. "I was one of the lucky ones."

"But what if someone wants to buy us, someone from a bad home. How will we know?"

"No one's going to buy us," Missy assured me. "We're going in as free agents. We make our own terms."

"But—"

"Don't worry. I know what I'm doing."

I wanted to trust her. If anyone could get us back to Penn, she was my best bet. But even though Missy was confident and strong, I still didn't trust her entirely.

The inside of the car had started off cool that morning, but over the hours it had grown hotter and hotter. By the time the train finally ground to a halt, the metal train car felt like an oven.

As soon as we were certain that the train had stopped for good, we cracked the door, gulping down deep breaths of fresh air.

Missy hitched her backpack up. "We're going to have to make a run for it," she said. "Follow me, okay? Even if someone spots you, don't stop."

Outside, the train yard was quiet.

"Can't we just wait until everyone leaves for the night?"

"The train isn't staying here. We don't have very long." She pushed the door open a little wider and swung her legs out, hopping down onto the gravel with a crunch. I squinted, trying to get my eyes to start working again, but the world was too big and too bright. I followed after Missy, stumbling a little as I jumped. My hands and knees hit the gravel at the same time.

"*Run*," Missy hissed at me, breaking into a run across the tracks.

I stumbled to my feet.

"Hey! Hey you, girls! Stop right there!"

I turned. We were parked next to another train and on the other side of it, a man in a dark blue jacket and a red baseball cap waved his arms at me.

My legs felt like stumps, too big, too blocky to actually move. They were still so sore from walking so long the night before and now the muscles not only felt tired, but cramped from sitting still for so many hours. I couldn't possibly run after Missy. I turned my head away from the screaming man and forced my body to follow her. Already she'd scrambled across two sets of train tracks and was making her way toward a dark wall of trees on the other side of the yard.

"Wait right there," the man called after me. "You're trespassing!"

Trespassing? If he caught me he would turn me into the police. And if the police found me, I'd be back at the congressman's house before I knew it. But not of my own volition. I'd be a prisoner again. And that wasn't how I'd planned this to go.

My arms pumped at my sides as I leaped between the tracks. My foot caught on one of the rails and I fell, catching myself on my hands again, but it only took a second for me to get to my feet.

Missy reached the trees and turned around. "Come on, come on!"

I crashed headlong into the woods. Trees slapped at my face and arms, grabbed out for my legs like they were trying to pull me down.

"This way!" Missy grabbed me by the elbow and pulled me down a small embankment. The dead leaves slipped beneath my feet, and I slid, grabbing onto thin trunks and branches. A few times I slid all the way down, but I was back on my feet in seconds. In front of us, a large outcropping of rocks jutted up out of the undergrowth and we dove for them, pressing our bodies into the damp earth.

My chest shuddered as I gasped for breath. Missy slid her hand over my mouth and held it there, listening. Her own breath was ragged next to my ear.

After a minute she peeked up over the rock.

"What did he say?" she asked, finally taking her hand from in front of my mouth and wiping her palm against her pants.

"Wait…he just said wait," I panted. "He said we were trespassing."

Missy rolled her eyes. "Well, no kidding." She shook her head. "I didn't even see him there. He must have been behind the other train when I looked."

"Do you think he'll call someone? The police? Do you think he recognized us?"

Missy stood back up, brushing the dirt and leaves from off her tights. "Nah, he was just some dumb railroad worker. He's not going to bother."

I sat a moment longer and rested my head in my hands. My body was still shaking. All of it. Even muscles I didn't know existed were cramped and trembling.

"Come on. It's time to get up," Missy ordered. "We can't just waste time sitting around in the woods."

I took a deep breath and stared up past the branches toward the bright blue sky above me. Why couldn't we just stay here a little bit longer? Rest. Breathe. The air was crisp and full of the loamy smell of life, so much nicer than the stale air inside the train. It reminded me of Penn's garden. I wished I could bottle it, take this perfume with me because something told me that the place we were headed wouldn't be anywhere near as nice as this.

The woods weren't wide, only a small stretch that separated the railroad from the rest of the town. We followed the cover of the trees as long as we could, but after a while they gave way to buildings and we moved out onto the sidewalk. The streets were lined with old brick buildings. A few had signs in the windows, but it was hard to tell whether they were open anymore or whether the signs were left over from years ago when it had actually been busy. Clearly, this wasn't the best part of town.

A car drove past and I stepped closer to Missy.

"Stop it," she snapped. "You can't cower at everything. It draws attention. You have to act like you're supposed to be here."

I scooted away.

"There it is." She stopped and jutted her chin toward the red brick building in front of us.

"That's it?" I didn't mean to sound so surprised, but it didn't look at all like what I was expecting. I had imagined a dark building underground. I imagined tunnels. But this just looked so…ordinary. It didn't look any different from the other buildings around it: a three story, red brick building with a few boarded up windows on the top floor and a bit of old peeling paint that must have advertised some old store that closed up years and years ago.

"What did you expect? A big sign with your face on it?" Missy laughed at her own joke. "It's a black market. You're not supposed to know it's here."

Missy turned to face me. She frowned, obviously not impressed with what she saw. "Don't say anything when we get in there," she said. She licked her finger and drew it underneath my eyes, rubbing in the makeup that must have smudged my skin. She raked a few fingers through my hair and sighed. "And wipe that stupid deer-in-the-headlights look off your face. It's just screaming for someone to take advantage of you."

I clenched my jaw, trying to fake a tough look as well as I knew how.

I followed Missy past the front door and paused, waiting for her to enter, but she kept walking, rounding the building to a side alley.

"Nobody uses the front door," she said, climbing the steps to a small blue door on the side. Further down the alley, a big white truck was backed up against the dock of the building. Was it loading something? Girls?

The blue door squeaked open and I followed Missy inside a dark hallway.

"Stay behind me," she ordered.

Look tough, I told myself, stepping behind her. I raised my chin even though it felt so much more natural to cast my eyes down to the ground. I was good at being meek and submissive. It's what I'd been trained to do. How was I supposed to rewire sixteen years of training?

Missy stopped at the third door. She paused and for a second her hand fluttered to her stomach. It was a small motion, but I saw the fear in it.

She would never want me to notice this small gesture of weakness, but I did.

With a slow, deep breath, Missy knocked on the door.

Chapter Five

"Door's open," a man's voice called from inside.

Missy squared her shoulders and turned the handle.

The room was small. A man sat behind a big wooden desk picking at his teeth with a letter opener. He wasn't a huge man, but his sharp features and jet-black hair made him appear to take up more room than he really did.

He looked up when we walked in. "Ahh." He smiled, showing long white teeth. "Look what the cat dragged back in."

Missy stepped one foot into the room. "Sorry to intrude, Tony," she said.

"No worries," he said, leaning back in his chair and putting his feet up on his desk. "I'm always happy to see your pretty face, doll."

Missy turned slightly and grabbed me by the elbow, pulling me forward.

A smile cut across the man's face. "And she comes bearing gifts..."

"We just need work for a day or two," Missy said. "A couple gigs."

His eyes traveled down the length of me. "I don't remember you. Have we had you on the Buffalo books before?" he asked.

I opened my mouth, unsure how to answer. I turned to Missy.

"She hasn't been here," she answered curtly.

"But you have papers?"

Missy swallowed. "No."

The smile slipped from his face. "Then I can't use her. No papers saying she's free, no gig. But you're welcome to stay. I've got a job you'll be perfect for tonight."

"If I stay, she can stay with me," Missy said, "right?"

He frowned and he uncrossed his feet, lowering them slowly to the ground before he leaned forward on his elbows. "You get some papers for her and she can stay."

Missy shook her head. "I told you, she doesn't have any."

"Then I guess you've answered your own question," he said. "We aren't in the business of housing and feeding homeless pets here. I'm not a member of the humane society."

"What if I work two gigs?" Missy said quickly. "I can do back-to-backs."

He cocked his head, considering. The calculating look in his eyes left a sour taste in my mouth.

"Let's leave," I said. "We don't need any of his work. I'm sure there's— "

"I'll give you a hundred percent on the second one," Missy said, shoving me behind her. "I won't take a penny. And you won't even know she's here. That's a damn good deal. You know it is."

I gasped. "Missy!"

She ignored me, staring sharply at Tony. He tapped his fingers together, considering her offer.

Finally, he said, "All right. But don't you tell anyone. I'm not a charity. Got it?"

Missy nodded, her shoulders trembling ever so slightly.

"Go ahead and head upstairs," he said. "There's a couple girls up there. They'll get you set up."

Missy pushed me back into the hallway, obviously in a hurry to get out of there before he changed his mind.

"And doll," he called after her, "you might want to rest up. You've got a long night ahead of you."

Missy closed the door with a *click* and leaned against it, letting her head fall back for just a moment. Her hand shook against the doorknob, but by the time she straightened her back, her body was stiff and strong again.

"We don't have to stay," I said. "You shouldn't have to—"

She raised a hand. "Don't. Just…don't."

At the end of the hallway she paused. To the right was the staircase that led up to the second floor. To the left, the corridor turned, leading to another long and narrow hallway. At the end of it was a single gray door, shut tight. It looked just like all the other doors, but something about the way Missy glanced at it told me that it was different.

"What's back there?" I asked.

Missy turned away from it and started up the stairs. "Those are just a few workrooms," she said. "But don't worry, you don't have to deal with any of that. Remember, no papers?"

My heart sank into my feet. I hated that she'd have to work harder because of me. Hated that I couldn't help when it was *my* fault we left Canada in the first place. Well,

I wouldn't let her carry our whole load. I'd just have to find another way to be useful.

She stopped at the top of the stairs. The room we'd entered was big, running the whole length of the front of the building. Four giant windows that would have looked out onto the street below were each covered with a dark colored sheet. A bit of light seeped around the edges, casting the room in an eerie, almost twilight, haze. Just below the windows, the floor was strewn with futons and pillows, a nest of bedding that looked both messy and perfectly wonderful after the long cramped ride that Missy and I had just endured. My stiff body ached to stretch out across the pillows and fall asleep.

When we walked in, the few girls who sat scattered underneath the windows, talking quietly to each other, turned to stare. It was obvious that they were all pets, although some appeared to be in better shape than others. A few of them looked like they weren't much older than me. What had they done to end up here? Had they run away like Missy, or had their masters grown tired of them?

One girl, who had been filing her fingernails on the far side of the room, stood and walked over to us. She was older than the rest. Time had settled over her in layers, padding the skin around her waist and upper arms.

"You're back," she said, stopping a few feet from us and folding her arms across her chest.

It was a defensive pose. Had Missy done something to make this girl dislike her? Considering it was Missy, this didn't seem too unlikely.

Missy moved right past her, leading me deeper into the room. "Hi Julia, it's good to see you, too."

Julia didn't look amused.

"I didn't plan on coming back," Missy said. "I've had an unexpected hitch in my plan."

It was obvious to me, if not to everyone else, that she meant me. I was the hitch.

"Don't worry," Missy said, stopping at a large rack of dresses that spanned the wall. "We don't plan on staying. You only have to put up with me for a day or two."

Julia's face softened a bit, obviously relieved.

Missy raked her hand through the wall of gowns. The sight of them made my stomach flip. They weren't exactly like the gowns that I'd worn at the congressman's house. Those had been sewn from fabrics in soft pinks and corals. These were brighter: reds and fuchsias and deep jewel greens. These dresses weren't quiet or well-mannered. They screamed. They flaunted. They were meant to turn the girl who wore them into a showpiece.

But none of the girls in the room were wearing gowns now.

"So, she's another free agent then?" Julia asked, nodding her head in my direction. "That'll make nine of us. That's kind of a lot for such a small market, don't you think? I don't know if Stan has that many jobs for us. That means we'll be—"

"She's not doing any jobs," Missy interrupted.

It was an odd thing to say, caged and vague. Why not just come out and tell them that I didn't have any papers? But her answer satisfied them.

We stood in uncomfortable silence for a moment. All those eyes searching my face, trying to map out my story there.

Finally Missy spoke. "This is Gigi," she said, catching my eye before she pushed me forward a little bit.

I smiled cautiously.

"She's going to lie low for a day or two," she went on. "Her old master died in a car crash a few weeks ago and his wife tried to dump her at the border, which didn't go well with the tightened security. Luckily, I ran into her. For now I'm going to show her the ropes so she doesn't get taken advantage of."

The lie rolled off of her tongue like she'd rehearsed it.

So that explained it. We couldn't trust anyone. Maybe it was naive faith in our similarities that made me want to trust them. I wanted to believe that we were all sisters. We could help carry each other's burdens. But maybe that wasn't the case. Maybe we each needed to look out for ourselves. Missy must have thought so.

"Are you still going to try to cross?"

"No." Missy shook her head. "It's impossible."

Julia nodded like she understood, but a small glimmer of disappointment flashed across her features.

"I think we're going to head back to one of the big markets," Missy explained. "Maybe we'll work there for a little bit, save up."

"Well, you both look like disasters," Julia said after a moment. As she drew closer to me, a strong floral smell drifted off of her. "Why don't you go back to the showers? I'll see if I can round you up a little something to eat."

The showers were at the back of the building. They were dingy and small, half a dozen stalls lined in a row. But they were stocked with soap and the water ran strong and hot.

As soon as the water was on, Missy drew the curtain and stepped in beside me.

"Don't trust anyone," she whispered. "Don't tell them who you really are."

"I won't."

"You have to promise."

I swallowed. "I do. I promise."

"Good." She smiled and let her head fall back into the hot stream of water, closing her eyes as the water washed away the dirt and makeup that had streaked her face.

After we were scrubbed clean and changed into clean clothes, Missy and I found a place on a few lumpy pillows near one of the windows. Julia had cobbled together a meal for each of us: an apple, half a granola bar, a cup of dried cereal.

We devoured the food, gnawing the apples down to the seeds and picking every last crumb of cereal off of the bottom of the bowl. I knew I should try to make it last, but I was starving.

The sun moved further west and the room grew darker. With the shift in light, the girls grew antsy. Legs uncrossed and then crossed again. Hands jumped from neck, to arm, to hair, moving to tangle strands in loops around fingers.

When two pairs of footsteps beat their way up the stairs, the girls froze. It reminded me of the game that Ruby had begged me to play with her over and over again, freeze tag. It seemed so strange to think that only a couple weeks ago I'd played it with her on the back lawn. She would run in circles on the grass, jumping and twirling until I yelled freeze and she would halt, trying not to fall while giggling over whatever silly position she had stopped in.

But these girls were not giggling.

The man who stepped into the room was the same one I met earlier, only now that he wasn't sitting behind his desk, the height of him appeared to have quadrupled.

Behind him, a pet followed, carrying a large, steaming pot.

"Good evening, gals. I'm glad to see you're keeping yourselves busy." He snorted a little as if he'd just told himself a little joke that only he understood.

From his back pocket he pulled a folded sheet of paper. "Let's see what we've got on the docket," he said. "I've got two potential buyers coming in. One is flying in from Ohio and the other is from upstate, I believe. Both seem pretty serious, so I want everyone out on thc showroom floor tonight."

There was a slight shifting around me as the energy in the room changed, but I couldn't tell if it was excitement or apprehension that made the air buzz and flex.

"On second thought…" He paused and looked around the room as if he were taking inventory. "You." He snapped his fingers, pointing to a pale blond girl in the corner. "You, you, and you." He pointed to a few other girls scattered throughout the room. "I want the rest of you to stay here. You still need to be presentable, but I'll only call you down if I need you. Got it?"

They nodded.

"Good." He shook out his paper again. "And it looks like a busy night for the rest of you, too. Some of you are double booked." He looked directly at Missy. His eyes were steely and unforgiving, as if challenging her not to follow through on her word. "We've got clients showing up at nine, so make sure you're down on the floor fifteen minutes early. I won't tolerate tardiness."

Around me heads nodded in agreement.

"All right. Line up for dinner," he snapped, and the group jumped to their feet.

The soup rumbled and gurgled in my stomach as I sat back and watched the girls get ready for the evening. Missy pulled an emerald green gown down from the giant rack of dresses and slipped it over her head before she plopped down in front of me.

"Zip me up."

I tugged on the zipper and the corseted bodice cinched in her already small waist. With her hair washed and combed out, she looked almost exactly the same as she had the day I first met her.

"Where will you go?" I asked. "What sort of jobs do they send you on?"

She turned to face me with a sour expression. "Don't worry about it," she said.

"I'm not worried. I only want— "

"Just remember what I told you in the shower earlier and let me deal with this." She motioned to the gown as if it was so much more than just a dress, as if inside the yards of fabric someone had woven together a dense tangle of ideas.

No one talked as they dressed. Instead, the room was filled with the quiet whispering of so many dresses swooshing past one another as the girls moved from wardrobe to mirror to vanity.

Tony stalked the room as the girls finished getting ready. One by one, they lined up against the wall for final approval.

"This dress is wrong. Go change," he ordered the girl at the front of the line before he continued down the row, pointing out flaws, the frown lines on his face growing deeper, as if these girls were purposely offending him.

He stopped in front of a girl wearing a short black dress and his eyes narrowed. The girl folded in on herself, visually shrinking in front of Tony's gaze.

"Look up at me," he huffed, jabbing a thick finger under the girl's chin and cranking her head up so that their eyes met.

The other girls shifted on their feet, as if they sensed a storm coming. I could feel it too, like lightning building, and I wished I could make myself smaller, wished I could disappear inside the pile of pillows.

"What's this?" he asked, pointing to the girl's face. "Who did your makeup?"

Even though she was across the room, I could hear the girl swallow, could hear her shallow breathing quicken.

"I did," she squeaked.

"Did I say you could do it by yourself?" Tony asked. "I can't send you out like this! You aren't a bunch of meth-addict whores! Is that what you want people to think? You want people to think you're cheap? You want us to lose all our business? Answer me!"

"No."

"It's no, *sir*. Got it? You won't be doing any jobs tonight," he said. "And no jobs means no privileges."

A tear slipped down the girl's red cheek, bringing a trail of dark makeup with it.

"The rest of you get out of my sight," he ordered, turning toward the stairs with disdain.

The room stayed heavy with silence. For a long moment

nothing stirred. Finally, they took a collective breath, a mass of girls drawing strength together as they moved to follow him.

I could tell, just from looking at them, which girls were going down to meet their potential new owners. It wasn't that they'd dressed any differently from the others. They all wore gowns. They all looked polished and expensive. But there was a fever that flashed in some of their eyes that had nothing to do with what they'd just witnessed.

I didn't need to be told why. While some of these girls would leave for the night to go do some untold job—a job that I couldn't begin to guess at—they knew they would return a few hours later. They would come back to this room and although it was dingy and stale, with brick walls that they were probably tired of staring at day after day, at least it was familiar.

At least they knew what to expect. For the other girls, who knew? The room that they were headed off to could contain anything.

The procession of them glided down the stairs, each one as light and graceful on her feet as if one of their own trainers had been leading them.

The rest of the girls who had been told to stay behind hovered at the top of the stairs. When the last of the girls had disappeared down the hallway below, they turned to face me. Even though there was space to seat fifty girls, I was suddenly worried that I was taking up too much space, or worse, sitting in one of their spots. I felt like an intruder. An imposter.

But it was like they didn't even see me as, one by one, they sank back down onto their stiff pillows. The girl who had gotten in trouble for doing her own makeup sat down a few feet from me, clasping her trembling hands in her lap.

A minute later she glanced up, suddenly noticing me. "Why aren't you dressed?"

"They told me not to."

"Are you sure?" she asked, glancing back toward the stairs as if she expected the man to come charging back up for me any second.

I nodded.

"Because you don't want to upset him."

That was pretty clear. They'd treated us sternly at the kennels. I knew a reprimand when I heard it.

She licked her dry lips. "I'm Kat, by the way," she said, sticking her hand out to clasp mine.

For a moment I hesitated, trying to remember the name that Ella had made up for me. "I'm Gigi."

"I know," she said, and her face softened with a small smile. "Missy told us, remember?"

I was surprised that they knew Missy's real name. Why had she felt compelled to lie about mine when she'd been honest with her own?

"Is Gigi your only name?"

I opened my mouth and then closed it again, stunned. Did she know?

"Kat is my first name," she went on, when I didn't answer. "I've had two owners, but the second one only kept me for a year. They called me Vera." She wrinkled her nose. "I never liked it much. Kat seems like a much nicer name and it suits me better, don't you think?"

She seemed so guileless, so open, that for a moment I felt almost guilty keeping my own name from her. What would it really hurt to tell these girls who I really was?

"I only had one owner," I admitted. There couldn't be

any harm in sharing such a simple fact about myself. Missy couldn't object to that, could she? And besides, it felt good to give a tiny piece of myself, even if that's all it was.

"You're lucky..." Kat said, "...that she didn't bring you here first, I mean. Most of them want to make some of their money back. That's all they're worried about. But it sounds like she was just happy to be rid of you."

"Yes, she certainly never wanted me around. Even from the beginning."

"Julia says it's better to be a free agent," she said. "But I'm not sure."

"So all those other girls are free agents?"

Kat shook her head. "Not all of them. Some belong to Tony."

"Do you belong to Tony?" I was trying to keep everything straight.

"Yes," she said, "but they've been here longer. Tony has a lot of permanent clients. Some come here to buy pets to keep, but others don't want that big of a commitment. If he can't find a home for a pet within the first six months, then he moves her to the temporary jobs, like the free agents. We're too expensive to keep on if we're not bringing in any money."

"What temporary jobs?"

She shrugged. "Just jobs."

"Like what?"

"Oh, I don't know. Like to go to parties and stuff. Most people can't afford a pet of their own, but they want their friends to think that they can, so they rent one."

Going to parties? That's what Missy wouldn't tell me?

"What else?"

Kat's face brightened a little. "There's this old man that

comes in a few times a week just to dance with one of us. He's really old and Julia complains that he smells like mothballs and urine, but I think he sounds sweet. His wife died a few years ago and he really misses her. They used to be ballroom dancers when they were younger. So now he rents out one of the rooms for an hour or so just to dance."

"That *does* sound sweet."

"Yeah," she said, smiling. "So they aren't *all* bad."

"What do you mean?"

The smile fell from Kat's face. "Oh...it's nothing."

"Are some of them bad? You can tell me."

She looked down at her hands, picking nervously at her nails, and her face darkened with unease. "We aren't supposed to talk about it. I shouldn't have said anything."

"But someone must have told you," I pressed.

"No. It's nothing. You probably just misunderstood me," she said. "All I meant to say was that if I don't end up getting sold, maybe I can be the one that dances with that old man. That was my main talent."

She continued to stare into her lap, refusing to meet my eyes. So that was it? She wouldn't tell me either.

"Do you want to get sold?" I asked, not wanting the silence to consume us.

She raised her eyes again, smiling softly. Was she relieved that I'd changed the subject?

"Some girls say it's dangerous to be in the market for a permanent home since we can't control who buys us next, but I don't know. The kennels didn't do a perfect job either. We all ended up here, didn't we? Maybe I'll be lucky this time." Her voice broke and she turned away.

I placed my hand on her shoulder. The tenderness in this small touch surprised us both. "I'm sorry," I said, pulling my hand away.

She shook her head. "I don't mind," she said, bunching up her skirts and scooting a little closer. "It feels nice sometimes. Just to know we aren't alone."

We hadn't been allowed to share affection with each other like this when we'd been in the kennels. They'd been afraid that we'd grow too attached to one another, that the separation once we'd been placed in our new homes would be too difficult for us, so they wouldn't allow friendships to grow between us. In the kennels we were equals. But we weren't friends.

Things were different outside the kennels. Take away the cold white walls that separated us, and it blossomed so easily, this affection, this want to be held, to be loved.

Kat lowered her head down on my shoulder. "I'm just going to close my eyes for a minute," she said.

It didn't take long for her breathing to slow. Her head grew heavy, dropping lower on my arm. The warmth of her body, so close to mine, opened an ache inside of me. The pain was deep, wedged between my ribs. It felt like it was breaking me open, trying to push its way out of me. I knew what it meant to be held. I knew it. I'd claw my way across five hundred miles for the chance to feel the weight of Penn's arms around my shoulders. Ruby's adorable head in my lap.

I glanced down at Kat, at the sweet, trusting smile on her lips that twitched while she dreamed. For the past week, all I'd thought of was finding my way back to Penn while innocent girls like Kat dreamed of having any future at all.

When had I become so selfish?

Chapter Six

Outside it grew dark.

Across the room, the other girls looked like they had fallen asleep, too. Gently, I lowered Kat's head down onto one of the pillows beside me.

Missy told me to be careful who I talked to, but she hadn't said anything about staying put. She might not trust me enough to be able to handle one of these stupid jobs, but she couldn't expect me to just sit here doing nothing. If I wanted to be useful, I'd have to leave this room.

The stairs creaked softly beneath my feet as I made my way down to the first floor. It was probably safer to poke around on the second level. It would certainly be easier to come up with an excuse if somebody caught me, but I also knew there wouldn't be anything worth finding up there.

I needed something valuable to add to my meager collection of belongings. I'd pull my weight any way that I could and if stealing was the only way, fine.

I paused at the bottom of the stairs. The corridor in front of me was dark, even though a bit of light spilled out from underneath half of the doors that lined it. Those were the workrooms. Missy had said so. My curiosity pulled me toward them. I wanted to know what was going on behind those doors, but I didn't have time for it. Not yet. If Tony had anything valuable, it wouldn't be in one of those rooms.

I turned left down the dark hallway. There was no light on in the office that Missy and I had visited earlier. I paused in front of the door and pushed my ear up against it. At the refugee center, I'd been surprised to learn how well you could tell if a room was occupied. Even whispers carried.

But there was nothing. No talking. No whispers. No soft shuffle of bodies. I tried the handle, half expecting the door to be locked, but it twisted beneath my hand and I slipped in, closing it quietly behind me.

My eyes adjusted to the dark. There was only one small window on the wall behind the desk, but I knew better than to turn on a light. I moved quickly and quietly across the room. Already my body was learning the tricks of this new talent: breath control, like singing; balance, like ballet; the fine art of observation, like drawing; and most importantly, nimble fingers, just like playing the piano. I smiled to myself. Who could have guessed that for all those years, our trainers had actually been cultivating thieves? Pets. The perfect little stealing machines.

The desk was cluttered with junk: papers and old soda cups, sticky notes and grainy photocopies. An ashtray overflowed with old cigarettes, and the remains of a half-eaten sandwich dried in the middle of an open notebook. I scanned the items, pocketing one of the many ballpoint pens that littered the desk.

Somewhere, not too far off, a man laughed. My heart quickened, reminding me that I didn't have time to be picky.

My eyes traveled down to the desk drawer. Is that where Tony kept his secrets? I tugged at the handle and it jerked open a few inches. Even in the dim light, I could see the shiny barrel of the gun. I'd never seen a real one before, but I'd seen enough of them on the Kimbles' television shows to recognize it. The bad guys always had them, didn't they? Even in real life.

I slid the drawer shut, wishing I'd never seen it. This wasn't the sort of thing I'd wanted to find.

I pulled the pen back out of my pocket and left it on the desk. I didn't want to take anything from this room. I just wanted to leave.

Back at the stairway I paused. Light still shone out from under the doors of a few workrooms, beckoning me.

I stopped at the first door and placed my ear against the wood. The muffled hum of voices buzzed back, but the words were too quiet to understand. If I could just make out a sentence or two… I held my breath, listening. My hands twitched at my sides. I could just crack the door a little bit, peek inside.

I twisted the handle. Ever so gradually, it turned beneath my hand. I knew how to do this. I would be so delicate with it that no one would ever even see it moving. Bit by bit the handle turned and after a minute I pushed the door forward ever so slightly, just enough to peer through the slit.

The room wasn't huge, just a small box no bigger than the rooms we'd grown up in. But the furnishings weren't anything like the ones at the kennel. The walls were a deep crimson red almost the same color as the thick Persian rug that lined the floor. In the middle of the room there was a bed mounded with expensive looking pillows. On it, a girl reclined. She wore only a silk scarf, draped delicately across her body. My face flushed as my gaze traveled over her, not because I'd never seen another pet undressed before, but because someone must be paying to see her this way.

The slit in the door was only big enough to see part of the room. Ever so slightly, I eased it further open. A chair came into view. On it, a man sat bent over a large sketchbook. His hand moved frantically, like it couldn't get the graphite down onto the paper fast enough.

"Move your chin to the right," he said. "Not that much. Good. Right there."

I stepped back, pulling the door shut.

One of the jobs was posing for drawings? We used to pose for each other back at the training center. Not with our clothes off, but I'd seen pictures of classical art. This wasn't anything new. Was Missy really so worried that I wouldn't be able to handle posing nude?

Kat was still asleep when I collapsed down next to her.

All I could think about was the gun. I could imagine the cold weight of it in my hand as I pulled it from the drawer. There was nothing stopping me from going back for it. I wanted it, more than any of the other things I'd ever stolen, but it frightened me too much.

After a while there was the soft shuffle of feet and the creak of stairs. Kat opened her eyes, rubbing them as she scanned the group that trailed into the room.

"They took Lacie?" she asked, sitting up. On the side of

her face there was a red crease from one of the cushions. It reminded me of the way Ruby used to wake in the morning with lines from her pillow creased across her cheeks.

The girls moved slowly to the wardrobe, helping each other climb out of their dresses. I could tell that they wanted to leave them there, wadded on the floor, but they were too accustomed to being responsible and so they lifted them, smoothing out the wrinkles before they hung them back on the rack for next time.

"Which one was it?" Kat asked.

"The man from Ohio," one of the girls answered, clearly understanding what Kat meant.

"Did he look nice?"

They looked at one another like they were trying to come to a consensus. Finally they all gave a small shrug. Maybe they were deciding to be positive. Or maybe they couldn't come to a conclusion at all.

"Was it bad?" Kat asked. She stood and shed her own dress, too.

"Do you remember last week, when that man with the black hat came?" one of the girls asked. "Remember how he made us open our mouths so he could check all of our teeth?"

"Yes," Kat said. "He wore those rubber gloves."

"This was like that," the girl said. She pulled on a pair of pants and a long-sleeved shirt and curled back up on a pile of pillows across from me. "It took a long time. He was very thorough."

"And the other man?"

"He didn't stay long," the girl said. "I guess he didn't see anything he liked."

We all sat for a long time in silence. Their faces were blank, but mine probably was, too. We didn't wear our emotions on our faces. Maybe they were trying as hard as I was to block out things that they'd seen, things that they'd done.

"Maybe *none* of us will get sold again," someone said quietly after a while.

Next to me Kat sighed. "Maybe," she echoed.

I fought to stay awake, but my eyelids were too heavy. The weariness from the past few weeks draped over me like a blanket. Thick. Suffocating. Each time I closed my eyes, I saw the glint of the gun barrel in Tony's drawer. Maybe it had been a mistake to leave it there.

I had no idea what time it was, but Missy still hadn't returned. Somewhere, she was doing a job as a free agent.

She could sing. I hoped that's what she had been asked to do. I pictured her, in her bright green gown, up on a stage with soft lights twinkling down on her. Behind her, a band would play and she would open her mouth and the words would pour out of her, clean and pure.

When I woke, Missy was standing over me. In the dim morning light that leaked past the sheets that covered the windows I could see that she still wore her green gown, but her hair was mussed and there were dark circles under her eyes.

I moved, sitting up stiffly. My back ached from lying in such a peculiar position for so long.

Sometime during the night, the other free agents had come in and gotten undressed, although I hadn't heard any of it. Missy must have been the last one. Two jobs. I guess that meant that she'd been out working all night long.

"Help me unzip," she whispered, turning around.

As soon as I'd freed her from the dress, she kicked it into a pile on the floor and collapsed onto the cushions beside me. She didn't bother to hang it back up. She didn't bother to slip back into her regular clothes. She simply tucked her arms beneath her head and closed her eyes and before I knew it she was asleep.

I scooted closer. It felt strange to stare at Missy while she slept, but I couldn't look away. She was different asleep. The mask that she wore during the day slipped away. Without the sassiness and bravado, she looked so much more vulnerable. She looked small.

I studied her face, wanting to find some clue there about where she'd been tonight, but it was blank, wiped clean.

One by one, the other girls awoke and by the time Tony brought up a pot of oatmeal for breakfast, Missy was just beginning to stir.

I grabbed a bowl and sat back down at her feet.

"You aren't going to get me some," she groaned, rolling onto her back.

She was still only dressed in her undergarments.

"Do you want to get dressed first?"

She glanced down at herself as if she'd forgotten what she was wearing and shrugged, rubbing at her eyes.

I handed over the food I'd just gotten for myself and she grabbed the bowl without so much as a thank you, shoveling a spoonful into her mouth. "I'm starving," she said.

"I see that."

"We've got to get out of here," Missy said. "Tony is driving to New York this morning to pick up two new girls that another market doesn't need anymore and he said he'd give us a ride."

"But we just got here."

"This is good," Missy said. She sounded annoyed. "You know, you could stand to be a little bit more grateful."

"I *am* grateful."

I just didn't want to leave before I had a chance to go get that gun. A gun was power. And that was exactly what we needed.

She set down her bowl with a *thud*. "Oh, give me a break. You don't even know what to be grateful for," she said. "You're completely clueless."

She stood and walked over to her bag, snatching out her old clothes.

"Then tell me." I followed close behind. My hands shook at my sides. "You refuse to share anything with me, and then you act like I should be able to read your mind. Like I should just *know*. Well, I'm sorry that I'm not as worldly as you, Missy, but you aren't protecting me by keeping things a secret."

"Trust me, you'd rather not know."

"I know it's not as bad as you're making it seem," I said.

"How do you—?" She reared around to face me, her eyes narrowing. "You went down there, didn't you? What did you see?"

I took a step away from her. "I saw a job."

"What? Tell me what you saw?"

"I saw a girl posing. A man was drawing her…nude."

Missy laughed darkly and rubbed a hand over her face. "Oh, there's far more to the black markets than just that."

"You don't have to try to protect me," I said. "I can pull my weight around here. I'm not stupid."

"Stop fighting me on this, Ella!" she snapped. "This is the last we're going to talk about it. No jobs! Got it? You ask again and I'm gone." She finished tugging on her tights and pulled her shirt over her head. When she finally looked back at me, the fight had drained from her eyes. "Grab something to eat. We'll leave in half an hour. I don't want to miss this ride."

Chapter Seven

The back of the box truck was even darker than the inside of the train car. Once the door slid shut, we were encased in darkness. There were two empty seats up front with the driver, but obviously we weren't passengers. Even as free agents, we were still considered property, objects that needed to be transported from one place to another. We could have been boxes of napkins or crates full of shirts, something to be used up and discarded. It's not like those objects would want to look out the window. It's not like those objects might like to see the way the trees rush past or to feel the warmth of the afternoon sun.

Luckily, the hard bottom of the truck had been lined with a few folded blankets. Missy shuffled around next to me in the dark, repositioning herself. She sighed and I imagined the way she was lying on her back with her arms folded gently across her chest as if she was simply lounging on the grass in the sun.

The engine flared to life underneath us, and the truck jerked forward and bumped down the alleyway, swaying back and forth as it pulled out onto the street.

There were so many questions that I still wanted to ask Missy, but I knew better than to speak right now. She was angry. Angry that I'd been careless sneaking around the market. Angry that I'd burst the protective bubble she'd tried to place around me. Angry that she couldn't dictate which parts of the world I chose to see.

And I was angry, too. I'd allowed Missy to take my power away, but I wasn't going to stand for it anymore. I'd lost the gun, but I wouldn't let something like that slip through my fingers again.

I tilted my head back and let my thoughts drift, instead, to Penn. It was easier to think about him, even if it was painful. I'd gotten used to pushing those thoughts away, but now all I wanted was to fall into them.

When I let myself think of him, the smell of earth and leaves and water rushed over me, as if the memory of him was the smell itself. Penn wasn't just a boy anymore. He was the cool press of water against my arms as I sank down into the pond. He was the sound of the wind rustling the ivy that draped the tall stone walls, and the soft silver light of the moon. He was the taste of chocolate on my lips. He was sweetness. He was heat. He was rest. He was the feeling of lightness in my limbs as I floated on the surface of the water.

Just thinking of him made my heart quicken, all the blood inside me rushing to remember him. It could consume me if I let it. This desire. Sometimes it felt like it could swallow me whole.

But for now, I let myself slip into it. I could get lost for hours playing and replaying the moments we spent together.

Sometimes it didn't even matter if they were real. I could make up new moments that existed only inside my head. I'd move the two of us across the stage of my mind and sometimes we would be ourselves and other times we would morph, turning into Eurydice and Orpheus. It almost felt as if we'd fallen into the story. Truth and fiction blending together.

I'd blink and we'd be standing on the bridge, bits of light and water shattering around us and I would freeze. *Don't turn around*, I'd tell myself. But I couldn't stop. Just like Orpheus, I would turn. I would turn and reality would come speeding back at me, plowing me down. The officers. Penn. That look of loss cut across his face. If only I hadn't turned. Then what? Would we still be together? Would we have made it out of the gates of hell?

I opened my eyes.

Darkness.

"Ella."

I blinked, but all the light was gone.

"Ella," Missy repeated.

"What?" My voice came out rusty and tired.

For the first time since I opened my eyes, I noticed how still it was. The truck, which had been bumping beneath us for hours, had stopped. Outside, cars sped past. Horns blared, and in the distance, a siren wailed.

"Sit up," Missy said, nudging me.

At some point during our drive Missy must have sat back up. Now I was slumped against her. I straightened, rubbing a hand over my face as the back door of the truck rumbled open. Light flooded the cab and Missy and I both raised our hands to our eyes.

"Are we here?"

"Yes." There was a strange hesitance behind her voice.

"Come on, gals," Tony said. "Let's not keep Mr. Bernard waiting. I can't afford to piss this guy off."

Missy and I crawled stiffly out of the truck and glanced around. We'd pulled up onto the dock of a building that looked very much like the one that we'd just come from. The dock door to the building was open and we stepped from the back of the truck into a storage room stacked high with boxes.

A tall man in a dark gray suit came through a door at the back of the room. He was quite a bit bigger than Tony, all shoulders and chest like a lumberjack from one of Ruby's stories, a massive beast standing on two legs. His eyes were deep set and so dark that from across the room, it almost looked like he had no eyes at all, only two dark holes. At his side was a younger man dressed in almost an identical suit, although the two men, themselves, looked nothing alike. The younger man was at least a head shorter. He didn't have any of the other man's bulk and even though he wasn't fat, he looked…soft. His ashy blond hair curled along his thinning hairline.

"Tony," the first man said, smiling as he stretched his hand out. "Thank you for driving out. Have you met my nephew, Seth?"

The two men shook hands, nodding.

"I believe we spoke on the phone," Tony said. His voice sounded so much smaller than it had before. I couldn't believe that he'd be nervous, but that's exactly what it looked like.

"Seth tells me that you folks have been lucky over there in Buffalo. You haven't been having the same problems we've been having."

"No, we've been lucky," Tony said.

"One of my best dealers flat out quit yesterday," Mr. Bernard said. "I'm not sure we can deal with many more of these...shall we say...unwanted packages."

Without making any sudden movements, Missy slid her hand next to mine and squeezed the soft flesh on the inside of my wrist. She didn't need to tell me. I knew what he was talking about. *Unwanted packages*. The words were terrible, so heartless, like he couldn't even be bothered to refer to them as girls. The weakness in my knees didn't surprise me anymore. The world just kept dropping out from underneath my feet. How could a girl survive like this, knowing that any second it could fall away? Gone.

"And what do we have here?" Mr. Bernard asked, eyeing us as if he'd just noticed us standing there.

His eyes narrowed on my face. In an instant, the blood felt like it drained from my head. Maybe I looked like one of the dead girls myself.

"I hope it's okay to drop these two off with you," Tony said. "They're strictly working as free agents with a 20/80 split. I spoke to your nephew on the phone this morning and he said it would be fine if I dropped them off. You might be able to use them."

"Normally I'd say no," Bernard said. "We have plenty of free agents. We actually make more money here moving sales than we do with trade. I know it's different over where you are. But I have a couple clients who'll be happy to see that this one's back," he said, cupping Missy's face in his palm. "What did I tell you, sweetheart? You should have stayed with me the first time."

Missy smiled. "You're right, sir."

"And who's this?" His gaze shifted to me, his eyebrows raised.

"Apparently these two come together now," Tony said. "She doesn't have papers."

Mr. Bernard slowly appraised me. Taking my chin in his hand, he tipped my head thoughtfully one direction and then the other. His eyes narrowed and his gaze slowly traveled over my eyes, my nose, my lips. I had no idea what he was looking for, but I didn't doubt that he had a checklist that he was mentally compiling. It was almost as if, with each feature that he studied, he was deciding just how much I was worth. After a moment he lowered my face and picked up a lock of hair that fell beside my cheek. He rubbed it between his fingers.

I stiffened. He'd noticed that my hair had been dyed. I knew it. That careful gaze of his unnerved me. What more could he tell about me?

He dropped my hair and turned back to Tony. "I can take this one, too. What do I need papers for? Half the girls I get in here don't have any papers." He laughed. "That's what my nephew's good for. You didn't think that I hired this boy for his intimidating physique, did you? I mean look at him." He patted Seth on his arm. "Nope. This boy's a genius. You ever need some papers done up, you come here, you got me?"

Tony nodded. "I'll remember that." The idea appeared to make him uncomfortable, but apparently Mr. Bernard wasn't the sort of person that someone said no to. "So..." Tony said, changing the subject, "you've got a couple of girls for me to take back to Buffalo?"

"I do," he said, turning to lead us out. "Sometimes I wonder if these customers are even more picky than the ones that buy from the kennels. You get these assholes thinking that they're so smart, working the system, getting the best deal, and suddenly nothing's good enough for them."

Mr. Bernard kept talking as he entered a large room with ceilings so high that I wouldn't be able to reach them even if I stood on the back of five men. In the center of the room was a small raised platform in front of which half a dozen chairs were arranged in a semi-circle.

"Seth, you take these dolls over to the bay and bring back the other ones while I finish up some business with Tony."

Seth nodded and I realized that I'd never actually heard him speak.

"And Seth?" Bernard called after us. "Don't screw it up this time."

We followed him across the room. His shiny black shoes *clack*ed against the cement floor with each step. In the corner, he stopped in front of a heavy curtain and glanced back across the room to where his uncle and Tony were having an animated discussion.

"I didn't think you'd come back here," he said to Missy, only glancing at her for a second before he looked down at the ground.

She seemed almost as surprised as I was to hear him speak.

"No," she finally said, "I didn't think I'd be back either."

"I know you're probably not…happy to be here," he said, glancing up at her. "But I'm glad to see you again."

Missy smiled. "Thank you."

The look on her face surprised me, such pure and honest happiness. I'd never seen her look that way before. But it only lasted a second. She blinked and the usual facade slipped back over her features.

Seth smiled shyly and pulled aside the heavy curtain that led into a small waiting room. The walls were lined with short padded benches. On the other side of the room, two girls sat with their hands folded in their laps. They looked up expectantly when we entered. Both looked as if they'd been crying.

"You can wait here," Seth said. "I'm kind of busy with things, but maybe I'll get to see you again soon."

"Maybe," Missy said.

"I hope so."

Missy nodded. Had I imagined it before, that look that crossed her face?

"You two, come with me," he said to the other two girls. His voice was still soft, kind even, but it sounded different than when he spoke to Missy.

When the curtain had closed behind them, Missy lowered herself down onto one of the benches and buried her head in her hands.

I sat down next to her. "Are you all right?"

"No." She didn't look up at me when she spoke.

My hand hovered above her arm.

"Is it that man? Seth?"

Her eyes were fierce when she looked back up. "No. It has nothing…" She shook her head. "It doesn't matter. I swore I wouldn't come back here and now I'm here. Just let me deal with it."

"I'm sorry," I said. "If you want to talk about it—"

"I don't."

I got up and paced the room. It wasn't what I'd expected. I'd imagined that they'd all be similar, but this place was different. So much larger. Yet it wasn't just the size that shocked me: the wide room just beyond the curtain, with its vast cement floors and expansive ceilings, seemed like part of a machine that could suck us in and crank us out. It made the other market seem like an amateur production.

The curtain parted again and Mr. Bernard stepped inside. Missy and I both stiffened. There was something about this man that frightened her, but I wasn't sure if she was just intimidated by the sheer size of him the way I was, or if there was something more.

He paused, studying us for just a moment before he spoke.

"This really is unexpected," he said, smiling. "You know, I pride myself on being a shrewd businessman, but I never should have let you go."

Missy didn't answer.

"I hope you're planning on staying longer this time," he said. "My offer still stands. I can guarantee that you're not going to get an offer like that from anyone else."

"It's very generous," Missy said.

Mr. Bernard studied her face.

The Missy I knew had a knack for controlling people, for manipulating them, but it was clear that her normal tactics wouldn't work on this man. The amused look on his face made me wonder if he could tell that she was avoiding giving him a straight answer.

"You really are a different one, aren't you?" He chuckled. "Don't worry. There's no need to answer me right away. Why don't you and your friend go back to the common room and get a bit to eat. Rest up. I need you looking fresh for tomorrow."

He turned to go.

"Wait…" Missy said.

His eyebrows rose as he turned back around.

Missy glanced uncomfortably in my direction. "She can't do any jobs."

"I'm sure we can come to some sort of arrangement." Mr. Bernard grinned. "Come to my office later and we'll finalize things."

The curtain swung shut behind him and Missy raised a hand as if she already knew that I was going to object. "Come on. I'll show you the common room."

The common room didn't feel a thing like the one in Buffalo. I followed Missy down a set of stairs into a large windowless room. The mood had been quiet at the other market, timid and somber. But here the atmosphere was chaotic. Girls bustled back and forth between the bathroom and the common room, in a constant state of motion. Some were returning from jobs, shedding their strange costumes and rushing to the showers as if they could wash away any remnant of the persona they had just discarded. Others lay passed out on cushions scattered throughout the room, somehow able to sleep through the commotion. It was impossible to tell which girls were free agents and which ones were owned by Mr. Bernard, but there was one thing that was obvious: there were a lot of them.

The noise was a constant jumble of voices and shuffling heels, of clanking plates and hangers screeching against their rods. No one paid us much mind. They looked to be worried about other things.

Missy led me back to a small, dark kitchen, grabbing us each a plate full of food out of the dirty fridge before we found a quiet place to hunker down.

"It's different than most of the other markets," she said, following the way my gaze darted around the chaos.

"It seems so much busier. How can there be this many girls for sale?"

"This is the hub," she said. "Mr. Bernard buys them from all over."

"He buys them?"

"It's not like it's easy to sell one of us, you know? You can't just put an ad in the paper. The kennels bred us to be lifelong companions, so people aren't thrilled to admit that they've turned out to be terrible owners. Besides, I'm not sure if it's even legal to sell us. I'm sure they're happy to just pass us all on to people like Mr. Bernard so that he can deal with it."

"Did he buy you?"

Missy bristled. "The first time, yes. My owners lived in California, but they shipped me out here pretty quickly when I got sick and not too long after that, I got sent to another market in New Jersey."

"Is that what he meant when he said he shouldn't have let you go?"

"No." She frowned a little. "I doubt he even knows that I came through here the first time. I wouldn't have made him very much money. I was so sick that they were pretty eager to just pass me on to someone else. Cut their losses. Well," she said softly, "there was one person who was kind to me."

"Seth?"

She picked absentmindedly at her fingernails and her eyes flicked up to my face and then back down to her hands.

"Yes. But I don't know why. It's not like I looked like myself. I wasn't beautiful. I was a mess. Frail. Sallow. I was so sick that I could only lie there on my back, staring up at the ceiling and wishing that I'd just die. I couldn't wash myself. Couldn't brush my hair. It got so matted and tangled that the people in New Jersey had to cut it all off."

"But they took care of you there?"

She snorted. "I don't know if I'd say that they took care of me. But I did finally get better."

"So you came back here again…after you ran away."

She nodded.

"And Seth… Did he remember you?"

She paused. "He did."

The answer seemed like a beautiful thing. He remembered her. Wasn't this a good thing? I wanted to ask her, but the way her voice had grown flat, her eyes dull, I wondered if maybe I misunderstood. To be remembered was the only thing that kept me going right now.

Chapter Eight

Missy stayed true to her word. She must have slipped off to see Mr. Bernard while I slept because the next day when a short man with thinning hair and a baggy suit came in with the day's schedule, my name was absent from any assignments.

Missy, on the other hand, was given an all-day job with three other girls.

I sat against the wall on a small stool while she finished pinning up her hair.

"I feel useless," I said.

She glared at me and drew a dark line above her eyelashes with a small brush.

"You want to do something?" she asked. "Stay out of the way."

She pushed past me and pulled on a tight blue dress. The other two girls were already wearing theirs. Apparently the client had requested girls with the same coloring. If they stood side by side, you'd think they were identical.

"You know, I'm not as naive as you think I am."

Missy laughed. "I have to go."

"Fine."

She leaned in close to my ear. "Be sure not to say or do anything stupid while I'm gone."

"I thought you said you had to go."

She glanced at herself one last time in the mirror, rubbing away a bit of lipstick that had smudged the corner of her mouth. "It's only stupid if you talk about yourself," she said. "These girls hear stuff. I didn't say you couldn't ask them questions. Who knows, maybe you'll learn something."

Missy's group was the first to leave for the day. I sat off in the corner as the others slowly completed their metamorphoses and followed suit until there were less than a dozen of us left in the room. A few of the girls sat in clumps talking, but mostly they were absorbed in their own small tasks, their own private thoughts. No one even noticed as I inched my way to the back of the room and slipped down the hallway near the bathrooms.

On the ceiling, a fluorescent light flickered, casting the cement walls of the long corridor in cold blue light. I glanced behind me, hoping no one had followed me, but I was all alone.

Maybe it would have been better to stay and talk to the girls, but I couldn't stand the thought of sitting still while Missy went away to another one of her jobs. If she wouldn't let me work, I had another way to be useful.

Maybe a part of me craved this new pastime. Already, my heart thudded that new familiar rhythm. I was addicted to the heady thrill, the power of my own small body to finally take instead of give.

In a place this large, this thriving, there would be plenty of things for me to take.

At the end of the hallway, a narrow staircase led back up to the main floor. I crouched at the top. The doors to a couple of offices across the hall from me were open. The lights were on in one of the rooms, revealing the edge of a glossy wood desk and a tall filing cabinet, but I couldn't see far enough in to know whether or not it was occupied.

Just as I poked my head out of the stairwell, two men rounded the corner. I slunk back down a few steps, retreating into the dark.

"I don't see why he'd care if you showed them to me," a man said. "He's told everyone anyway. It's not like it's a secret."

The *click* of their shoes drew closer.

Just then, I saw movement in the unlit office. A young man crept ever so slightly forward out of the dark, pressing his back against the opposite wall as the other two men approached. He was obviously spying on them.

I leaned forward, studying him in the near darkness. He wasn't a huge, hulking man in a suit, like most of the other men I'd seen, or brainy and businesslike, like Seth. But there was something…different…about him. Maybe it was the way he held himself, with quiet confidence and power, which seemed out of place on his smaller frame.

"Then why don't you just ask him yourself?" one of the men said, coming to a stop only a few feet away. They must have been right outside the office.

I recognized that voice. It belonged to Seth. For some reason, this bit of information made me bolder. I slowly climbed back up the steps until my head rested right out of sight at the top of the landing.

"Come on, man, you know Bernard. Don't make me ask him. I want to see what everyone's getting so worked up about."

"Fine," Seth sighed, his voice diminishing a bit as they moved into the office. "I only have the ones from New York. The chief told Bernard that they've found some in Jersey and Connecticut, too. But I don't know what you're going to be able to tell from the pictures."

"I might surprise you," he said. "They call me eagle eyes."

"I'm sure they do," Seth said.

A drawer squeaked and I imagined him opening the tall filing cabinet and shuffling through the papers until he found whatever it was he was looking for.

"Holy shit! They weren't kidding. This is bad, man! This is some CSI shit," the man said. He talked tough, but something in his voice had changed, an undercurrent of fear that left him almost breathless. "They're all like this?"

"Not all of them," Seth sighed. "I mean, yes, they're all bad. Disfigured. But each one's a little different."

Disfigured? My stomach flipped. They were talking about the dead girls. Right now, they must be holding pictures of them in their hands. My fingers trembled, seeking out the pendant in my pocket. I rubbed the smooth center, feeling the small indents where my name was etched into the surface.

Across the hall the young man reacted, too, but instead of cringing, what looked like a smile flickered across his features. I drew in a deep breath, bringing my hand to my mouth. His gaze drifted from the hallway to the stairwell and for a second, his eyes met mine. I pressed back further into the shadows. Had he seen me?

Slowly, he brought a finger to his lips. And then he melted back into the shadows like he'd never been there.

"Man, Mr. B's just paying to cover this shit up and he expects us to just go on like normal?" the man said. The cocky bravado from a minute ago had all but disappeared. His voice lowered even more, mumbling something I couldn't quite understand.

"As far as I know," Seth said and then he must have turned because his voice became too quiet to hear.

I wanted to follow. Needed to hear what they were saying, but I could still see the satisfied smirk flicking across that man's lips. Could still feel the way my hair rose on the back of my neck. I squinted into the darkness where he'd been, but there was only empty shadows. Had I imagined him? Or was he just waiting for me to step into the hallway so he could grab me?

Indecision warred inside of me. I had to know about the dead girls. I *had* to. My heartbeat thrummed in my ears and I scooted up a little further on the stairs, staying out of sight while trying to make out what they were saying.

"I'm sorry," the man said, "but I can't believe these are just pissed off owners, or whatever Bernard thinks. I mean look, they're all cutting out the chips, right?"

"They aren't stupid enough to leave them in," Seth said.

"Maybe not all of them. But look, the cut is clean. You'd think it'd be more—"

"Listen, I don't really have time for this," Seth interrupted. He sounded upset. Was that anger? Fear?

"Oh, okay," the other guy said. Did he hear it, too, the

change in Seth's voice?

The floor groaned as they moved around the office. "We should probably get back," Seth said, his voice suddenly loud as they reappeared in the doorway.

I scooted back into the dark stairwell, willing my heart to calm as I waited for their footsteps to retreat down the hallway. There was still no sign of the other man. When the footsteps finally rounded the corner, I sprang from my spot. I couldn't sit and think about what I was about to do. If I focused on it too long, I'd be paralyzed.

My arms and legs buzzed, practically moving on their own as they swept me across the hall and into the office. I didn't pause to look around me. My eyes focused on the filing cabinet, locking on the top drawer, which still sat open, just a crack. I tugged the handle, steeling myself for what I knew I'd find, but it was impossible to prepare myself.

"It's not something people usually go out of their way to see," the young man from the shadows said from the doorway.

I whirled around and stiffened. "Stay away from me. I'll scream if you get any closer."

"Don't worry," he said, keeping his distance with his hands raised. "I'm not here to hurt you. I'm just part of the system like everyone else."

I studied him in the full light. He looked too young to work for Bernard. Too small. Despite his size, with his almond shaped eyes, strong cheekbones, and thick curly hair, he was strikingly handsome. I hadn't seen any boys working the black market, but if there had been, I imagined they'd look like this man.

Cautiously, I looked down at the photographs and my stomach turned, twisted, recoiling. I was going to be sick.

"You know about this?" I asked, choking back the urge to fall to my knees, to crawl under the desk and curl into a ball. I couldn't lose it. Not now. I needed to be strong.

The glossy images were so much worse than I ever could have imagined. How could they be real? These had been girls. Only a few short days ago they had breathed air in through their lungs. They had sipped cold water and felt the breeze against their skin. Maybe they had even let themselves dream. But not anymore.

"A lot of people know," he said, taking a step closer.

"Did you do it? Did you kill them?"

His smile disappeared. "No."

I studied him again, watching for any sign of deception. "But you know who did?"

He nodded.

"Who?"

The man's face lit up, even as he shook his head. He knew but he wouldn't tell me? Girls were dying, and yet again, someone else had decided I wasn't allowed to help.

I dumped the stack of photos on the desk and fanned them out across the polished wood. There were too many. Eight. Ten. Twelve. How many girls had died? My eyes darted over the photos. Pieces of girls. Remnants. I didn't want to see, but how could I look away? If I'd done this to them…if this was my fault… I couldn't close my eyes.

"You act like it's okay," I snapped.

His eyes narrowed, his face hardening into a fierce look. Was that the face of a killer? "I never said that."

"Who are you?"

"If you don't want to get caught, you should leave now," he said, ignoring my question. He moved forward, stepping so close to me that I could feel the heat of his chest against my side. He reached around me, plucking a few photographs off of the table, and pressed them into my hand. "Here, take these."

I sat in the corner, thumbing the edge of the paper inside my pocket. For the past hour I'd let my fingers drift to the photographs, rubbing the stiff paper across my fingertips until they felt raw, but nothing could erase the numbness. Or the anger.

That man hadn't given me all of them, even though I'd almost wished he had. It felt like I was abandoning them, like it was my job to free them, even if it was only a picture.

The images were gruesome, but I felt the need to study them, not just to acknowledge the terrible thing that had happened to these girls, but to see if I could find a common clue, some thread that tied it all together. But every time I thought about pulling them out, the man with the baggy suit came in and rounded up a few more girls.

A girl that just returned settled back down on the pillows next to me and opened a pad of paper.

"Do you mind if I sketch you?" she asked.

Her hand hovered above the paper, waiting for me to give my approval.

I shrugged, already missing my invisibility. "Sure."

"Thanks." She smiled, not just a tiny grin for courtesy's sake, but a real smile. I wasn't sure that I'd seen one like that in days. "I'm Carlie."

I hesitated. "I'm Gigi."

"It's nice to have a new face," she said, flipping through

her notebook. "I've drawn everybody else already."

The pages were dense with drawings. They covered every square inch of paper; faces, some sleeping, some awake. Some gazed directly off the page, but others only captured a profile. These images were so different from the ones inside my pocket.

"Where did you get that?" I asked, nodding to the sketchbook. I hadn't seen anyone else with anything like it. It seemed nice to have a way to occupy time.

I craved the piano. There must have been one in one of those rooms upstairs. I would have been happy just to sit in front of it, to forget about all the pain and gruesomeness in the world. For a second I had to close my eyes, imagining it. Feeling the keys beneath my fingertips would be almost as exquisite as touching Penn.

Her face flushed. "They let me keep it. My master felt guilty about getting rid of me. Maybe this was kind of like an apology," she said as she stroked the leather cover. "I've tried to make it last, but I only have seven more pages."

I sat stiffly, thinking about the last time I'd seen someone drawing.

"Just relax," she said. "Can you sit the way you were before, when I walked in? You looked like you were concentrating on something. I liked it. Most of the girls look sad in my pictures, but you looked…" She searched for the right word. "Determined, I guess. I'd like to remember that."

Determined? Not angry? Not disgusted? Not sick?

I held still, trying to concentrate, the way I had been before. I thought of the girls. What was Seth hiding about them? And who was the man who gave me the pictures? It felt like I'd been close to understanding something, but now that Carlie was watching me, I couldn't focus.

"I saw you leave before. Did you go out on a job?" I asked, hoping she could give me a little bit more insight into the jobs they did at this market.

Carlie stopped sketching and the happy look on her face faded. "No, I'm still looking for a new home. If they don't find a buyer here, I think I might get sent somewhere else."

"I'm sorry," I said. "I shouldn't have mentioned it."

She shook her head and started sketching again. Out of the corner of my eye I watched the image take shape. It was beautiful, not just the drawing that she was making, but the way the pencil moved. Each stroke had a purpose. Sometimes she moved slowly, taking her time with a line, pressing down with the lead so that the mark she left looked heavy, weighted. But other times they were only soft wisps, merely a suggestion.

She finished the drawing and held it up for me to see.

I reached out and traced my finger over the lines. The girl in the picture looked like a stranger. It wasn't just the short, cropped hair, although that was certainly some of it. I didn't recognize the person that she'd captured on the page. She looked strong in a way that I didn't feel. Her chin was raised, her eyes set in a look of concentration. More than determined. She looked fierce.

I was ready to be that girl.

Life inside Mr. Bernard's market existed in a vacuum. Downstairs, in the windowless room, time melted away. Without a view to the outside world, there was only now. No morning. No evening. No bright sun and pale moon. Only dank cement walls and the harsh white glow of the lights that hung from the ceiling.

I had no idea what time it was or how long I'd been asleep when Missy nudged me awake. I sat up groggily, my hand moving instinctively to my pocket to check for the stiff paper of the photos still hidden there.

"Rub my feet for a second," she said, kicking off her shoes before she flopped down on the cushion next to me and plunked her feet in my lap. "I have all of ten minutes before I'm supposed to be ready for my next gig."

I kneaded a thumb into the bottom of her foot. "You're not done?" I asked. "I really wanted a chance to talk to you."

I needed to show her the pictures. I needed to talk to someone about them. And that man, the one who'd been spying on Seth, too… Did Missy know who he was?

"At least the next one won't be too long," she sighed.

"Why? Where are you going next?"

"Don't worry about it," Missy snapped, pulling her feet away from me. "I have to change and freshen up my makeup. You can go back to sleep."

She stood and made her way over to one of the vanities, switching on the bright light above the mirror. A few of the girls moaned and rolled away from the light, shielding their eyes with their arms.

"Don't go," I said, trailing after her. "Can't you say you're sick or something?"

She rolled her eyes and pulled on a tight red dress. "No. As far as Bernard is concerned, if we can stand, we can work. Actually, in his opinion, standing probably isn't even that important." She popped the lid off of a tube of lipstick and dabbed the bright color across her lips.

"But there are bad things happening out there," I said. "Really bad things. I think we need to—"

Missy stood up with a start, her chair clattering to the ground. "God! You don't shut up, do you?"

"But you need to listen to me."

"Save it," Missy hissed "I have someplace I need to be."

She glanced in the mirror, frowning, before she turned on her heel and marched away from me and up the stairs.

I waited ten minutes, enough time for Missy to check in for her next gig. All the while, my blood boiled. Missy was impossible. Insufferable. And I wasn't going to put up with it anymore.

We couldn't stay here any longer. If we needed money this bad, I'd find it. A man like Bernard had to have plenty of it lying around somewhere. I just needed to figure out where.

No one seemed to notice when I climbed the dark staircase that led to the showroom. Off to the left, a long hallway was cast in warm light. This wasn't a hall full of offices like the ones I'd seen earlier. It was surprisingly similar to the hallway in the last market, and it was easy to believe that the rooms behind these doors were painted the same gaudy red, decorated with plush carpets and oversize furniture.

From down the hall, I heard whimpering. I held still, listening, but the sounds confused me. They were small, muffled. Was someone crying? It was hard to tell if the sound was coming from the first door or from somewhere further down. From where I stood, it almost sounded like it was coming from a few different rooms.

I crept further down the corridor and put my ear to the first door. Maybe I was pressing my luck, but I couldn't just walk away without knowing what was going on. I was done with being naive.

The whimpering sound continued, but now that I was closer, I could hear a thumping noise. It was rhythmic, like the beating of a drum. A man's voice mumbled something and the whimpering stopped.

My stomach knotted.

I should leave, that's what my gut was telling me. Step away from the door. Go back downstairs. But I couldn't just run away, not now that I'd made this decision. And now my curiosity had gotten the better of me.

Maybe it wasn't a girl crying at all, I told myself as I placed my hand on the doorknob. A wave of relief struck me with this idea. It must have been another one of those sad old men, missing his dead wife. Maybe Missy was in there right now comforting him. She would hold his head against her shoulder and stroke the soft wisps of white hair off of his forehead. Maybe she would sing him a song that his wife used to sing to him and he would leave here feeling happier than he had in months.

I twisted the knob and pushed. Inside, the room looked almost exactly the same as the ones in Buffalo. The walls here were painted a deep plum, but everything else was the same. A bed sat hulking in the middle of the floor.

I scanned the scene, almost excited to see the old man.

But there was no crying old man. There wasn't even an artist and his sketchpad in here. Nothing about this was what I'd expected to see.

A man's broad, sweaty back faced me from where he lay on the bed. The blankets were pulled up, covering his lower body, but I knew that below it there was only flesh and heat.

The man reared back and slapped the girl's face. "Shut

up! I didn't pay a grand for you to cry the whole time!"

The thing happening here was wrong. Wrong. Wrong.

My head spun thinking of Penn's warm body on top of mine. I knew how it should be and this wasn't it. This wasn't love. This was violence.

I stepped back, my eyes traveling down the bed to the red dress crumpled on the floor and as I did, the man moved. His broad back no longer blocked my range of vision and Missy's face came into view. Her cheeks were streaked with mascara and the bright pink lipstick that she'd applied not very long ago was smudged and faded. For a split second our eyes met and a single tear dropped down her cheek before she shut her eyes.

I wanted her to leap up and yell at me. I wanted her to shove me out of the room, to tell me that there was some mistake. This thing I'd seen wasn't what it looked like. But she only lay limply on the mattress, drained of anything that even resembled the girl that I knew.

I turned, not bothering to close the door as I ran.

Chapter Nine

I stopped at the top of the stairs and collapsed against the wall. What was I supposed to do? If only I had that gun. If only. If only. I almost ached to clutch it in my hand, to point it at that man's broad, sweaty back. I wouldn't let him do that to Missy! She deserved more.

On the other side of the showroom, the lights switched on and a second later, a man in a baggy suit rounded the corner, followed by two other men with clipboards. He stopped when he saw me.

"You're not supposed to be up here yet," he said, shaking his head before he turned to one of the other men. "Take her to the holding room while I grab the others."

"Wait. I'm actually supposed to be downstairs," I said.

The man stared at me like I was speaking a foreign language. "It doesn't matter," he said. "Go wait for the others."

One of the men grabbed me by the elbow as the other two trudged down the stairs.

"I need everyone to gather by the doors," I heard one of them say. "Even if you were told to get ready for a showing later, you're still being asked to come now as well."

"There's been a mistake," I told the man who steered me away from the stairs toward the curtained room that I'd waited in when I first arrived.

He glanced at me for just a second and grunted, shrugging.

"No, I don't think you understand," I said. "I'm not supposed to be doing any jobs. Mr. Bernard knows. Ask him."

The soft humming of voices drew closer and still he ignored me. A moment later the curtain parted and a stream of girls filed into the room beside me. Most of their faces still looked groggy from sleep. Carlie spotted me and hurried to my side.

"What's going on?" I whispered.

She shook her head.

"Remove your outerwear and take a seat. We'll be bringing everyone out as a group for inspection in a few minutes," the man with the clipboard barked, checking something down in his notes as each of us stepped past him into the waiting room.

Bodies moved, arms and legs bending and stretching as clothes fell away. I mimicked the rest of them as best I could, but I could hardly see. My head swam as I tucked the photographs and pendant securely in my pocket before I pushed my clothes underneath the bench. I couldn't chance them finding my things. What would they do to me if they found out I stole those pictures? Worse, if they found that pendant, the one with the congressman's address on it, I was as good as dead.

I shivered, crossing my arms over my chest. How was I supposed to follow their instructions when I knew that they were allowing girls to be used this way?

There were more than two dozen of us, stripped down to our underwear. Our worried gazes flicked across one another. There couldn't have been more than ten years that separated all of us in age, but those ten years had been hard on some of them. Skin sagged. Waistlines widened.

I knew from listening to the congressman's conversations that the kennels had been raising pets for about twenty-five years, even though they hadn't started selling them until ten years ago, when those girls turned sixteen. Back then, it had only been legal in a few states, but now that the bills had been passed making it legal almost everywhere, I wondered how many of us there were in the world. How many of those girls found homes to live in for the rest of their lives and how many ended up in a room like this? How many had been forced to do things against their will?

Carlie fidgeted next to me.

"Is this normal?" I whispered.

She shook her head. "Not really. Normally it's just three or four of us. They don't like to overwhelm the clients with too many choices. That's why they get their preferences beforehand."

Clients? My head spun, thinking of Missy in that room. The man with her was a "client." So were the men who liked to draw nude girls and dance with us. What would these clients want me to do?

Worse, would Mr. Bernard's men try to sell me to a new owner?

The curtain whooshed open and all of us raised our heads, standing up straight. Like actors on the stage, we'd been taught how to look when there was an audience present. As my body followed suit automatically, the realization of just how ingrained our training had been made my stomach turn.

"Okay, I need you all to make your way to the viewing platform," the man with the clipboard said.

I followed behind Carlie, the group ahead of me moving seamlessly, elegantly. Now that there were eyes watching, the girls moved as if performing a dance. Feet glided across the floor. Backs stood erect. Arms balanced perfectly to our sides. So many of these girls had been treated poorly. They'd been used and rejected and still they could walk across a cold cement floor with so much grace that the room transformed around them. Did any of the people watching us even realize what a gift this was?

One by one we stepped up onto the platform, standing shoulder to shoulder. Around me, the other girls held their chins high, but I couldn't do it. I wanted to fold in on myself, to curl into a ball.

The chairs set up in front of us were still empty, but the sound of voices carried over to us from across the room. I turned to see a group making their way over to us.

One of Mr. Bernard's men led the group. There were only three of them: two men and one woman, all dressed in crisp, tailored suits.

As they neared us, the woman's eyes locked with mine, narrowing as she appraised me. My stomach knotted. I hadn't had very much experience with people, but something told me not to trust her. Not to trust any of them. There was a cold apathy that emanated from them, an indifference that sent a chill down my spine. I took the smallest step away from them. Maybe if I stood with poor posture I would make a bad impression.

"Please, make yourselves comfortable," the man with the clipboard said, gesturing to the seats.

"No need," the woman said, shaking her head. "We won't be long."

"But there are twenty-seven of them," the man with the clipboard said. "It will take at least an hour to get through them all, even with only a small sample of their talents."

The woman dismissed his comment with a wave of her hand. "We aren't interested in talents," she said.

The floor dropped out from under me. A sale. This was a sale.

The man looked down at his clipboard. "I'm sorry, Ms. Gibson," he said. "I didn't realize."

"We're more interested in health," she said, as if he hadn't spoken. "These are the youngest ones you have?"

"These are all of them. I was told that you wanted to look at them all," the man said. "But I can assure you, we only keep the best. Mr. Bernard is very discerning. If he doesn't think that one of them is fit, he's got connections with other dealers who'll take them."

"So you say," the woman said, "but this one here is certainly over twenty. Look at her." She poked at the girl's upper thigh. "We won't be needing this one. Or this one." She moved down the line, pointing out the girls with a derisive nod of her head.

Hurriedly, one of the men in suits corralled the rejected girls and whisked them back to the waiting bay. My legs twitched, watching them slip away without me.

Less than a dozen of us remained.

Next to me, Carlie stood as still as a statue, barely breathing. I hardly knew her, but I wanted to reach out and grab her hand. I needed someone to hold onto, someone to steady me. And to steady her in return.

The woman stopped in front of us. "You," she said, staring

coldly into my eyes. “Step down for a moment.”

I did as I was told.

“Take all their measurements,” she said to the man beside her.

He pulled out a tape measure. The cold plastic only lingered on my waist for a moment before it moved down my hips. Quickly he jotted the numbers down in his notebook.

“When you’re done with that, move on to the oral exam.”

He pulled on a pair of white rubber gloves. “Open your mouth.”

I swallowed. “I’m not one of the ones you should be looking at. I’m not for sale.”

He cocked his head, staring at me as if he didn’t understand the language I was speaking. “Open your mouth,” he said again.

“But there’s been a mistake—”

“The only mistake is you not listening when you’re given instructions,” the man said. He reached up and grabbed my cheeks, gripping the hinge of my jaw to force my mouth open. My head snapped back with a jolt.

He peered inside my mouth and I squeezed my eyes shut tight, trying to ignore the whistling sound of his breath. A tear dripped down my cheek and into my ear, but I concentrated instead on taking deep breaths through my mouth. I wouldn’t think about the way he touched me. I wouldn’t think about the fact that they hadn’t even bought me yet and already they were treating my body as if it belonged to them.

A moment later, he let go of my face and uncapped a marker that he pulled from his shirt pocket. Hastily, he scrawled two big, black numbers on my upper arm before he moved on down the line without a second glance in my direction.

Please let them think I'm not good enough. Please, please, please.

They moved down the row, measuring waists and hips, carefully examining the insides of our mouths and then writing down their findings in a notepad.

"This one has signs of neglect," the man said. "I don't recommend using her."

It didn't take long for them to examine us all. The woman flipped through the men's notes before slowly taking us in one last time. She walked down the aisle, glancing from the notebook to the number scrawled on our arms.

"You," she said, pointing to a girl at the end of the line. "Step forward. And you. You. You." She worked her way closer to me. "You," she said, pointing to Carlie. "And you." She looked me in the eye before she turned to the man in the suit.

No. I shook my head, even though no one was paying any attention. I could yell. I could argue. I could claw at them with my fingernails and they wouldn't listen to me. That much was clear. But I wouldn't let them keep me. The most I could hope for was to escape when they tried to take me away. And if I couldn't, I'd escape when we got to wherever they were taking us.

"We were hoping for more, but you'll inform us if you receive any new ones with our specifications. The kennel needed them yesterday."

The kennel?

My heart stopped and my head spun as the image of the red door materialized behind my eyes. The red door where they sent imperfect pets. Wasn't that who I was now? An imperfect pet?

There was no escaping the red door.

The weight of a thousand hands pressed down on my chest. I couldn't breathe. All sound rushed away, as if a drain had been pulled and now all the noises that had once filled the room were being sucked away. Funneling. Spinning. Swirling.

Far away, I heard the sound of screaming. Was it me?

I blinked at the other girls, trying to focus. Their mouths were shut tight, but their eyes were large. Their necks craned toward the back of the warehouse.

"Norraaiiitttoooottttaaaaeeekerrrr…"

It sounded like my head was underwater. The thick roar of it filled my head, but underneath it I heard that sound. They were words. Those sounds. They were words.

"I made a deal with him, you bastards! Are you listening to me? She isn't yours to sell!"

The tide pulled back and sound rushed back at me, crashing over my head. Missy stood on the loading dock, once again wearing the red dress, pounding on the chest of a tall man with spiky blond hair. Her tiny arms flailed, but it didn't even seem to faze him. He swatted her away, frowning.

"Listen to me!" she yelled.

But clearly he wasn't listening. He picked her up and started carrying her across the warehouse toward the doors that led down to the common room.

The woman turned her nose up in disgust and glared at the rest of us, as if we had been the ones who had made the outburst. As Missy continued to yell, the distaste on her face only grew more apparent.

"I would recommend having that one put down," she said to the man in the suit. "That sort of behavior is toxic. It has to be extinguished the moment it's spotted before it contaminates the group."

Put down. Put down. Put down. The words knocked against the inside of my head. I needed to do…something. But I couldn't move. Couldn't think beyond the red door.

Across the warehouse, a door opened and Mr. Bernard's nephew, Seth, stepped out, obviously concerned about the outburst.

I saw his lips move, and a moment later he was sprinting across the warehouse. He ran awkwardly, flat-footed and loping, but his face was determined.

"Put her down, Vic," he said.

Missy's face, tight with rage, relaxed a little as he set her down.

"This is highly unprofessional," the woman from the kennel said. "Can we please wrap this up? We're on a tight schedule."

"Certainly." The man in the suit nodded. "You have a way to transport all of them?"

"The truck is parked in your dock," the woman said. "You can load them up now."

"All right then," the man said, addressing us. "Those of you who haven't been selected, head back to the common room. The rest of you, come with me."

He shoved me forward. I dug in my heels, but I couldn't stop him from moving me.

"Would you like them to get dressed before you leave?" he asked the woman, nudging my back with his clipboard.

She glanced back at us and shrugged. "No need. We'll be dressing them in uniforms at the facility."

Behind me, someone choked back a sob. It was a lonesome sound, hopeless and heartbreaking. How could a person stand it? To have their soul pushed down this way.

Broken over and over again.

Anger spiked inside of me, spearing through the weakness. They couldn't treat us this way. They couldn't prod our bodies like animals. We weren't cattle that they could brand and herd, driving us to slaughter. This was *wrong*.

"You have no right to treat us like this," I spat back at him.

The clipboard dug deeper into my back and the man let out a snort of a laugh. "I don't have the right?"

In front of me, one of the men from the kennel pulled open the back to a large truck that was backed into the dock. The door rumbled open. One by one the girls in front of me stepped into the dark interior of the truck.

"I hate to tell you this, sweetie, but you have no rights. You're a pet. What did you expect would happen?"

The realization that he was right was like a dagger straight through my anger and hatred. The clothes, the pictures, the things I stole… Everything I'd done to get this far, gone. How could I be so stupid, to think things had changed for me, to think I could make my way back to Penn? Wanting something wasn't the same as being able to make it come true. Wanting—*hoping*—wasn't enough. It never had been.

Maybe that had been my problem from the beginning. I'd hoped for something more. I'd hoped to be something that I wasn't, and time and time again I was shown how wrong I'd been. I just needed to accept the truth. I was a pet. My life had never been my own. I'd been created in a lab to benefit humans. I'd wanted to believe that life itself was a gift, something magical that I owned, but the sooner I realized that it didn't belong to me, the sooner I could stop feeling this pain.

Through the gap between the truck and the loading dock, a cold gust of air knocked into me. The man shoved me between the shoulder blades. I stumbled, stepping from the cement slab into the gritty metal bed of the truck.

The man in the suit reached up, pulling down on the handle to the door and it rumbled back down into place, locking us in darkness. The truck shook to life beneath us and I sank down onto the cold floor.

Seven other girls huddled next to me, but none of us spoke. Each of us was alone in our fear. Each trapped in our own dark cage.

We were husks. Empty bodies. The image of the dead girls swam in front of my eyes. Girls blackened and burned. Girls drowned. Girls cut. Girls who'd had their lives stolen from them until there was nothing left. Behind the roar of the engine, the sound of voices rose and fell. The door thundered open, we all reeled back, startled by the sudden burst of light.

"...willing to pay more than she's worth." The woman stood silhouetted in the square of light of the truck's open door. Her voice had climbed to a high octave and her body shook with anger.

Seth shook his head. "I'm sorry," he said. "I can't allow it. Of course, you can still take the others."

He stepped into the back of the truck and reached his hand out to me. "Come on, now," he said, pulling me to my feet. "Let's get you back inside."

Standing in the shadow of the doorway, Missy stood with her arms crossed defiantly over her chest. I couldn't see her face, but I guessed it must look fierce.

I held my chin high, trying not to let the pressure in my chest overcome me. I wouldn't look back. I could feel the eyes of the other girls in the truck watching me. It didn't seem fair, that I was being led away, while they were being taken back to the kennel. I didn't know them, but my heart shattered, little pieces splintering off for each one of them.

Seth's fingers were shaking against my arm where he clasped me above the elbow, leading me back into the warehouse. It seemed impossible that he would be frightened, but I could feel the fear trembling through him.

Behind us, the truck bumped out of the parking lot.

Seth stopped next to the man with the spiked blond hair. "I won't tell the boss what almost happened," he said. His voice sounded sharp, confident.

The man nodded once. "Hey, thanks man," he said, clearly shaken. "It was an honest mistake. You know how it is, right? Once their clothes are off, these girls all look the same."

The man chuckled, but Seth only stared at him, his jaw clenching.

The man shrank back. "I'm sorry. I was just joking."

Seth didn't respond. Instead, he tightened his grip on my arm and pulled me back into the warehouse toward his office. Missy trailed behind.

"We don't have a whole lot of time," Seth said in a low voice. He opened the door to his office and ushered us both inside.

"What do you mean?" Missy asked.

He closed the door behind him and sank down into one of the chairs near the door. "Shit," he said, burying his head in his hands. "This is bad."

"I don't see what the problem is," Missy said. "I made a deal with Mr. Bernard. This was all just a big mistake. You didn't do anything wrong."

"No." He rubbed his temples. "I've overstepped my bounds. He couldn't care less if he made a deal with you. He cares about the money. That's it. And we just cost him over a hundred grand."

"That...bastard!" Missy said, choking on the word. "You mean I...I..." She brought her hand to her throat, like she was trying to protect some tender part of herself. "For nothing! I did that for *nothing*!"

Seth's face was pale and he looked like he might be sick. "I'm sorry," he whispered.

"Now what?" I asked. "We can't stay, can we?"

"No!" Missy snapped. "Of course we can't stay, and now we have nowhere to go. I doubt I've even earned enough money for a ride. Not that it matters. He hasn't paid me yet and he sure as hell isn't going to pay me now. Maybe he wasn't ever planning on paying me."

"It doesn't matter," Seth said. "We've got to get you out of here."

He moved to his desk, rummaging through his drawers. He pulled out a stack of papers. "How quickly can you get your things?"

"What do you expect us to do?" Missy asked. "We can't walk back to Connecticut."

"Don't worry about it now," Seth said. He glanced at me. "Get some clothes on her and be back here as fast as you can."

Missy grabbed my arm and pulled me out of the office. She moved like a storm, a blast of air. She moved with the kind of passion that boiled up inside me. It was the kind of passion that I was used to pressing down, but inside her it overflowed. It spilled out and into the world.

"This is a disaster," she said, once we were clear of any

listening ears. "You were supposed to stay in the common room. I gave you one task, Ella. One task and you couldn't even do that!"

I ripped my arm away from her grasp. "You make it sound so easy," I said. "Stay in the common room. Don't do any jobs. Make yourself invisible. Don't share any secrets. Well, you can blame me all you want, but it's not going to do us any good now. How could you possibly keep a secret like that from me?"

Missy threw back the curtain to the waiting room and I snatched my clothes up off the ground.

"A secret? I was protecting you!"

"I never would have come here if I'd known," I said, wiggling into my clothes as quickly as I could.

"You don't think I know that?" Missy asked, turning away from me. "This was the only way. It's imperfect, but what other choice did we have?"

"That's not how it's supposed to be. The things those men are doing to you. It's not supposed to be that way. That's not love. Love is about two people sharing—"

"No one said anything about love," she snapped, and stomped toward the stairs.

I followed her. "But it is. I know it is," I said. "That's how it's supposed to be."

"Well, there's your problem," she said, "thinking that there's a way things are supposed to be instead of the way that they just *are*. People are cruel. People hurt each other. Get used to it."

"Not everyone hurts you!"

"This whole thing is pointless," she said. "We're both fools if we think we're going to actually get you back. And even if we do make it…what then? What good is it going to do us?"

I lifted my chin. “Penn will help us.”

“Yeah? What’s he going to be able to do? He’s trapped by his father. I’ve seen him on TV. He’s practically the new spokesperson for pet inequality. And don’t tell me that you don’t know it! What difference is it going to make if you’re there? Nothing will change.”

We reached the common room, Missy’s words ringing in my ears. Maybe she was right. Maybe it was useless to try to get back to Penn when the whole world was working against us.

Chapter Ten

Missy ripped off the red gown and began stuffing her things in her bag. On the cushions in front of me, Carlie's sketchbook sat in exactly the same spot she'd left it. The tiny nub of a pencil had rolled off of the top and underneath a pillow. I dropped to my knees and picked it up.

I wondered if she'd realized yet that it had been left behind. There was no way to get it to her now. Even if there was, they wouldn't allow her to use it at the kennel. She'd been lucky to have something that was hers, even if it was just for a little while.

I opened it up and flipped through the pages, past images of girls that I'd never seen before, yet their faces looked so familiar to me. In all of them, I saw a bit of myself. Carlie had captured their essence. Some appeared curious, others thoughtful, but what struck me most was the sadness. The emptiness she'd sketched into all of their features.

On the final page I found my own face, as unrecognizable

as it was to me. I traced my finger over the lines. The graphite smudged, bleeding into the white page. She'd drawn me differently than she had the rest of them, but it was hard to distinguish exactly how. I flipped back through the pages. The eyes were different. Not the shape really, but the soul of them. She'd given me life.

"It will make a difference," I said quietly.

Missy looked up from her bag. "What?"

I tore Carlie's picture of me from the notebook and held it defiantly as if the determination in that portrait's face could fortify me.

"I'm going to get there," I said. "Once we're all together we can make a plan. We'll find a way. But I'm not going to stop. I can't."

She rolled her eyes. "Wouldn't it spare us all a lot of trouble if we just faced reality and gave up now?"

"You want to see *reality*?" I asked, digging into my pocket for the photographs. I shoved them against her chest. "This is what reality looks like now! Do whatever you want," I said. "I'm not going to get this close and then just turn around. It isn't just about me anymore. Maybe it never was."

I stepped back and she turned the photographs over in her hands. For a moment she didn't move as her gaze skittered over the glossy image, absorbing it. And then her mouth opened, a strangled choking sound rising out of her as it hit, the truth of what she was holding.

She shook her head. "No," she whispered. "No. No."

She flipped through the pictures, her eyes clouding. "Where did you get these?"

"I took them."

"From where?" She looked up at me, her eyes fierce.

"I found them in one of the offices while you were gone." I paused. "Seth's office."

She shook her head.

"How do you know we can trust him?"

Seth looked up from his papers, startled, when we walked back into his office. "That was fast."

"Yeah, well…we don't have much," Missy said. Normally, this sort of remark would sound biting and condescending, but when she spoke to Seth, it only sounded like the sad, honest truth.

"Are you sure you can help us?" I asked.

His eyes traveled between the two of us, finally coming to rest on Missy. "I can," he said.

They were the words that I wanted to hear, but the way he said them made it sound like he was losing something. And maybe he was.

He stuffed the papers he was working on in an envelope and took a deep breath, standing. "I've made new papers for each of you. In case you need them. This way, if someone stops you, it'll be harder for them to track down your real history." He held out the envelope to Missy. "I'll tell my uncle that the two of you left out of the blue. He'll be pissed. I know he was hoping to get his hands on you for good this time, but it'll be a dose of reality for him. It's not healthy for a man to get everything he wants all the time."

Missy took the envelope tenderly. For a moment her fingers rested against his. "Thank you. You're the only one who's ever truly been kind to me," she said. "I'm afraid I'll never get a chance to repay you."

The longing on his face broke my heart. "It's been my pleasure."

Missy rose on her tiptoes and placed a soft kiss on his lips.

His face flushed and I turned away, not only because it felt like I was intruding on a moment that didn't belong to me, but because it hurt too much to watch. Seth was such an unlikely person for Missy to love, but she did. And I understood. You couldn't choose whom you loved, just like you couldn't choose if you were born a pet or a princess or a poor boy in India. It just happened to you.

"Well, I guess we should get you two on your way," he finally said. "I paid a cab to take you wherever you need to go. It's waiting for you down the street. I'll walk you to the back door. You should be safe to leave from there."

Across the warehouse, the men in suits were already wrangling together another showing. A handful of girls once again stood on the platform being examined by a couple in expensive-looking clothes.

Seth cracked open the back door and I slid past him out into the back alley. Missy turned around, pausing in the threshold.

"I wish things had been different," she said.

He nodded. "Me, too."

"Come with us," she blurted.

Seth froze, soaking in her question. He closed his eyes as if he were letting himself imagine what it would be like to say yes. When he opened them again his face looked pained. "I can't," he said, softly.

"It's not worth it. When he finds out you let us go…" Her voice trailed off.

"I have to take my chances," he said.

"But I need you," Missy said. Her voice sounded so small, like a fragile baby bird teetering on the edge of its nest. Full of fear, but *wanting*.

Seth swallowed, shaking his head. "I can't."

The cab sat idling on the corner, just like he said it would be. The driver glanced in his rearview mirror at us as we slipped inside, squinting his eyes appraisingly before he turned around to get a better look.

Missy glanced back over her shoulder toward the warehouse.

"We need to go," she said. Her voice still sounded shaky. Small.

The cab driver frowned at us. "You sure I'm allowed to be driving you two?"

Missy tapped her hand against the seat. "Yes, get a move on it."

"You look like those pets. Aren't you supposed to be with someone else?" he said. "I talked to a guy on the phone. Where is he?"

"He arranged to pay you, didn't he?" Missy asked.

The driver nodded.

"Then what's the problem?"

He sat for a minute staring at her. He didn't look like the smartest man. Maybe it was the way his jaw hung a little limply so that his mouth was slightly open. Finally, he smacked his lips and nodded, like he'd come to a decision. "Well, I can't go anywhere if I don't have an address," he said, still eyeing us warily. "Where to?"

Missy looked to me.

"Congressman Kimble's house. In Connecticut," I said.

Missy turned again to look out the back window and her face went white. "We've really got to hurry," she said, pressing against the back of the driver's seat as if she could actually push the car forward with the strength of her hands.

I turned to look out the rear window. A black sedan pulled to a stop outside the warehouse. The windows were tinted, but the dark head that loomed behind the driver's seat looked like Mr. Bernard. If he found us, I doubted that he would let us go so easily again.

"You want to go to a congressman's house?" the cab driver asked.

Both of us nodded.

"I still need an address," he said. "I don't just have the direction to famous people's houses memorized. This isn't Hollywood Tours."

"Well, we don't have the address," Missy said, panicking a little now. "Can't you just look it up?"

"Doubt it," the driver said. "Those political types don't usually like people to know where they live."

"Wait!" I said. "Will this work?"

I dug deep into my pocket. I hadn't shown Missy the collar, but I didn't have time to worry about her judgment right now.

"Here." I shoved the necklace into his hand. "That's where we need to go."

He held the pendant between his fingers and turned it in the light, admiring the way the tiny diamonds glinted in the sun. Missy's mouth dropped open, but she quickly recovered.

"Does it work or doesn't it?" she asked.

He squinted at the engraved words. "Yeah, I can get you there," he said, pleased with himself as he jotted them down in a little notebook on the seat next to him. "But it's outside the city. It's going to cost a lot."

"We've given you the address! The payment is already arranged!" I yelled. "Why are we sitting here talking about it? Just go! Go!"

Both he and Missy jumped a little at my outburst. It wasn't like me to yell, but it felt good. Maybe Missy was rubbing off on me.

The driver gave me an annoyed grimace, but he didn't argue. Instead he turned around in his seat and put the car in drive. The engine purred beneath us as the car bumped forward into traffic.

Missy slumped back into the seat. "I can't believe you kept that…*thing*."

"It didn't feel right to leave it behind," I said.

She shook her head. "I couldn't wait to leave mine behind."

"I guess I wanted to remember."

"What could you possibly want to remember? That collar represents everything that's ever gone wrong in my life," she said. "Every decision that was made for me, every dream I didn't get to follow, every person I've had to say good-bye to. Why would you possibly want to remember that?"

I stared out the window.

"That's exactly why I wanted to keep it," I finally said. "It wasn't because I wanted to remember it fondly." Although there were the good things. Penn. Penn had been good. And Ruby. "It just didn't seem right to leave it behind.

To forget."

Missy shook her head. "Forgetting is all I want to do."

Maybe that was true, but I didn't believe her. If she really wanted to forget she never would have agreed to come with me. Besides, she didn't seem like the sort of person that could forget, not when there were other girls who were still living through it. To forget would be to turn a blind eye. To forget would be a lie.

"What's going to happen to him?" I asked after a while.

She turned away from me, looking out the window. "I don't know. If Bernard finds out that he was responsible for me leaving again…" She shook her head.

"What?"

"He'll kill him."

"But I thought they were related!"

"It doesn't matter," Missy said. "No one's safe. Not with Bernard."

We stayed silent. Missy's hand rested on the seat next to mine. I scooted closer to her. There was nothing I could say to make her feel better. There were no words that could fix this thing. And so I sat. I sat and let the warmth of my body next to her be enough. It was what I could give her. My silence.

It seemed impossible that we were finally on our way to Penn. I closed my eyes and let myself think of him. I'd spent hours imagining him, yet somehow at a distance, afraid that if I let myself get too close to the memory of him, I wouldn't be able to pull myself away. I could get trapped there, inside one of those memories: the way it felt to run my fingers through the soft hair at the base of his neck; the heat of his hands on my back; the velvety touch of his lips against my own.

We wove our way through traffic, getting lost in the sea of cars that surrounded us. The taxi passed sidewalks full of people moving in such a hurry. I wondered where they were going. Was it really as important as the looks on their faces suggested?

After a while, the city gridlock gave way to bridges, and finally to the wide stretch of the highway. Beside us, thick patches of trees rushed past. The golden slant of the setting sun made their shadows stretch long. It would be dark soon, but the day didn't know it yet. The orange light looked like it had set the world on fire. It flashed off of windows and glowed atop shingled rooftops.

Missy and I both tensed as we drew nearer. The taxi slowed as it approached the narrow driveway that led to the congressman's house.

"Don't pull in," Missy said, tapping the driver on the shoulder. "You can drop us off down the street."

The car bumped off of the road, stopping near a dense tangle of trees.

"You want me to leave you here?" the driver asked. "Are you sure you know where you're going?"

"We know," I assured him.

He eyed us warily as we climbed out onto the gravelly shoulder of the road.

"You two be safe," he called back to us. "I can always come back for you if you need me to."

The car idled as the driver drummed his fingers nervously against the wheel. Maybe he was worried to leave us alone, but his gallantry only lasted for a moment before he must have realized we weren't his problem. The tires skidded on the gravel, kicking up a cloud of dust, and a minute later the car disappeared around the corner, leaving us alone. I started off toward the tall hedges that lined the driveway back to my old home.

"What are you doing?" Missy asked.

"It's this way."

"You can't just walk down the driveway and ring the doorbell," she huffed. "And we can't just stand out here on the road, either. Someone could see us."

She pulled me over a low stone wall, ducking into the branches behind it.

"I wasn't thinking. I'm sorry," I apologized.

The closer we got to Penn, the fuzzier my mind became. My limbs trembled, so full of excitement and fear and worry that they hardly felt like they belonged to me anymore.

Missy rubbed her hand over her face. The night was coming on fast and I could hardly make out her expression in the dim light that filtered through the trees.

"We need a plan," she said. "It feels like we're walking into this thing blind."

"I guess we can't really do anything yet," I said. "We'll have to wait until everyone goes to sleep. Then I'm pretty sure we can sneak up to Penn's room."

"Are you sure you can get in there without anyone seeing you? There might be security cameras and stuff."

"There aren't any."

"There aren't or there weren't?" Missy asked. "You have no idea what he could have put in since you've been gone."

"Fine," I said. "I won't go through the house. There's a trellis I can use to get to the second floor."

Missy sighed. Obviously my meager plan didn't fill her with confidence. "And then what? You're just expecting that he'll come with you?"

"Yes."

It must have sounded absurd to her. Maybe it was crazy to think that I could climb into Penn's room like one of those princes in Ruby's fairytales and just sweep him away with me.

"Okay," she said after a minute. "Let's just say it all goes smoothly and you can waltz in there without getting caught and then convince him to come with you. I sure am hoping that he's going to have some grand plan for us after that, because this is as far ahead as I've planned. You asked me to get you here and I did it."

"And I'm really grateful to you," I told her.

"Well, I hope your gratitude comes with a place to sleep and food to eat."

"I wish I could promise you that."

"Oh never mind." She shrugged. "Right now we just need to find a place to hide for a couple hours. We're way too close to the road right here."

She began walking through the undergrowth, pushing aside branches as she went. The ground sloped a little, opening up into a small drainage ditch. Beside it, a large pine tree rose into the sky.

"This is perfect," she said, motioning for me to follow her as she stooped beneath some boughs. The lowest branches reached all the way to the ground, forming a shelter. Inside, it was dark, but with what little light that shone through, I could see that the ground was clear of almost anything but pinecones. The blanket of dried needles that covered it all was surprisingly soft as we lowered ourselves onto it.

"Do you think you could find this tree again if you needed to?" Missy asked.

"I think so."

It was a tall tree, taller than most of the others that grew around it. But even if I couldn't spot it from a distance, I was pretty sure I'd be able to make my way back to it.

"Good," she said. "This is where we can meet up later."

"You're not coming with me?" The panic in my voice was clear.

I don't know why I had assumed that she'd go with me. But the thought of returning to the congressman's house by myself made me lightheaded. I leaned back against the prickly bark of the tree trunk and took a deep breath.

"You'll be fine," Missy said.

"But wouldn't it make sense for you to come?" I asked in a small voice. "You could keep an eye out just in case someone sees me."

"You'll be fine," she said again.

"Do you *want* me to get caught?" I blurted, as surprised to hear the idea spring from my lips as Missy was.

"No."

Her answer was flat, devoid of the normal spark that usually annoyed me. It was a dull answer and I couldn't tell whether she was bored by me, or whether she was lying.

My throat felt dry, parched, as I tried to swallow back the fear that was creeping up inside me, but it only climbed.

It didn't make sense for me to trust Missy, but I had. From the moment she'd shown up at the refugee center, I'd let my need to get back to Penn blind my suspicions. I'd been so focused on getting back here, that I'd pushed away my doubts and fears, not giving enough thought to *why* she'd agreed to help me.

But now, I couldn't help but wonder again.

Above us, a gust of wind blew through the trees and I tensed at the sound. I'd never realized how noisy these woods were. The crack of sticks, the rustle of leaves, each sound made me bristle. I thought I'd gotten used to the sound of these trees at night, but that had been before.

It was funny to think how dangerous the world had seemed when I'd lived here. I'd been so afraid that someone would find out about my feelings. Back then, that had been the thing that frightened me most, but now I knew better. The whole world was dangerous. I'd been so afraid to be sent back to the kennel, so afraid of what lay behind that red door. But death could find you anywhere. Girls like me were dying. And who even cared. Who would protect us?

There was no real way to know how much time had passed. Our legs and backs grew stiff from sitting on the cold ground, but finally I crawled out from underneath the dark boughs.

"You're going already?" Missy asked, crawling after me. She sounded nervous, even though I was the one who should be scared. "Don't you think you should wait a little bit longer?"

"No." I studied her face in the pale light, looking for some sign that she was about to betray me, but her features gave away nothing.

I turned my face toward the sky where the bright crescent moon shone against a clear black night speckled with stars. "It seems pointless to wait too long. If I'm going to get caught, a couple of hours won't make a difference. I can't sit around worrying any longer. If I'm going to do this, I need to do it now."

She crawled out from under the tree. In the moonlight,

I could see the bits of needles and leaves that clung to her tights and stuck out from her hair. She looked like a mess, imperfect and real and just as vulnerable as me. For just a moment I let myself truly hope that I'd see her again.

"Be careful," she said.

"You'll be here when I get back?" I asked.

"I'll be here."

I nodded, not even attempting to speak anymore over the lump that was forming in my throat.

The leaves crunched under my feet as I walked away from her, following the path that the drainage ditch cut through the trees. Luckily the sky was clear, the light from the moon bright.

The smell of damp leaves and dirt perfumed the air. It reminded me of the smell of Penn's garden. Penn. The thought of him pulled me and my legs moved faster. Branches snapped under my feet and clawed at my face, but I didn't slow. I couldn't.

Penn was so close. Just past these trees. Just beyond the next rise.

My lungs burned, but I hardly cared. I could already imagine him, asleep in his room. I could see the soft rise and fall of his chest as he dreamed, not knowing that I was almost there. I wondered if he could feel me getting nearer. Did he see me in his dreams, dashing toward him?

In front of me, I came to the slatted fence that marked the Kimbles' property. It was hard to tell exactly where I was because the trees were still thick, but I guessed that I was just down the hill from the carriage house. Through the trees, I could make out the yellow glow of a light.

My breath was raspy and loud from running. I paused at the fence wishing that I could just leap over it and burst into the house without caring who saw me. But I wasn't stupid. Now wasn't the time for valiant acts of courage. It was time for patience. And so instead of crashing into the house, I waited for my breathing to slow and when I could once again hear the sound of the wind and the chirp of the crickets instead of the rush of my own blood in my ears, I ducked between the slats of the fence and stepped onto the path that led up to the house.

I'd walked this path a hundred times with Penn, but it felt different now. Even though this house had never truly felt like my own home, I hadn't felt like I was trespassing. But now I'd encroached on some invisible barrier, a bubble that sat unseen, suspended around the house. I stepped forward, moving past the thin film into the center of it.

I neared the carriage house and the blinking red light of a camera caught my eye. The black box was tucked up underneath the eaves. The house had never had cameras before, but like Missy had said, things had changed. Something told me that security cameras weren't the only thing.

I moved off the path, keeping close to the bushes that hugged the side of the house. Even in the dark it still looked beautiful. I hadn't been away long, but already I'd forgotten the simply majesty of it: the whitewashed bricks, the wide windows, the tall, pointed roof reaching into the night sky. It was still the most beautiful house I'd ever seen.

I had no idea how wide of a view the camera could capture; no idea, for that matter, how the camera really worked. Did it turn on if it sensed me or was it always going, recording every second in case something showed up? I moved slowly, hoping that if someone were watching, they wouldn't notice me.

I reached the side of the house and pressed my body up

against the tall windows that used to belong to my room. It had only been a couple of weeks since I slept inside those walls, but it felt like a lifetime ago. But I didn't have time to think about that now. Even crouched beside the bushes, the side of the house felt too exposed.

The trellis was only a few steps away. It sat on the other side of the corridor that connected my old room to the rest of the house. It was a sturdy white structure that reached almost all the way up to the roof. The climbing roses that had adorned it during the summer were almost done blooming for the season, but a few white flowers still blossomed near the bottom of it.

I stayed to the edge of the trellis, careful not to grab the sharp thorns that studded the branches that poked out in all directions. The twigs snagged my pant legs as I climbed, scratching the skin around my ankles.

I'd almost reached the top when the sound of voices made me freeze. They were coming from the driveway, two deep voices that I didn't recognize.

"...wants us to stick to the rear post, but it's a waste of time if you ask me."

"Nah, he's not going anywhere."

I clung onto the trellis, trying to push my body against the wall, but if someone walked around the corner of the house, there wasn't going to be any hiding. Even the bushy green leaves from the rosebush wouldn't do anything to hide me.

Feet crunched on the gravel only a few yards away.

My sweaty hands gripped the trellis harder, but I couldn't stay here forever. I was losing my grasp, slipping. From the other side of the garage, the men's footsteps continued to crunch closer. Were they going to follow the path up the driveway or turn left toward the back of the carriage house? If they did, they'd be coming into view any second.

The beat of my pulse throbbed in my neck, my heart trying desperately to escape through my throat, but I didn't take my eyes off of the side of the house. Any second the men would turn the corner and then I'd have a choice to make: jump eight feet to the ground and make a run for it, or pray that they wouldn't notice me perched in the shadows.

Chapter Eleven

My hands and legs twitched, ready to jump, but just as I prepared to leap, the voices began to get quieter. The crunch of footsteps receded into the distance.

My body, which had been clenched so tight in fear, felt suddenly weak. I pulled myself shakily up the last little bit of trellis and onto the roof, collapsing onto the rough tile. I panted, rolling onto my back so that my arms and legs were spread across the small slope, grounding me as I stared up into the night sky. Penn's room was less than twenty feet away, but from here, the ledge that led to it looked so narrow those last few yards seemed impossibly far away.

I stared down the ledge, willing my breath to still. I couldn't just be stuck here, so close. I'd made it hundreds of miles, what were a few more feet? I closed my eyes, trying to will just a little more strength into my shaky limbs. When I opened my eyes, my gaze traveled to Ruby's room. The roof where I clung butted up almost perfectly to her window, which was cracked open to let in a breeze. My heart swelled.

I slid open the window and pushed on the screen. It popped out easily and I climbed inside.

Ruby. Sweet, little Ruby. I'd never even gotten a chance to say good-bye to her. How could I have told her that I was leaving and never coming back, that I'd probably never get a chance to see her again? It must have hurt her that I didn't even try. I'd been her friend, one of the only ones, and I'd let her down. But maybe this was my chance to make up for it.

The room was exactly the same as the last time I'd been in it. The far wall was covered with an enormous bookshelf and the floor in front of it was littered with piles of books that Ruby was either in the process of reading or had just finished. The fat, red collection of fairytales that we'd been reading still sat beside the foot of the armchair. I could almost feel the creamy pages between my fingers.

The big canopied bed on the other side of the room was covered with pillows and the little lump of Ruby's body rested in the center, sleeping soundly. Quietly, I climbed onto the bed and curled up next to her. She snorted softly and wriggled down into her pillow, but she didn't wake.

I brushed away a stray curl that had fallen down in front of her face and took her in: the soft mess of freckles that dusted her cheeks; the tangle of brown hair that fanned around her head like a halo; the impish little smile that pricked her lips even as she slept. She might not grow up to be the great beauty that her parents hoped she would be, but to me, she was the loveliest ten-year-old in the world.

I loved Penn with all my heart, but Ruby might have been the best thing about this house and it broke my heart that I couldn't take her with me.

"Ruby," I whispered.

"Hmmm," she mumbled in her sleep.

I nudged her arm. "Ruby."

Her nose scrunched and her eyes blinked open. For a few long seconds she squinted at my face, unrecognizing, and then her eyes widened.

"Ella?" she said groggily, rubbing her eyes.

"Shh," I whispered. "We've got to be quiet. I only have a minute."

She reached out and touched her fingertips to the blunt edge of my hair where it fell just below my ear.

"You cut your hair," she said. "It's pretty." She wiggled closer and wrapped her arms around me. "I knew you'd come back," she mumbled into my neck.

"I came to tell you how much I love you," I said, stroking her hair.

She pulled away just enough so that she could look into my face. "Can't you stay?" she asked. "It's not the same here without you. No one's happy. Not even my mom."

"I can't," I said. My voice cracked. "But I have something for you."

I reached deep into my pocket and fished out the drawing that Carlie had done of me. I wished that I had something more to give her, some bigger part of myself that she could hold, but I didn't have anything, only this picture and my heart, and I'd already given her that.

I unfolded the paper and smoothed my hand across the image.

Ruby sat up. "This is for me?"

I nodded. If I spoke, I was afraid I'd start crying.

Lightly she touched the portrait. Her finger lingered for a long moment before she folded the paper back up and held it against her chest. "I don't want you to go, but

I understand," she said. "Nobody thinks I get it. They think I'm too little and just assume that I'm not going to understand all these big ideas, but I do." Her eyes filled. "I don't want to keep you here. I don't want to hurt you."

I wrapped her in my arms. Her tears soaked into my shirt, hot against my chest, and I rested my head on top of hers and let myself cry, too.

"Maybe someday things will change and we can be friends," Ruby said, settling back down into her bed.

"Oh, Ruby, we'll always be friends," I told her, pulling the blankets back up around her chin. "Don't you ever forget that."

She smiled sadly. "You won't forget me, will you?"

"Of course not." I leaned down and kissed her forehead. "My whole life, you'll always be my first best friend."

She smiled, nodding. I climbed off the bed, pausing at her door.

"Ella," she whispered.

I turned back around.

"I love you."

"I love you, too."

I stepped out into the dark hallway, closing her door quietly behind me. Already my heart felt raw and I hadn't even seen Penn yet.

The house was quiet, the hallway dark and empty. I let out a relieved breath. I don't know what I'd been expecting, an army of men like the ones outside guarding the doors? But the inside of the house looked exactly the way it had since the day I'd first arrived.

Down the hall, the door to Penn's room sat in shadows, closed tight. I stopped in front of it and rested my hand on the knob. If I closed my eyes, would I be able to hear the soft strains of Ray LaMontagne drifting under the door the way I had the very first time? All the memories of what lay just beyond the threshold flooded my mind: Penn's hands moving across the strings of his guitar, the sticky ice cream sundaes, the feel of his sheets beneath my skin. My skin prickled with excitement, as if my body could already sense the presence of him there, the magnetic pull of him.

The handle creaked ever so slightly as I pushed my way inside, but I wasn't worried. I was a thief now. Silently, I pulled the door shut behind me.

The blinds on the window were pulled shut, shrouding the room in black. Only a small beam of moonlight slanted across the floor, inching partway up the bed so that it illuminated Penn's hand where it dangled over the side of the mattress. It was too dark to see his face, but even the sight of his beautiful fingers made my throat constrict. I hadn't even realized how much I'd missed those hands. Those beautiful hands, strong and capable and tender. I'd missed watching the way they plucked the strings of his guitar. I'd missed the way he lifted them to his face to push away a stray lock of hair that had fallen into his eyes. I missed the way he would trace them across my nose, my cheeks, my mouth.

In a moment I was at his side pressing that hand to my lips. How had I gone so long without touching him? His hand was warm, the skin a little rough. I wanted to savor every inch of him; to kiss each finger, to feel the calluses on their tips, worn smooth from the strings of his guitar.

But my kiss only lasted a moment. My touch woke him and he pulled back, startled, fumbling for the lamp at the side of his bed. He flipped the switch and light spilled across the bed, bathing him in a warm yellow glow.

He blinked, allowing his eyes to adjust to the brightness. His face was still disoriented from sleep. A few crease marks from his pillow lined the left side of his forehead and cheek, and his dark hair stuck up a bit on one side. I wasn't used to this short cut. Even messed up from sleep this new haircut looked too tame, too adult. He was only a year older than me, but it seemed like he'd aged ten years in the few weeks we'd been apart.

He rubbed his eyes. It was the most vulnerable I'd ever seen him and the scene made my head spin with a pure and burning love, so overwhelming that I couldn't think, couldn't speak.

He blinked one more time and a look of recognition dawned across his face.

"Ella."

My name on his lips, so soft, so sweet.

In the time it took to draw a breath, he slipped from the bed and cupped my face in his hands, kissing my eyes, my cheeks, my lips, my chin. He kissed me like he was drinking me in, like he'd never be able to get his fill. Unquenchable.

He pulled back a few inches, just enough to take in my face. His lips trembled as his hands traveled down past my neck, drifting over my shoulders and arms. They stopped at my wrists and he took a deep breath, slowly turning my hands so they lay open, cupped like I was waiting to hold onto something. He brought his mouth to them, brushing his lips across the lines that creased my palms.

And then his mouth was on mine and the time that we'd been separated melted away. That empty space inside my chest, which had felt so cavernous, so expansive, filled with the shape of him, the smell, the taste, as if I'd opened the barred cage of my ribs and he'd crawled inside me, making a home beside my heart. And like my heart, it felt like he'd always been here, as essential as the blood running through my veins.

"Oh God, Ella, I..." He moaned and then, as if the words had startled him, he drew back, holding me at arm's length.

The happiness that had shone from his face disappeared with a shake of his head. The small circle of light that enveloped us seemed to shrink, darkness pushing in from all sides.

"You can't be here," he said. "You've got to leave."

He scrambled to his feet, pulling me up by my elbow as he dragged me toward the window.

"What are you doing? I just—"

His large hand covered my mouth. His eyes had gotten big, but it wasn't surprise, or love, or even lust that I saw in them. There was only fear.

"You can't be here," he whispered.

For the first time since I'd entered his room, I looked around. I'd been so consumed by Penn that the whole world could have fallen away, but I saw it now. Most of the room was deep in shadow, but even the small amount of light given off by the lamp was enough for me to notice the difference.

It hardly even looked like his room anymore. Every bit of his personality had been wiped away. The wall that had once been covered with instruments was now bare. Even the nails that they had hung on were gone. All the posters and signs that had given the walls life and color had been stripped away and a new coat of paint blocked out every scratch or scuff, leaving the room bare except for furniture.

Penn watched me take it all in, but he didn't explain.

Instead, he fumbled to open the window. His motions were rushed and he glanced back over his shoulder toward the door.

He lifted me, pushing me through the window. "Meet me in the garden," he whispered, his words hot in my ear.

I grabbed onto the frame, fighting to keep my balance on the small ledge. From the hallway came the unmistakable sound of footsteps and I ducked down just as the door to his room opened. With one quick motion he pulled the blinds shut, and the room disappeared.

"What are you doing up?"

The congressman's voice caught me off guard. I would never forget the deep grumble of that voice, the way his vowels seemed to crunch like gravel inside his mouth. I wouldn't forget it if I lived for a million years. My head spun and I pressed myself against the side of the house to keep from toppling over.

It was his house. I should have known that there was the chance that I would see him, but I'd only been thinking about Penn. The sound of his voice, so clear, so close, made my stomach turn.

Through the open window, the ground creaked softly as Penn moved to block the window. "I couldn't sleep," he said. "I'm sorry. Did I wake you?"

He hadn't pulled the blinds closed all the way. A small gap about an inch wide still gave me a small glimpse of the room. My legs quivered, weak with fear as the congressman stepped further into the room and came into view. The lamp cast a shadow across his jaw, deepening the lines in his face and making the salt and pepper stubble that grew along his chin appear even darker. And even though I could only see the side of his face I knew that his black eyes were piercing.

Get away! my brain screamed. Like a siren. Like an alarm. Jump. Run. Fly. Whatever I needed to do to put distance between the congressman and myself. But I couldn't move. My body was frozen.

"The sensor went off," the congressman said, glancing around the room suspiciously.

I pressed myself closer to the house.

"I had a bad dream," Penn said. "I must have been mumbling in my sleep."

The congressman stared at his son. I had no idea what was going on inside his head, but the look that passed between them was brutal. Each glance felt like a blow, the blunt force of their egos knocking against one another.

Finally Penn looked down.

"Are you holding something?" the congressman asked, staring down at Penn's balled fists.

"No."

His jaw flexed. "Is it a phone? You know you were forbidden to have one."

"I don't—" Penn started to say.

"Have you been calling someone?"

"No! You took it away. How was I even supposed to get another one? It's not like I even go anywhere anymore."

"Show me your hands," the congressman ordered.

I knew that they were empty, but even so, my heart skipped. My touch hadn't actually left a mark on him, but it felt as if his hands should have been stained. After all, I could still feel his touch on my arms and my face as tangible as a second skin.

"I don't have anything." Penn held up his empty hands.

The congressman sighed. "I'm sorry," he said. "You know I'd like to be able to trust you again."

"I know," Penn mumbled.

"This isn't going to last forever," the congressman said. "A month or two and there's not going to be anything to worry about anymore. This whole problem will be extinguished and we can get things back to normal."

"What do you mean extinguished?"

A cold wind blew up from the lawn, making the curtains flap and the congressman's shoulders stiffened.

"Why is the window open?" he asked, completely ignoring Penn's question.

I scooted back from the window. The ledge was narrow, less than two feet wide, but I flipped around and pressed my back to the wall trying to make myself as small as I could.

Above me, the congressman pulled the curtains back with a *whoosh* and some of the light from the room shone out into the night. I pulled my legs closer to my chest, trying to make myself as small as I could. I looked to my left. The window to Ruby's room was only about fifteen feet away. Maybe I could crawl along the ledge and make it back into her room before the congressman saw me…

"You can close it," Penn said. "I woke up in a sweat. I just opened it to cool off."

I was too afraid to turn my head. If I looked up would I see the congressman peering down at me? The seconds ticked past. One. Two. Three. An eternity of waiting. I waited to feel his hand tighten around my shoulders, tugging me back into the room.

Instead, the congressman sighed. Above my head, the window slid shut and the curtains closed once again. I didn't have time to feel relieved. I scrambled back to the trellis.

When my feet hit the ground I bolted down the path toward the garden. The house disappeared behind me, replaced by arched branches of oak and ash. I moved farther down the path, past the hydrangea bushes and the gnarled tangle of the fruit orchard.

Despite the urgency of the situation, I felt at home. Penn and I had followed this same path down to the garden almost every night. Maybe my body kept the memory of this trail stored somewhere deep inside. It remembered the curve of the earth beneath my feet. It remembered the soft padding of woodchips and the crunch of gravel. I could have walked it blindfolded.

The tightness in my stomach began to release, just enough so that I could breathe. It didn't make sense that fear and love could feel so similar, but they did: this pounding in my chest, the unsteadiness in my legs, the feeling that each and every nerve in my body was alive and on fire.

At the entrance to the garden I slowed, stopping in front of the wrought iron gate. Funny that a place could seem almost human, but the garden did. I hadn't had a chance to say good-bye the last time I was here, but maybe tonight was for all sorts of good-byes.

I pushed on the gate and it squealed softly, welcoming me as I stepped inside.

"Hello," I said under my breath.

The wind brushed across the tops of the walls, making the ivy flutter like a thousand tiny hands waving.

Around the perimeter, the flowers had mostly come and gone. Their tall stalks hung heavy with fading blooms. In the air, there was a new smell. The garden had always smelled of moist earth and blossoms and decaying leaves, but now it smelled like change. Summer was dying.

The top of the reflecting pond was littered with fallen leaves. I sat down next to it and ran my fingers across the surface. If I brushed away these leaves would I be able to see the memory of Penn and me reflected in the surface? I wanted to believe that we were still here somewhere. That we always would be. I wanted that one perfect moment to exist forever. For years to come this water would hold the image of me floating on my back staring up into the sky, up into the constellation of Penn's eyes.

But maybe memories were the only things that could exist here now. Maybe I'd been wrong to come back. I was putting Penn in more danger. Clearly, things had changed since I left. His room was proof of that. His father had wiped away every trace of who he'd been only a few weeks ago and those were only objects. That was just a room. What must he have done to Penn?

The thought made me shudder. He couldn't have changed him that much. The way he'd touched me. The way he kissed me. That was the real Penn. I'd felt him there, even if the outside had changed.

Behind me, the gate groaned softly.

I jumped to my feet and turned to see Penn. The moon lit his white shirt so that it almost glowed, framed by the dark outline of the gate behind him. He looked almost too beautiful to believe, standing there still rumpled from sleep.

"Ella?"

He said my name like a question he was too afraid to ask, staring at me from across the garden as if he'd seen a ghost.

"You came," I said.

"Of course."

He closed the distance between us in a heartbeat. Standing before me, he reached out and stroked the blunt ends of my hair.

"As I was walking down here, I wondered if maybe I'd dreamed you. If it wasn't real. But here you are."

With his thumb and his forefinger, he gently lifted my chin and pressed his lips to mine. His mouth moved slowly, tenderly. Time slowed. Melted. Broke away. The moments stretched, as fluid as water, flowing forward: a drop, a river, an ocean, until I was suspended inside it. Lost.

He pulled away and the world rushed back into focus, time crashing down around us.

"Your father—" I said.

He shook his head. "Don't worry. He won't follow me out here. No one will."

"But inside… He knew!"

Penn shook his head. "He has the house bugged. He listens to everything: all my phone calls, all my conversations. He has a chokehold on me, but it's safe out here."

"What about those men?"

"His henchmen?" Penn chuckled, but it was a sad sound. "They won't come, either. I've been coming out here almost every night since he hired them. They're lazy. They got sick of following me after the first few nights. Once they realized that I was just coming out here to sit, they gave up."

He pulled me into him again, holding me so tight against his chest I could feel the thrum of his heart against my cheek.

"I can't believe you're really here," he said. "I didn't think I'd ever see you again." I looked up at him and he turned away, his face contorting. "I thought about trying to come to you a thousand times, but I didn't know how. My dad is watching the borders and I think he almost expected me to go running after you. But he never could have dreamed that you'd come back."

"I came as fast as I could," I said. "I saw you on TV. You looked so…" What could I say? So beaten down? So empty?

"But how? It's hundreds of miles and…" His voice trailed off and he shook his head.

There was so much to tell him about: Missy, my escape from the refugee center, the train, the horrible things I'd seen in the black markets.

"There's no time now, but I promise, I'll tell you later."

He sighed. "At least I got this chance to hold you one more time. To touch you. But you can't stay. It's too dangerous. If my dad knew you were here—"

"What has he done to you?" I ran my fingers through his cut hair. Even after he'd been sleeping on it, it looked too groomed, like his father had managed to suck the wildness right out of the top of his head.

"I'm fine," he said. "I can handle it as long as I know you're okay."

"But I'm not okay without you."

He closed his eyes. He wasn't okay either.

"Come with me," I said.

He swallowed. "Ella, he's way worse now. I know he was a little obsessed before, but now… If he got his hands on you…" He shook his head. "I don't think it would be enough to just own you again. He wants revenge. And if that means that he has to destroy you, it's what he'll do."

I closed my eyes, trying not to imagine the photographs, but it was impossible. If the congressman got his hands on me, would I be next?

"That's why we have to get out of here. *Both* of us," I said. "This isn't revenge? What he's doing to you? I saw your room. Every piece of you is gone. You can't last like this. You can't keep pretending."

"Well, I can't just leave," he said. "He'd find us. I never realized how strong his connections were, but since you've been gone, I've seen the worst come out in him. And it's not like he's just sitting home crying into a tub of ice cream. He's got powerful people working for him. Police. Lawmakers."

I lifted my chin. "Then we need to stop him."

"He and NuPet have more than half of the government wrapped around their little finger."

"So we just give up?"

Penn sighed. "At least you're free. That's something isn't it?"

"Not if I can't be with you. Not if terrible things are happening to girls like me all over the country."

"We can't help them, Ella." His face looked so sad in the moonlight. Defeated.

"Come with me," I said again.

"And do what?"

"You can't already have given up," I said. "We haven't even tried yet."

"I haven't given up," Penn said. "But I can't just think about what I want. I have to think about you, too. Maybe the best thing is for me to stay, learn things from the inside. Maybe I can make a difference here. I'll study law. I'll make sure that his stupid bill gets overturned."

"Are you listening to yourself? That would take years. *Years*. And he'd be controlling you the whole time."

"No he wouldn't. I'd— "

"You'd lose yourself," I interrupted. "And you'd lose me, too. I know what it's like to let someone else choose the course of your life. I know what it's like not to have a voice. Not to have a future. And I won't do it anymore."

Penn took the smallest step away from me. His brow

furrowed, studying my face as if I was some new creature that he'd never seen before. I didn't care. I hadn't come all this way just to have him give up on me. On us.

"And I don't care if it's dangerous," I went on. "You need to stop trying to protect me and let me protect myself. I'm stronger than anyone gives me credit for and if that's the one and only advantage I have to fight them with, fine. I'll take it."

I couldn't read the look in Penn's eye. It looked like fear, but of what, I had no way of knowing: fear of his father, fear of losing me, fear of losing himself. Fear of the unknown. Fear of the future. Maybe that's all that life really was: the fear of moving forward toward events we had no way of truly knowing.

"When you showed up in my room earlier. It was like seeing a ghost," he said. "The ghost of you. And for a second I really thought I was going crazy. I've seen you everywhere. In everything. It's like my house was haunted and not just with memories of you. I'd walk into a room and I'd swear I'd see you there, sitting by the window or on the couch and then I'd blink and you'd be gone. But tonight… I blinked, and you were still there."

He sighed. "Why can't we just stay inside this garden forever? You and me? We could forget the rest of the world and be together."

He wrapped me in his arms and kissed me long and hard, as if he truly believed that it could happen. If he wished hard enough, the magic of this place would envelop us and keep us safe.

"You wouldn't really want that," I said, staring up into the deep galaxy of his eyes. "You don't want to be trapped. Even if it is with me."

"I don't know if I can lose you again."

"Then don't," I said, taking his hand in mine. "Come with me."

Three words, but my future hung on them. *Come with me.* They were a prayer. They were hope flung from my lips into the endless sky above us. They were a dream. They were a wish.

Come with me.

"You want to leave now?" Penn asked.

I nodded. "I can't stay much longer. It's too dangerous."

He looked down at his clothes. He still wore the white undershirt that he slept in plus a pair of jeans and shoes he'd slipped on before he came down. But that was it. He shrugged and shook his head as if he was realizing that if he chose to come he was now wearing the sum total of everything that he owned.

"It would kill my mom. And Ruby."

"I'm sorry," I said. "If there was any other way…"

"No, I know." He shook his head and closed his eyes. It was impossible to hide the pain on his face. He'd already chosen to leave them once, but somehow this time it seemed worse. The permanence was more real. To leave now wouldn't just be a strike against his father; it would be a declaration of war.

He opened his eyes. "Okay."

Chapter Twelve

Okay? The word knocked the air from my lungs.

"You'll come?" I whispered.

A smile broke out across his face, shattering the fear that had lingered there all night. "It wasn't ever a question really, was it? Maybe we're being stupid. Maybe we're fools to think we stand a chance, but if it means I can be with you, I'll try." He looked down at his clothes again, then around at the garden. "So this is it then? I guess I can't go back to the house and pack a bag."

I shook my head.

"Well, at least I've got clean underwear," he laughed, pulling me into his chest. "And I've got you. That's all I really need."

His warm lips rested on the top of my head while we stood in silence in our garden one last time. At the other end of the reflecting pool, the stone angel lifted her head skyward. It was a hopeful posture and I lifted my head to copy her.

Stepping out of the garden felt like leaving one of Ruby's fairytales. In it, I could almost believe magic existed and protective spells could keep us safe, but it was time to move into the real world.

The gate groaned a lone note, a good-bye song, and we stepped onto the path.

"We need to get away from my house as fast as possible," Penn said.

I pulled him in the direction of the pine tree. "There's somewhere we have to go first."

How long had I been gone? It felt like the world had held its breath along with me. Since I stepped back onto the Kimbles' property, I had lost all sense of time. Hopefully Missy was still waiting for me.

The pine tree was even easier to find than I'd imagined, but when I pulled back the bottom boughs, Missy was gone.

"What is it?" Penn asked, concerned.

I shook my head. How could I tell him? How could I say that even though I never really expected Missy to stay, I wanted her friendship to be real? I *needed* it to be real. She'd only promised to get me here and she'd done that. But even with Penn at my side, I felt lost without her. She was a pet, like me, and maybe that's what I liked about her. As much as it irritated me, her strength and will, all the qualities that we'd been taught to push down, were the things that made me love her.

"He came?"

I spun around to see Missy emerge from behind a tree with her backpack dangling from one hand.

"*You?*" Penn asked, glancing from Missy to me.

She shrugged.

"I told you he would come," I said.

The two of them stared at each other.

"Penn, this is Missy. She helped me get back here."

She slung her bag up over her shoulder. "And now we're here and we've got you. Isn't that great?" she said. "Ella was so convinced that you were going to help. So now what?" She sized him up, but the look on her face told me that she didn't have much confidence in him.

"You're asking me?" Penn said.

"Yes."

"I don't know," he said. "I just woke up to a slight change in plans. It's not like I've really had time to think things over."

Missy looked down to the place where his hand held on to mine and rolled her eyes. "I'm so glad you're happily reunited, but right now we don't exactly have the luxury of time to mull things over, do we?"

"Enough," I snapped. "You're right. We don't have time. They could find out any moment that Penn is gone."

"And if they find him, they find us," Missy said. "You still think it was such a good idea to come get him?"

"Look, I realize that none of this is ideal," Penn said. "But I'm here and I'll try to help, so let's make do with what we've got."

"And what's that?" Missy asked. "Because it doesn't look like you've got much of anything."

"We've got each other," Penn said hopefully.

Missy snorted. "A fat lot of good that's going to do me. How about a plan? Do you have that? Or food? Or a car?"

Penn shook his head. "No."

"What about a place to stay?"

He shook his head again.

"Well, I suggest we start walking," Missy said. "Because it isn't doing us any good standing around here waiting to get caught."

She started tromping through the woods and Penn and I raced to catch up with her.

"Where are we going?" I asked.

"I need to make a quick stop," Missy said. "Your boy didn't come with anything useful, so we're going to have to get creative."

We clawed our way through the woods, finally scrambling up a small bank and out onto the quiet road.

"This way," Missy said, turning left.

"But that will lead us right past my house," Penn said.

"Then we better hurry."

The street was silent, except for the sound of our shoes hitting the pavement. In front of us, the entrance to Penn's driveway grew close once more. I slowed as we neared the dark hedges, every cell in my body screaming at me to run.

But first, there was something I needed to do.

I reached in my pocket and fished out the gold pendant. Without stopping to think it through, I ran up to the tall brick mailbox and draped the necklace over the handle.

"What are you doing?" Missy asked. "They'll know you were here."

"As long as I keep that, he's going to own a little piece of me," I said.

"So, chuck it in the woods. Flush it down the toilet. I don't care. Something. But don't let him know you were here."

"No," I said, stepping back from the necklace. "I want him to know. He's going to figure it out soon enough. With Penn gone, he'll know. And this way he can be sure. Let him know I was here. Let him know I slipped through his fingers one last time. He doesn't own me anymore."

I turned, heading away from the congressman's house one last time. The others trotted along behind me, but I didn't slow. The more distance I put between myself and that house, the more free I felt. The chains that had been holding me down for weeks, months, years, were finally falling away.

"I don't know what he's going to do when he finds that," Penn finally said, catching up to me. "But it's going to piss him off. He's not used to people standing up to him."

"Well, he better get used to it."

Missy jogged ahead of us. "You see that bend in the road up there?" she asked. "There's a ditch by those telephone poles. You two wait for me there, okay?"

I nodded. My gaze swept past the spot in the road that she was pointing to toward the smaller road that curved off of it. Even in the dark, I recognized it. She was heading home.

"You're not going to do anything stupid are you?" I asked.

"Not any stupider than anything you've done."

Her words sounded tough, but a hint of worry wavered beneath them. "Be careful," I whispered.

"Don't worry about me," she said. "If I'm not back in an hour, I want you guys to leave. Understand?"

"No, we're not just going to—"

"Don't argue with me," she interrupted.

Penn grabbed my hand, leading me toward the side of the road. "Fine," he said. "One hour."

Missy paused, studying him, and the smallest smile lifted the corners of her mouth before she spun on her heel and took off at a trot down the road.

Penn held my hand to steady me as I slid down the steep embankment. He followed after me and settled down amid the tall dry grass, patting the ground next to him. I folded myself into his side. As good as it felt to be with him, it didn't feel right to let Missy go off by herself.

"So Missy, huh?" Penn said. "I've got to say, it seems like an unlikely match, the two of you."

"That's putting it nicely." I laughed. "I can't tell you how many times I've wanted to strangle her."

Penn chuckled. "She doesn't like me much, does she?" he asked, gesturing back in the direction that Missy had disappeared.

"I'm not sure if Missy likes anyone."

"She must like you. Why else would she have come?"

"Honestly, I don't really know," I said. "I sometimes wondered if she was just leading me back to some trap that your dad set up."

Penn raised his eyebrows. "You don't think—"

"No!" I shook my head. "No, I don't." How could I tell Penn about the things I'd seen? The things she'd done to get us here? Missy had proved herself to be a brave and honest person, even though the reason she'd chosen to help me might always be a mystery.

I snuggled into his side. The warmth that he gave off made me want to close my eyes right there. This peace that I felt next to him was at such odds with the constant worry that had taken up residence inside me. If only for a few minutes, I wanted to let the anxiety of being found fall away, peeling back so many other fears with it. If only I could let myself forget that pets were dying, that girls were languishing in black markets that only valued them for their bodies, that now I was responsible for Penn's safety as well as my own. If only I could let those thoughts drop away and focus instead on the heat from Penn's hands, on the closeness of our bodies.

"Is it crazy that this feels right?" Penn asked. "I mean, we're in a cold ditch on the side of the road, basically running for our lives," he said, "and I still think that there's no place in the world I'd rather be. Tell me that's not crazy."

"Maybe it's a little crazy." I smiled. "Or maybe it's..." I searched for the word. "Masochistic."

Penn snorted. "It is, isn't it?" He shook his head. "You know, you never cease to amaze me. People underestimate you, don't they? Your whole life they've told you that you're just a pretty face. They thought they taught you to parrot big ideas, but that's never what you were doing. You soaked it all in. You remembered it all. All their big words. All their big ideas. And now you're going to crush them with it."

"I am?" I giggled, a little terrified and a little thrilled that he thought so much of me.

"They aren't going to know what hit 'em."

I shouldn't have worried about Missy being gone for long. Hardly half an hour passed before we heard the slap of her feet against the pavement as she appeared on the road above us. The moon lit her from behind, making it impossible to see her face as she kneeled down next to the side of the road.

"Come on," she called down to us. "We've got to get a move on."

Penn and I scrambled up the side of the hill. "Where are

we going?" I asked.

"Unless you want to sleep in that ditch, I think we better go find a place to stay."

Already, she was a few yards ahead of us, moving briskly. The two of us quickly brushed off our pants and shook our stiff legs, then rushed to catch up with her.

"Do you have a place in mind?" Penn asked.

"As a matter of fact, I do," she said. "And believe it or not, you're actually going to come in handy."

Penn shot me a concerned glance. "I don't have any friends we can stay with, if that's what you're thinking. I've already run the whole thing through my mind a million different times. If there were someplace I could go, someone that would actually help me, I would have already gone. But believe me, my dad would find us in a heartbeat."

"I'm not stupid," Missy said. "I don't know your friends and I'm not sure if I'd trust any of them anyway. They're probably all rich and arrogant and entitled like everyone else around here. We're going to stay at a motel. I've already slept in these woods once and I really don't want to do it again. There's no way someone would give a room to me or Ella, but they'll give one to you."

"That's nice, but I don't have any money," Penn said.

In front of us, a pair of headlights rounded the corner and, together, the three of us dove into the bushes, pressing our bodies as flat as we could against the ground. The car didn't even slow as it passed us. We all waited in silence until the red of its taillights had disappeared before we stood again.

Penn and I turned to go. "There's probably someplace that we can sleep. Maybe there's a groundskeeper's shed at the country club we could sneak into."

"We need someplace safe," Missy said. "Ella and I need sleep. We need a bed. We're going to the motel." She bent over her backpack. "Anyway, money isn't something we need to worry about. Where'd you think I went, anyway?" she said, pulling a thick stack of bills out of her bag. She fanned the wad of cash in front of her face.

"You just stole that?" Penn asked. "God, as if we weren't in enough trouble before. How much is that anyway? That's, like, thousands of dollars."

"Don't get all dramatic," Missy said, shoving the money back in her bag. "I only took one little stack. He has dozens of these. He's not even going to notice until he sits down to count his treasure and reconfirm to himself that he's the most powerful, potent, mighty man in the world." Her shoulders relaxed. "It's actually kind of funny when you think about it."

Penn gave me a sideways glance, raising one of his eyebrows as if to say that he seriously doubted it.

A cool breeze rustled through the trees and Missy chuckled just a little before she started talking again.

"My old master is kind of obsessed with his money. To say he's compensating is an understatement. So maybe if he was a little bit less obsessed with his net worth and was a tad more observant, he would have thought twice about opening his safe in front of me." She snorted. "I can't tell you how paranoid he is about his safe. He keeps it hidden behind a false panel in his study. He's gone to all sorts of trouble to make it so no one but him is able to open it. I'm not sure his wife even knows it's there, but I do. That's the funny part. You know what I mean, Ella. You're a pet. You know what it's like to be overlooked. But at least it paid off."

She patted her bag.

I smiled. So we had another thief amongst us. "So you just snuck in and opened the safe? There wasn't an alarm?"

"Oh, I knew the code to that, too," she said with a flick of her wrist.

Penn's mouth dropped open, but I just laughed. She'd stolen way too much money, but I loved her fearlessness, her tenacity, her irrepressible belief that she was right.

Our whole lives, we had been bred to give.

Now it was time to start taking.

We'd been walking for a little over three hours when we finally straggled up to the motel. The sky wasn't pitch black anymore, but it wasn't light out either. Morning was just an idea that night was considering, a blush-colored dream.

We stopped at the edge of the parking lot and stared up at the shabby two-story building with its rows of faded orange doors and flaking metal railings.

"You steal thousands of dollars and you choose to stay here?" Penn asked. "There were a bunch of places that were way closer and ten times as nice."

Missy completely ignored him as she sat down on a low cement railing and began counting out twenties from her stack of bills.

Penn just shook his head.

"I think it's perfect," I said. "We would have looked kind of suspicious showing up in the middle of the night at someplace too nice. This..." I looked up at the faded sign. The bit of neon writing below it fizzled on and off and back on again. "This looks like the kind of place where people come to hide."

"Well, let's just hope my father doesn't think the same thing."

"Here," Missy said, shoving a stack of bills into Penn's hand. "Stop complaining and go get us a room. Just be sure not to put it in your real name."

"I'm not that clueless," Penn said with a smile. "Don't worry. These places don't care about names as long as you've got cash, which we definitely have, thanks to *you*."

He winked at her, stuffed the money in his pocket, and trotted off across the parking lot.

Missy lifted her chin, a satisfied smile tugging at the corner of her lips. "Your boyfriend's not *completely* terrible."

If I wasn't so exhausted, I would have laughed.

The room was on the bottom floor, just down from the Dumpster with a view of the parking lot, but none of us cared. We hardly noticed the stained carpet or the dingy comforters after we closed the door behind us and collapsed onto the beds.

Missy didn't even bother kicking off her shoes. "Don't wake me up," she said, pulling the covers up over her. "Ever."

Penn scooted up onto the pillow and pulled me in close so that my back was pressed against his stomach. His arm curled tight around me and before I even had a chance to pull the blankets up over us, his breath had slowed. His hand stretched out across my stomach twitched softly.

I closed my eyes. "I love you, Penn," I whispered.

He moaned and buried his face into the back of my neck. "Ella," he breathed, as if my name alone was enough. And it was.

It didn't matter that the room was dark and musky and smelled of stale smoke and too much air freshener. This was the only place I wanted to be. Outside, an orange light flickered, hypnotizing me. I closed my eyes, too, letting myself rest as if I'd finally found my way home.

When I woke, sun was streaming through the crack in the blinds, and Penn was propped up on one elbow, smiling at me.

"If I could wake up to this view every morning for the rest of my life, I think I'd die a happy man," he said, brushing a wisp of hair off my cheek.

I rolled onto my side, facing him. "Good morning."

"I hope I didn't creep you out…just staring at you like that."

"No." I smiled. "I like it."

"Good," he said. "Because I'm going to be staring at you a lot today. It was dark last night, so I didn't get the full effect of this new look." He ran his finger across my forehead, tracing the fringe of my hair. "You look different."

"A good different?"

He laughed softly. "Yes, a good different. I don't think there's anything you could do that I wouldn't adore." He stopped talking and studied me, cocking his head just a little to the side. "You kind of look like a badass. I either see bass player in a punk band or assassin as viable career opportunities in your near future."

"Hmmm..." I tapped my chin, considering. "You don't see classical piano playing assassin?"

He laughed. "Hey! I don't want to pigeonhole you."

I stared up at the ceiling, smiling. For a second it seemed possible to imagine that my future was wide open.

Penn pulled me closer. "I freaked out for a second when I woke up," he said.

"Why?"

"You know when you first open your eyes and you're still stuck in whatever dream you were just dreaming and it takes a minute for reality to sink in?"

I nodded.

"I guess I was waiting for that to happen. Like everything that happened last night was just a dream. But it wasn't."

He pinched my arm.

"Ouch," I giggled, pulling it away. "Why are you doing that?"

He pinched me again. "I know I'm supposed to pinch myself to see if I'm awake, but you're much more fun to pinch."

I squealed, pinching his arm in retaliation and he rolled onto his back, pulling me on top of him.

"Will you two stop acting happy," Missy moaned from her bed. "Some of us are still trying to pretend that we exist in a different reality."

"All right," Penn said, kissing me gently on the forehead before he scooted out from under me. "I don't know about you, but I'm starving. There's a little gas station next door. I'll go see if I can rustle up something resembling a breakfast."

"Good idea," Missy mumbled. Under the covers she dug into her pocket and pulled out some of the leftover money that Penn hadn't used on the hotel room, tossing it blindly at him before she pulled the covers back up over her head.

Penn shook his head, gathering the money off the ground before he came to stand next to the bed. He cupped my face in his hand.

"It's hard to leave," he said. "Even though I know I'm coming right back."

I pressed my hands over the top of his and closed my eyes, trying to breathe him in. I knew he'd be back, but by now I also knew not to count on anything. Each moment was its own tiny wonder, but that didn't mean that it would last.

When the door latched behind him, I rose and pulled back the two layers of blinds, watching as he strode across the parking lot and disappeared around the side of the building.

The parking lot was full of cars. A few rows away, a man and woman leaned against the trunk of a blue sedan. They were too far away to see the expression on their faces, but I couldn't take my eyes off of them, the relaxed way they stood next to each other. The woman reached out, placing her hand on the back of his neck. It only rested there for a moment, the most fleeting gesture, but from the ease of it, I guessed that she'd touched him that same way a thousand times.

I had no idea what sort of lives normal people lived, but I wanted to know. It was almost impossible to believe that out of all the people in the world, these two had found one another. It seemed impossible, but I wanted to believe it.

Chapter Thirteen

Half an hour later, Penn returned with three bags full of food.

He dumped the contents out in the middle of our bed. "I might have gone overboard, but this is what happens when you ask a guy to go shopping when he's hungry."

Missy sat up, throwing the blankets off of her as if the packages spread out on the bed were actually plates full of fine meats and steaming loaves of fresh bread, drawing her to them with their irresistible aroma.

Penn sat down on the edge of the bed. "All right, let's see what we've got. I might not have covered the four main food groups, but I think I at least came close."

I sat at the head of the bed, tucking my legs up underneath me.

"For our grain group we've got two kinds of granola bars, goldfish crackers, and a box of cereal," he said, plucking the items out of the pile and laying them in front of Missy like an offering.

"For our all-important meat group—at least, I think that's a group—the meat group. It sounds right." He laughed uncomfortably. "I learned this in like third grade, so I can't totally be expected to remember. Anyway, for the meat group, we've got a jumbo bag of beef jerky—Teriyaki flavored, of course—and a bunch of these beef stick things, although they look a little sketchy, and a can of sardines, which I realize might be gross, but I don't know what you guys like."

Missy and I stared at him, transfixed.

He blinked at us and cleared his throat. "So, um…okay. Fruits and vegetables were kind of tricky, but I got a couple bags of trail mix that has dried fruit in it, and some of these yogurts with fruit on the bottom. That's gotta count for fruit and dairy, I think."

He finished organizing his haul and leaned back on his palms, looking at all the packages a little sheepishly.

I reached for his hand. "I think you got enough food to last us for a month."

"Are you kidding?" Penn snorted. "We'll be lucky if this lasts until dinner."

Missy rolled her eyes, but she was smiling. "I didn't realize we were going to be feeding an elephant when we brought him along. I should have stolen the gold bars, too."

"Be thankful that you didn't," Penn said. "I bet those things are heavy."

I grabbed one of the cups of yogurt and an individually wrapped plastic spoon and leaned back against the headboard, peeling back the yogurt's thin silvery wrapper. I'd never tried one before. I'd had plain yogurt with flaxseeds, but this was different. It was the softest shade of pink and when I dug my spoon in, a dark, purple syrup rose to the surface. I licked the sweetness off of the spoon and closed my eyes. Maybe I was just hungry, or maybe now that Penn was with me again, the world had regained its color, and brightness, and beauty, because it was the most delicious thing I'd ever tasted.

Missy grabbed a box of granola bars and switched on the TV before she plopped back down on the bed.

"I can't tell you how long I've wanted to be able to do this," she said, unwrapping one of the bars and shoving half of it in her mouth.

"What? Stay at a crappy motel?" Penn asked.

"I couldn't care less if it's a piece of crap," she said. "I've stayed in some of the nicest hotels in Europe and never once was I able to do this."

"Eat on the bed?"

"No! This!" she said, pointing to herself and then to the rest of the room in wide circling gestures, as if she was trying to scoop the whole scene into her arms. "This! This! This! There's no one here expecting me to be anything or do anything. I mean look. Look at that," she said, pointing to the TV.

On the screen, a woman was spinning a huge colored wheel while a man with a microphone stood next to her. The colors on the screen didn't seem quite right. The people were too orange and the blues all looked muddy.

"*The Price is Right*?" Penn asked.

"No!" Missy shouted. "I mean yes, whatever. It doesn't matter what the show is. What matters is that I picked it and no one is going to come in here and tell me to turn it off, or switch the channel to the thing they want to watch because their opinion matters and mine doesn't."

She scooted to the end of the bed and took another big bite out of her granola bar.

The morning passed in a lazy haze of game shows and sitcoms. Missy and I had spent our lives learning how to be idle, but this was different. We knew how to be beautiful doing nothing at all, but we'd never known how to enjoy it. We could be the perfect showpiece while our master did the most mundane tasks. We could sit still for hours with impeccable posture and a content look upon our faces while he talked business with colleagues or plucked his eyebrows. It didn't really make a difference to us. But that was a different sort of idle.

Now we lounged back across the bed without thinking about the shapes our bodies made. Instead we thought about comfort. Missy lay on her stomach with her arms dangling off the edge of the bed while I lay on my back with my feet propped up on the headboard, my arms crossed behind my head.

"I could get used to this," I said, reaching out to run my hand through Penn's hair for the hundredth time.

I couldn't stop touching him. Sometimes my hand moved on its own accord, like my body wanted reassurance that he was still next to me even though my eyes could see him there.

"I almost feel like a normal person," Missy said.

"Yeah." I nodded. "Me, too. But I bet normal people don't even know what it's like to be normal. They probably just take it for granted."

Of all the millions of people in this country, how many of them even thought twice about their freedom? Or did they just move through their days thinking of all the things they didn't have—the jobs, the cars, the big TVs—instead of all the things they'd already been given, just by being born who they were? Maybe they thought of their lives as a prison, too, not knowing how lucky they were just to be able to drive their beat-up cars and shop in grocery stores and wake up next to the people that they loved.

"Maybe we could stay here," Missy said. "At least for a few more days, while we try to figure out what to do. There was a commercial for a Chinese place nearby that has takeout. Or we can order pizza."

It sounded perfect. I wouldn't mind sealing off the door and living inside this little room for ages. Let the outside world keep spinning. Let the sun rise and fall, let the cars rush past on the freeway, let the kids go back and forth to school while husbands and wives fought their million tiny battles. None of it mattered inside this room.

Missy crumpled up the wrapper to her fifth granola bar and tossed it at the garbage can. It bounced off and rolled onto the floor.

Penn sighed, rolling off the bed to pick it up. "You know none of this can last, right?" he asked.

Missy groaned. "Oh, come on, don't spoil things."

"I'm sorry to interfere with your 'vacation,'" he said. "But someone has to be realistic."

Missy switched off the TV and the room went silent. From somewhere above us we heard the muffled sound of voices and the hollow thud of feet. Pure silence would have been better. Then, maybe we could have kept pretending that we were alone in the world, that our actions didn't have any consequences.

"Penn, do we have to—"

"I'm not trying to be mean," he said, "but we can't keep pretending that we've gotten to some happy ending. We might be together for a minute, but none of this is going to last. It's not."

I opened my mouth to argue, but I couldn't find any words. He was right. Missy and I both knew it, even if we didn't want to admit it. How long could we hide in this motel? A week maybe? At some point people would start to get suspicious. At some point we would have to move on. And then where would we go?

"So let's make it last," Missy said.

"How?" Penn asked.

"We get back to Canada. It'll be safe there for both of you."

"Yeah. We tried that once already," Penn said.

"Fine then, not Canada. I don't care where we go, just so long as we get out of this stupid, messed up country," Missy said.

"I think Penn's right," I said.

Missy folded her arms and raised her eyebrows. "Big surprise there."

"If we run now, we'll just have to keep running. Our whole lives. I don't know if I can live that way," I said. "I want a real life."

Missy's jaw clenched. She turned away from me, pulling back the sheer blinds so that she was staring out into the parking lot, like she was going to find an answer there amid the oil stains and bits of gravel.

"So what do we do?" she asked.

"Fight!" Penn said.

"The three of us?" Missy said. "Look at us. What good

are we going to do? Two pets and a teenager."

I dangled my legs over the side of the bed. They didn't quite touch the ground. I stared down at them. Yes, I was small, but I wouldn't let that define me. Yes, I was a pet, but that wasn't who I was, that was someone else's idea of what they wanted me to be.

"I think you're underestimating us," I said.

Missy snorted. "I guess it's my turn to be the realistic one here."

"Maybe this isn't the sort of thing to be realistic about."

"Come on," Missy said. "You don't even have a plan."

"Not yet." I shrugged. "We may just be two pets and a teenager, but maybe we can use that to our advantage. I mean, who's going to expect people like us to make a difference? Nobody, right? But all that means is they aren't going to expect it. They aren't going to expect us to fight back."

"What does that even mean?" Missy said. "You say fight back, but I don't know what you're talking about. Do you mean guns and tanks? Do you mean war? Are you planning on blowing something up? Because it's not like we can plant a bomb in every NuPet Kennel in the United States. There are hundreds of them."

Penn studied me. "Maybe it means blowing things up a different way."

I nodded, grinning. "A figurative explosion. One that blows things up from the *inside*."

Penn and I left Missy in her snack food induced stupor and walked outside into the warm sun. We needed time to think and the motel room's stale air and fluorescent light weren't doing much to inspire us.

I grabbed Penn's hand and we meandered across the parking lot. The street was busy with traffic, hundreds of faces passing by. Each one looked like a threat.

I pressed myself close up to Penn's side. "Maybe it's not safe out here."

He paused, and glanced around us. "No one will see us back there," he said, and pulled me behind the rickety fence that ran between the motel and the gas station parking lot. Behind the buildings, a narrow canal wound through the slender trees.

We sat down on the edge of the bank, removing our shoes, as if out of habit, so that we could dip our toes into the cold water that flowed past. Time and again we seemed drawn to water: the pool, the pond, and now this.

"We need a scandal," Penn said. "One so big my dad won't be able to hide from it."

"But we can't just make up a scandal," I said.

Penn shook his head. "We won't need to. Look at NuPet! He's their puppet. He worked harder to get their stupid bill passed than just about anything else. I've heard the way he talks on the phone with them. He's wrapped around their little finger. They're all hiding something, and they're terrified that someone is going to find out. I just wish I knew what it was."

One by one, the faces of the murdered girls wavered in and out of my memory, each frozen in one final pose, immortalized on film, and now, inside my head. Those faces. I couldn't shake them. It didn't matter whether they were pressed down in the dirt or partially covered with matted hair, charred by fire or waterlogged and swollen, I saw the girls they must have been and they haunted me.

"I think I know what they're trying to hide," I said.

I pulled the pictures from my pocket. They were crinkled and bent, but the images were still clear. I smoothed my palm over what was left of the girls and handed them over.

His fingers shook as he stared at the top photograph. "I can't…" He shook his head, his jaw clenching tightly before he shoved the pictures back into my hand. "I can't look at these. I think I'm going to be sick."

"I'm sorry," I said. "I thought you'd want to know."

"Where did you get those?"

"I stole them," I said. "From an office in one of the black markets."

"Wait, what?" He jumped to his feet and took a step back. "The black markets are real? And you…you *went* to one?"

"It was the only way," I said. "I'm sorry."

His hands clenched. "Did they hurt you? Did they—"

"No." I shook my head. "Missy did all the jobs. She's been there before, knew how it worked. It was the only way to get back here."

Penn closed his eyes and his shoulders slumped. "I didn't even think those things were real. I mean, I've heard people talk, but I always assumed it was a rumor." He took a few steps down the bank, then spun around, his eyes a little wild around the edges. "This is so messed up, Ella! And now that I've seen those pictures, it's getting really, *really* scary. Shouldn't we give those to the police?"

I placed the pictures gently on my lap. The images didn't scare me anymore. They had taken up residence inside of me. These girls were a part of me now.

"The police already know. Someone is paying them to

keep it quiet. The people at the market don't know what's going on either. Missy said they think it could be the owners, but would they really spend all that money on a pet and then just kill her?"

Penn digested my words and his eyes clouded. I could almost see the thoughts churning in his brain. I wanted him to shake his head and tell me no, of course not. No owner would ever kill their own pet. But we both knew what people were capable of when they were scared of losing whatever they valued most. Their secrets. Their money.

Their power over others.

"Nothing they could do would surprise me," Penn said quietly. "Ella, we can never let my father find you. *Never*. Do you understand?"

I nodded and stared down at the water, seeing the red door instead of the swirling grays and whites. "I think the kennels have something to do with this."

"Why?"

I tried to think of the best way to tell him about what I'd seen in the black markets. About the jobs and the sales and how close I'd come to being sold back to the kennel. "It's like someone *wants* people to believe that the owners are doing this," I said, "but I just don't believe it. Not this many girls. Not all at once. I just can't shake the feeling that it comes back to NuPet."

Penn rubbed a hand over his face. "I don't know. Look at those pictures. They're brutal. The kennels would have a better way of getting rid of bodies. Cremating them or something."

I didn't want to think about the ashes of burned girls. About mutilated bodies or who was responsible. I wanted to lie back in the soft leaves with the boy I loved. I wanted to hold him, and to only think about the feel of fingers on flesh.

But I couldn't allow myself that luxury. Not when girls were dying.

I had to fix this.

"When I was in the black markets," I said carefully, "girls weren't only being sold to do jobs the way Missy was. And they weren't just being sold to new owners either. There were people from the kennel there."

Penn frowned. "Working at the black market?"

"No. They were there to buy girls. I don't know why, but they were looking for the youngest and healthiest. They had us strip down. They measured us, looked in our mouths…" I cringed, remembering the feel of those rubber gloves pressing into my jaw.

Penn cradled his head in his hands and balled his fists, moving them in front of his ears like if he concentrated hard enough, he could block out all the terrible things that had happened to me, that could ever happen.

"What if we broke back into your house?" I asked suddenly. "Is there a file your dad kept on NuPet? Anything that we could use to point us in the right direction?"

Penn shook his head. "It's too dangerous. Plus, he wouldn't keep stuff like that at the house. He's too smart to have anything incriminating lying around."

"But there's got to be something," I said. "Have you overheard any of his calls with NuPet?"

"Bits and pieces, but not enough to use against him," Penn said.

I almost wished I were back in the congressman's office. Maybe if I heard some of those calls firsthand I could untangle this riddle, but it was impossible. If I ever set foot in that office again, I was as good as dead. Which only left us one option. "We have to break into one of the kennels."

Penn stomped toward me, his eyes wide. "Are you crazy? Breaking into my house was dangerous enough. Look at those pictures. If it is the kennels, what makes you think I'm letting you go anywhere near one of those places?"

I stood and poked him in the chest. "First of all, I'm free. This is my decision, not yours." It hurt to say the words, to devalue his need to protect me, but I couldn't let him stop me. This was too important. "If we're going to figure this out, we have to do something bold. Something dangerous."

Penn ran his hands through his hair and tugged at the shortened strands. "I know that. I do. But you can't expect me to like the idea of you doing something like this." His hands dropped to his sides. "I just got you back, Ella."

I wrapped my arms around his waist. "I know. And I love you. But I have to do this, and it will be a lot less dangerous if you help."

He sighed into my hair, his arms tightening around my shoulders. "I'll help. Of course I'll help. But how are we going to do this? It's not like we can just march up to their front door and ask for answers."

I smiled into his chest. "When I was trying to get back here to you, Missy hid me in plain sight," I said. "Nobody really saw us there. They only saw pets. They only saw two girls they could exploit."

He stepped back and stared at me for a few moments, frowning. Finally, his shoulders slumped and he sighed. "We're going to march right up to their front door, aren't we?"

I grinned.

Missy sat on the edge of the bed. Her mouth hung slightly ajar as her gaze shifted between the two of us. "Are you crazy?"

"So we just shouldn't try?" I asked.

She sniffed. "Not if you want to stay alive."

"It's the only way to find anything out," I insisted. "And I know they'll buy me. They were desperate for girls. You saw it. Once I'm inside I'll be able to figure out what's really going on. We can't do anything from the outside."

Missy stood and began pacing the room. "You don't even know you're going to find anything in there," Missy said, her arms flying around as she spoke. "And if they're the ones killing pets like you seem to think, what's going to stop them from killing you? I do *not* want to see a picture of you cut into a million pieces. Not after how hard I worked to get you here."

Penn held up his hand. "I could've done without the image, thanks."

Missy spun on him. "I can't believe you, of all people, are on board with this."

"Oh, believe me, I'm not." He sighed, but a hint of a smile tugged at his lips. "But as Ella so plainly put it, I don't get to decide what she can and can't do anymore. As if I ever could."

Missy cocked an eyebrow at me. "I liked her more when she followed directions."

I rolled my eyes, though I couldn't contain the flush of pride in my cheeks. Maybe I was turning into Missy now. If being with her for the past week had taught me anything, it was spunk, and endurance, and bravery.

"I want to live," I said to Missy. "And right now, being a pet doesn't look too safe regardless of where you are. So I'm not going to run away. You're the one who's always calling me naive." I lifted my chin. "Well, I refuse to stay blind."

"God," Missy moaned. "Enough with the dramatic pep talk. If we're doing this, I can't stomach your change-the-world attitude."

I blinked. "We?"

"Well you don't think I'm letting you go in there alone, do you?"

Chapter Fourteen

By that evening we had everything we needed. Penn's old clothes were stuffed in a plastic shopping bag and he was decked out in a new pair of khakis and a sports coat. He had a part to play and a dingy white T-shirt and jeans weren't going to cut it. Neither were the grungy clothes that Missy and I had been wearing for the past week. Even though my things were smudged with grass stains and dirt, I was sad to give them up in exchange for a dress again.

Missy had fussed and pouted, but besides paying for the clothes she'd also given him a thousand dollars to go buy an old, beat-up sedan. She hated to part with the money, but we couldn't walk all the way to the kennel in Greenwich and she couldn't argue with the fact that taking a taxi was a bad idea. We needed our own transportation. There was just no other way around it.

"Don't you think it's a little late to be going tonight?" Penn asked as we all climbed into the car.

Missy and I both hesitated. Just looking at her, I knew she was dreading this plan as much as I was, but if we didn't act now, we might not actually have the nerve to go through with it. I glanced back at the motel room. It was dumpy and dark, but it had been an oasis. I knew each one of us was sad to go.

I turned away from the faded orange door and locked eyes with Missy. "If we leave now, we can get there before they close for the day."

"We do it quick," Missy said. "Get it over with."

Penn nodded and sighed before he cranked the key. The car sputtered to life, coughing and jerking as we bumped out onto the road.

"I still don't feel good about this," he said, glancing over at me with pleading eyes.

"It's the best we've got," I said. "What else can we do?"

"I don't know. That thing Missy said about using bombs is actually sounding pretty good at the moment."

"As much as I hate to admit it, you know Ella's right," Missy said. "If there's something going on, we're not going to find out staying on the outside."

"But what if it's nothing?" Penn asked. "What if you get in there and find out that it's all just a dead end? That the kennels have nothing to do with the dead pets? What if you get in and there's no way to get back out?"

"It doesn't seem like a dead end," I said. "I have a feeling about it. I can't explain it, but it's scary and very, very real."

"But it's not enough to just go on a feeling."

"It's more than a feeling," Missy said. "If your dad's upset, there's probably a pretty good reason why. And I know my owner's upset. I'd bet a whole box of granola bars that they're upset about the same thing."

Penn tightened his grip on the wheel, but he didn't

argue. For a minute we all stayed silent, thinking our own private thoughts, concocting our own private fears.

"Do you remember it at all?" Penn asked me after a while. "I mean this is the kennel you came from, right? Greenwich?"

I wasn't happy to be returning, but it was the closest kennel. "I don't remember very much about it."

Most of what I remembered blended together with the training center: the austere white bedrooms, the sound of shoes on the linoleum floors, the long hallways lined with doors. I could have told Penn about those things, but I was afraid to. When I let myself remember the kennel, my mind jumped to the red door. Bad things happened behind that door. Girls went in and they never came out.

The red door was the answer. It had to be.

"So, you don't remember the babies?" Penn asked.

I shook my head. "We were only kept with the girls our own age. Each year they moved us to a different dormitory, so we didn't get a chance to see many of the others."

"I've just always wondered." Penn shrugged. "When that whole bill was getting passed, my dad made this huge deal about how pets were different from people and how it was okay to buy them since they were made in a laboratory. It made them different."

"But we aren't different, are we?" I asked.

"Of course not," Missy snapped. "Look at us. I don't care if you hand-selected my genes and grew me in a test tube. I know what I am."

"And so do I," Penn said, sensing her anger. "My father drilled it into my head and maybe I sort of believed it…until I met Ella."

I smiled and pinched his thigh. "Human is human."

I just hoped that would be enough.

It only took half an hour to find the compound that belonged to Greenwich Kennel. The entrance was nestled at the end of a narrow stretch of wooded road only a few miles past the center of the city and before we knew it, we were pulling past the unmarked brick gate onto the driveway. On either side of us, the woods gave way, opening up onto a wide stretch of grass, neatly mowed and lined with rows of spindly new trees.

"Are you sure this is it?" Missy asked, peering out her window at the sprawling brick building that appeared over a small rise. "This place doesn't look right."

"What's it supposed to look like?" Penn asked.

"I don't know. But not this," she said, flipping her hand dismissively at the long, squat building. "This looks like one of those places that sells bulk rolls of toilet paper."

Penn laughed. "Clearly you've never been to a warehouse club."

Missy rolled her eyes. "So what?"

"Well, they don't look like this," Penn said. "At least, I've never been to one that has a water feature."

We stared out the driver side windows at the fountain situated in the middle of a large circular driveway. At its center, a thick column of water shot into the air before cascading down the marble sides. Quite the display, considering we were the only ones around to impress.

Slowly, Penn eased the car to a stop in the small parking lot. "Hopefully they don't have cameras out here," he said, turning off the car. "We won't be fooling anyone if they see this thing."

"I guess you'll need these," Missy said, pulling a couple of envelopes out of her bag and handing them over to him. "Keep an eye on my bag, okay? I want it back when we're done with all this."

"Don't worry. I won't lose it."

"And I know how much money is in there," she said. "So don't think you can just go on a shopping spree or anything."

"Got it." He forced a smile, but it didn't fool any of us. We each turned to look at the entrance. The NuPet logo was etched in the center of the two tall, frosted glass doors, beckoning us.

"How will we know how to find you...when we get back out?" I asked, suddenly worried that even if we did manage to get inside and find something, that we'd never be able to find Penn again.

"Don't worry. I'll be waiting in my car out past the front gate. The bushes are plenty thick and this car is small enough to hide."

"You promise you'll be there?" I asked.

"I'll be camped there all day and all night until you come."

Our lips met and for just a moment the worry and the fear lifted. There was only warmth and the sweet hum of wanting him. Kissing Penn felt like a warm summer night. It felt like a soft breeze on bare skin, like a clear sky and a bright moon. If only I could carry this feeling with me. If only I could live inside one of those kisses.

Missy cleared her throat. "I'm sorry to break up the love fest, but if we're going to do this thing, we need to get going."

Penn pulled away and squeezed my hand. "You ready?"

"Ready."

He straightened his collar and ran a hand over his jacket before he swung open the tall doors that led into the kennel.

Behind him, Missy and I had already composed ourselves, wearing our persona as pets as easily as we wore our dresses.

It was surprising to me how quickly I could still slip back into this identity; as if it was a piece of clothing I could slide over my head. Or maybe I was more surprised by how easy it had been to change out of. A lifetime of training and I had cast it aside like a dirty shirt.

Behind the sleek metal counter a woman looked up from her desk. "Can I help you?"

"Hello," Penn said, putting on his most charming smile. "A family friend referred me. I was told to speak to one of your buyers."

The woman cocked her head, considering. Her eyes flicked over to me and Missy for just a moment before she pressed a button on her desk and leaned down to talk quietly into the speaker.

"Sorry to bother you, Ms. Leaver," she said. "But there's a young man here to speak with you." She stopped talking and sat back up with a plastic grin set on her painted lips. "If you'd like to have a seat, she should be out in just a moment."

Penn thanked her, turning toward the row of stiff modern chairs that lined the wall. He eyed them warily. Instead of sitting he leaned up against a large cement column. I could tell he was nervous from the way he kept licking his lips. I wanted nothing more than to feel the assuring squeeze of his hand in mine, but I kept my distance from him, imagining that we really were the people we were pretending to be.

A few minutes later the clacking of heels down the hallway made us all turn. Penn straightened, once again sporting that easy, confident smile that looked so convincing.

He stretched out his hand. "Ms. Leaver?"

She didn't need to introduce herself for me to know that we had the right woman. She looked like she'd been cut from the same mold as the woman I'd seen at Bernard's market: the crisp, tailored suit; the cold, piercing eyes. She even had the same look of concentrated derision on her face.

She glanced disinterestedly at Penn's hand, not bothering to shake it, before her gaze turned to me and Missy and her eyebrows lifted just a little.

"And what's this?" she asked, stepping closer to Missy and me.

For a moment Penn looked flustered. The smile slipped from his lips. "I…was referred by a family friend," he said, finally snapping back into form. "We were hoping to get rid of our pets. They just aren't working out."

For the first time, Ms. Leaver turned and studied Penn. Her eyes traveled slowly over him, much the same way she'd appraised us.

"You're young," she said.

Penn shrugged. "They belonged to my grandpa, but he's too sick to come. Dementia," he said, as if that explained it. "My mom would have come, but she doesn't think he should have gotten them in the first place."

Ms. Leaver narrowed her eyes for just a second before a new expression transformed her face. Was it compassion? Pity? "It happens fairly often," she finally said, nodding. "Nothing to feel ashamed about. We're happy to take them off your hands."

"Oh, good," Penn said. "I brought their paperwork." His hands shook as he reached into his breast pocket, but Ms. Leaver had already turned away from him again.

"Your grandfather should know that we don't offer a full refund."

"Of course not," Penn said.

She circled us slowly, her arms crossed in front of her chest as she studied us. "This one?" she said, picking up my arm by the wrist to study my hand. "She's new?"

Penn swallowed. "Yeah, sort of new." Maybe we should have come up with a better story. Maybe we should have spent more time rehearsing. "My grandpa got her last year."

"From one of our facilities?" she asked, raising an eyebrow.

"I…I…" Penn stuttered, fumbling with the envelope. He'd read over both the documents before we came, but he must have forgotten. The paper shook in his hand as he unfolded it. "No…he got her from Texas. I guess he had her shipped in."

"Ah…" She nodded. "They did a nice job," she said. "I could have mistaken her for one of ours."

Penn laughed uncomfortably.

"And the other one?" she asked. "She looks older. We're not really in the market for these."

"My grandpa really needs to get rid of them both. He's not in the condition to care for them and my mom won't let either one of them back in the house."

"Well, for the right price, I suppose we can come to an arrangement."

Next to me, Missy clenched and unclenched her hands, an indignant expression plastered across her features.

"Would you care to follow me back to my office and we'll work something out?" Ms. Leaver asked, already walking back down the hallway that she'd come from.

Penn nodded, casting me a quick sidelong glance before he strode after her. I grabbed Missy by the arm, squeezing the soft skin above her elbow in the hopes that she'd wipe the sour look off of her face.

Ms. Leaver paused at the desk and the woman with the bright red lips looked up attentively. "Allison, take these two back to intake while I finish the paperwork," she said, not even bothering to glance back at Missy and me.

Penn stiffened. "Wait, you're taking them now?"

Maybe he could hide the panic in his voice from Ms. Leaver, but he couldn't hide it from me. It swelled and multiplied in my ears, filling up my whole head. That was it? Of course, I had known that getting sold back to the kennel would mean leaving Penn, but I hadn't thought about how it would feel.

Ms. Leaver turned around. "Is there a problem?"

"No. No problem," Penn managed to say, although when he spoke, it sounded like the air had been kicked from his lungs.

"Fine, then follow me," she said, not even offering for him to bid us good-bye.

I locked eyes with Penn. For one last moment we held each other's gaze. I wanted to let it fill me. I wanted it to give me courage, but it only felt like a knife was being plunged deeper inside me. As if a piece of me was being sliced away. How many times could a person be cut open before they couldn't take it anymore?

I slumped into Missy. Her hand reached out to find mine and I clung on to keep myself from toppling over. The girl behind the desk wrinkled her nose, eyeing us suspiciously. She opened her mouth as if she was considering calling after Ms. Leaver, who was disappearing around a corner with Penn, but she reconsidered, giving her head a small shake and pursing her lips before she turned back to us.

"You're not sick, are you?" she asked. "Because we can't

have you infecting the others."

I swallowed. "No," I managed. "I'm fine."

"Okay." She sighed. "Follow me."

I straightened my back, mustering as much strength as I could. The woman pushed open a pair of swinging doors and Missy and I followed her back into the kennel.

There was no turning back now.

The doors swung shut behind us with a *whoosh*, and we followed after the girl still clutching each other's hands. Now that she wasn't sitting behind the desk, I could see just how tall she was. She towered over us, balancing on high red heels that made her legs look like they went on forever. I'd been around men that were taller than her, but she made me feel smaller than I'd ever felt before, staring down at me impatiently as she waited for us to catch up. At the end of the hall, she opened the door to a small room and ushered us inside.

"You won't be needing those dresses anymore," she said, opening a small cabinet next to the door. She grabbed two white jumpers and shoved them into our hands. "Put these on. You can toss your old clothes in the bin in the corner."

My head spun. This felt wrong. So wrong.

Maybe it was the feel of the fabric between my fingers, so familiar it made me weak. It was the same fabric that had covered my body for almost as long as I could remember.

Maybe it was the smell of bleach mixed with the flowery scent of soap. One whiff of that smell and a thousand memories washed over me. I felt the tepid water of our nightly baths, tasted the grainy oatmeal that they served us every morning at the narrow metal tables in the dining hall, heard the lonely squeak of my mattress as I curled up alone in my cot each night.

And even though I wanted to push it away, wanted to bury it deep underneath every other memory that I'd ever had, I saw the bright red door looming at the end of the hallway, waiting to swallow me.

"Did you hear what I said?" the girl asked, clearly annoyed.

I shook my head, trying to get my head to surface above so many memories.

She sighed. "Someone will be here shortly to check you in."

"Thank you," I said.

She didn't bother with a good-bye, simply rolled her eyes and left, shutting us in the room alone.

Missy clutched the jumper, staring down at it with an expression that must have mirrored mine.

"I never thought I'd see one of these again," she murmured. "God, when we're done with this, I'm going to burn this thing."

I imagined what it would be like to see one of these jumpers go up in flames. My arms and legs, which had felt weak and tingly, surged with a bit of new energy. "Come on, we need to get dressed. Or do you want them to send you straight through the red door?"

Her back straightened. "You know about the door? I…I thought maybe they only had one at the kennel where I was from," she said in a breathy whisper. "I didn't want to think about it, but…" She rubbed her hands over her eyes as if she was trying to wipe away the vision.

"I know," I said, turning her around so that I could unzip her dress. "But it's impossible, isn't it?"

She let me pull off her gown and I wriggled the new jumper over her head.

"It's just…I feel like a child again. Small and weak," she

said, shaking her head.

"It's not just you," I told her, slipping out of my gown. "That door was painted red for a reason. They didn't want it to look like every other door. They wanted us to remember it. They wanted us to fear it, didn't they?"

The door rattled and I quickly pulled the new jumper over my head and sat down next to Missy. The man who entered the room looked up from his clipboard. A skinny man in a long white coat followed behind him.

"Ah, there are two. Wonderful!" the thin man said. "Maybe we'll have enough for the new trials."

He didn't bother to introduce himself. Just pulled me to my feet and began examining me, calling out notes for the other man to jot down as he looked into my eyes and ears. He pressed his fingers along my throat and ran a hand up my spine.

"Good. Good." He couldn't contain his smile. "Mark this one down for phase one. We'll get started right away with the HGC injections," he said before he moved on to Missy.

I lowered myself back down into the chair, trying to settle my shaking legs. I'd never been afraid of our yearly vaccinations, but this was different. Phase one? HGC? These weren't phrases I'd ever heard before.

"This one looks to be a few years past her prime, but she's strong. I think we'll use her anyway."

"The mortality rate is almost ninety percent in the first trimester for ones we've had at a comparable age," the man with the clipboard said. "You sure you don't want to move her to one of the other trials?"

"No. Leaver promised me two-dozen new subjects and she's way behind this month. We have to make do with what we've got. It'll still give us some useful data, regardless," he said dismissively. "Move them to the dormitory and we'll finish the paperwork in the morning."

The man in the white coat nodded once, satisfied, and left without another word.

Alone with us, the man with the clipboard looked at his watch and sighed. "I don't want to be here all night. Let's get going."

We left the room behind, padding barefoot down the tiled hall. I'd never spent any time in this part of the kennel. Growing up, I'd never dreamed that it was so expansive, but the building seemed to go on forever, a never-ending stretch of hallways. Most of the doors were closed, but every once in a while we passed an open office or supply room.

I glanced over at Missy, hoping that between the two of us, we might be able to plot out at least a general map of the building. Getting hopelessly lost while searching for what we needed wasn't going to help our plan.

We took one final turn and the hallway ended at a large metal door that separated this wing of the building. The man with the clipboard lifted a small hatch on the wall beside the door, revealing a keypad, and I stood up ever so slightly on my tiptoes, trying to peer past his shoulder without seeming too obvious. Fortunately, he didn't even bother to check whether we were spying before he typed in his code. The lock clicked and released with a small puff of air.

The hallway we entered looked exactly like I remembered. It couldn't have been one of the ones from my childhood. There were no little girls here. But it didn't matter. It was an exact duplicate. To the right, we passed the empty bathing room where dozens of wide basins sat empty. They looked exactly as I remembered. Even the bottles of shampoo that rested on the porcelain edge looked as if they'd been plucked directly out of my memory.

We passed the empty dining hall and turned left into what I had expected would be another hallway lined with doors leading into the small bedroom units, but instead, we came to another door. The man with the clipboard pushed it open and Missy and I froze behind him.

The room that we'd just entered was gigantic. Instead of a couple dozen individual rooms it was one giant dorm, lined with cots and interspersed with medical equipment. In the beds nearest to us, a dozen girls—*pets*—lay staring up at the ceiling, their eyes empty, their faces slack. Long, clear tubes stretched from their arms to the machines sitting next to them. Beyond them, several girls reclined in their beds, looking just as ashen, but slightly more alert.

Missy clutched the back of my jumper. "What the hell," she hissed in my ear.

Zombies, I thought, remembering Ruby's fairytales.

But these girls weren't zombies. And we certainly weren't in a fairytale.

Forget the cryptic phone calls that Penn had overheard, forget any of the hints or hunches. I'd expected NuPet was up to something, but we never could have imagined… whatever *this* was.

The door clicked shut behind us.

Next to us, a machine beeped and the girl attached to it grimaced, clutching her stomach.

"Don't stop there," the man with the clipboard said, motioning for us to follow him, but neither of us budged.

Across the room, an attendant waved him over and he shook his head, giving up on us. He handed over our papers, motioning in our direction as he spoke. Another attendant scooted past us, pushing a red button on the machine. The beeping stopped, but the girl's grimace didn't fade.

Missy grabbed my arm. "We've got to get out of here. Now."

"It'll be fine," I said. "Just stay calm."

"If they hook us up to one of those things, we're never getting out." She didn't look at me as she spoke, instead, her eyes were trained on the four square pieces of rubber that were suction cupped to the girl's stomach out of which a tangle of wires connected to the machine.

When I looked back up for the man with the clipboard, he was disappearing behind a curtain that ran the length of the room. The attendant he'd been speaking to strode over to us, taking us in head to toe in one long glance.

"All right, let's get you two situated," he said, leading us down the row of beds toward some empty cots. "Someone will be down shortly to take your vitals."

Missy and I eased down on the edge of the beds facing each other, barely scooting back enough to wrinkle the stiff, white sheets. Across the aisle, the reclining girls stared at us.

I raised one hand in an awkward wave. "Hi, I'm Ella."

The girls frowned, shaking their heads ever so slightly.

"What's the matter with them?" Missy whispered. "Do you think they can talk?"

From behind me came a weak, "Shhh."

I turned around. Unlike some of the girls across from us, her skin looked like it still had a little bit of color and her eyes weren't framed with dark circles. Other than the plastic tube that ran from her arm to a container of clear liquid that dangled on a metal rod next to her bed, she looked normal. Almost exactly the way I remembered her.

"Carlie?"

She lay curled on her side. The sound of her name made

her grimace and she glanced back at the attendant who was digging through a drawer on the other side of the room before she turned back to me.

"They don't like us to speak to one another," she whispered. "And don't let them catch you using names. You'll be reassigned a number. If you have to speak, use that."

I nodded. "Why don't they—" I started to say, but her eyes widened and I turned around to see the attendant wheeling a cart in our direction.

"What?" Missy hissed on the other side of me. "Did she just say that we weren't going to be able—"

"Quiet," the attendant snapped, stopping his cart at the end of the beds. "Unless you'd like to have your vocal cords numbed, I'd suggest keeping your speaking to a minimum. This is a room of science, not socializing. As you'll soon find out, your bodies will need to reserve every ounce of strength for much more important tasks than talking."

He pulled out a marker and grabbed a whiteboard off of the end of the bed, scribbling a large number twenty-two in the middle of it. Missy's bed was next. Twenty-three.

"These are your new numbers. Remember them," he said.

So that was it. With a quick swipe of his marker he'd erased our names, and with them, he'd taken the one bit of humanity that our masters had given to us.

A cold chill spread over my limbs as the attendant moved briskly between Missy and me, taking our temperature and measuring our blood pressure. I recognized the way he looked at me, like I was a chore that needed to be completed.

He hummed quietly to himself as he moved down our charts, checking boxes and scribbling numbers in the columns. Finally, he opened a small plastic container and pulled out two syringes. He grabbed my arm, pulling me closer to him and a whiff of garlic on his breath made my stomach turn. I twisted away, but he only clamped his hand harder around my upper arm.

"Wait! What is that?" I asked.

He frowned. "It's none of your concern."

"But the man before…the one with the white coat… He said to start the injections tomorrow. I don't think you're supposed to—"

He yanked my arm and I winced from the pain.

"Don't tell me how to do my job."

"At least tell me what you're doing."

"I'm trying to do my *job*," he grumbled. "Now, stop moving." He jerked my arm forward and jabbed in the needle, releasing the fluid with a quick press of his thumb. "You're not someone's pet anymore. You belong to the kennel now and if they want to poke you with needles all day, that's what's going to happen."

He pulled out the needle, but the spot felt cold, the chill spreading down my arm like ice water.

My head spun.

Was this what had caused the numbed look in all the girls' eyes? Or were they simply filled with a flood of panic so overwhelming it smothered them?

I tried to steady my breathing but it felt like a heavy weight was being lowered down on my rib cage. It was crushing, not just the heaviness in my chest, but the fear, the feeling that I was trapped again. Caged. And this time, I wasn't getting out. Missy was right. This was a mistake.

I opened my mouth to talk, but my lips only trembled, useless.

I thought I would be smart enough to get away. I thought I could outwit them, but I'd only been inside their walls for an hour and already they had won.

For a moment I had the audacity to dream that I had any control over my own life, my own body, my own future. But that had been a reckless hope. Foolish. How many times would I make that same mistake?

The cage doors clanged shut.

"Ell…a?" Missy's voice. Slurred, but familiar.

I couldn't answer. Couldn't do anything but droop across the bed while the room grew dark around the edges until only a pinprick of light remained.

Chapter Fifteen

When I next opened my eyes, the room was dark, except for a few lights that glowed underneath a stretch of cabinets on the far side of the room, lighting the rows of doctor's tools, neatly packaged and stacked on shelves.

My head still felt strange, foggy and loose, like it might float off my head and up onto the ceiling tiles like one of Ruby's balloons. I sat up, holding my forehead to keep it from flying away.

Next to me Missy groaned, opening her eyes.

I swung my legs over the side of the bed.

"I wouldn't get up." In the dark, I could just make out Carlie's face. She lifted her head from her pillow. "They'll be upset if they find out. They'll punish you."

"Who will?" I whispered.

"The orderlies," she said. Slowly she propped herself up on one elbow and glanced cautiously around the room.

"Where are they?"

"There's an office down the hall," she said.

"Will they be coming back soon?"

She shrugged. "Maybe. If someone presses their button."

I shuffled around the bed and knelt down in front of her. "You have to help me." I rubbed my arm. It was sore, but I wasn't sure if it was from the injection or from the attendant's rough grip. "What's that stuff they gave me?"

She shrugged and shook her head. "I don't know. They gave it to us all when we got here."

"Have you heard any of the doctors say anything about it?"

She shook her head again.

"Do you have any idea what they're doing here?" I asked. "What are these tubes? Are they drugs?"

"I'm sorry," she said. "I don't know. I don't even remember what's happening half the time."

"What about these other girls?" I asked. "Some of them have been here longer than you. They must know."

She shrugged. "They won't speak. It's too dangerous."

"Why?"

"I shouldn't be talking either," she said.

"Why? Please, Carlie, you've got to help me."

She gave her head another small shake before she lay back down, closing her eyes.

"No, you don't know? Or no, you won't tell me?" I asked, but she didn't move. "Please." I shook her gently.

"I can't…" she whispered, keeping her eyes shut tight.

I tried one last time. "Please. I'm not trying to get you in trouble. I'm trying to help."

Her lips barely moved. "Be careful," she whispered.

I scanned the room full of small bodies and medical equipment. It was clear that the girls weren't going to be much help, but there were cabinets everywhere, just begging to be explored. My heart quickened.

The tiles were cold against my feet, but the shock of them made my head feel a little bit clearer. I knew how to do this. I didn't make a sound as I made my way over to the small cart full of medical supplies.

A month ago, I might have gone for the row of cabinets, hoping that they'd hold something big I could use to protect myself: a knife or a stun gun. But that would have been a mistake. It was the little things that I could hide inside a fist or a pocket that I needed.

A month ago, my hands would have shaken as I lifted the lid to the case full of needles. I would have held my breath the way I had the first few times I'd taken things. But I knew better now. I let the breath go, breathing out the way I did right before I played the piano. My hands moved slowly, steadily, plucking one of the glass syringes off the top of the stack without a sound.

I tucked it in my pocket and plucked one more off the pile. It was small, but I'd seen the power in that bit of clear liquid; could still feel the remnants of it in the corners of my mind.

Behind me, Missy moaned again, clutching her head.

I shuffled back over to our beds, trying not to move too quickly. "Come on," I said, shaking her. "You have to get up."

"My head hurts," she mumbled.

I lowered myself down on the edge of her bed and she blinked up at me. "What's going on, Ella?" she said. "This isn't what I expected. I never would have come." She shook her head, her eyes traveling around the room.

"I know we thought we'd have time to figure things out," I said, "but we need to find something now. I don't know what they're doing to these girls, but it's something scary."

She nodded, propping herself up on her elbow. "Did you hear that?" she asked, glancing toward the curtain that ran down the center of the room.

I shook my head.

"There's something back there," she whispered.

I froze, waiting to hear the sound of footsteps or the gruff voice of one of the attendants ordering me back to bed, but it wasn't that. Now that she pointed it out, I could hear it too, a humming sound like someone was speaking just below the buzz of all those machines.

"You don't think there's more of them?" I asked, looking back toward the girls sleeping in the rows of beds beside me.

If there were more, I didn't want to know what the doctors had done to them. Why would they put up a curtain to separate us? My stomach twisted at the thought. They must be so much worse than these girls if they were being kept hidden.

I tugged on Missy's hand. "We need to look."

"I don't want to," she said. "This is getting bad. It's way worse than I expected."

"The sooner we find out what's going on here, the sooner we get out, okay?"

That was all I wanted. To get out. My body screamed for me to run. There was an exit somewhere nearby, there had to be. And not too far down that road, Penn was waiting for me. If I left now, I knew I could get to him. But if we stayed much longer…

She nodded. "All right."

I glanced back toward the other girls, hoping that they were sleeping soundly. But even without looking, I sensed that Carlie was watching. She blinked once and her eyes bore into me. Was it a warning? Was it a plea for help? How was I supposed to know if she refused to tell me anything?

I wanted to trust that she was still good, that she was still the person who had seen fierceness in me. But the spark had drained from her. There was something wrong with these girls. Something terrifying. Seeing their bodies tethered to these beds was bad enough, but the look in their eyes was even scarier. Empty. Broken. What if one of them pushed the call button and summoned an attendant? If they caught us out of bed I was pretty sure we'd end up with another shot in the arm and next time, I was afraid it would be days before we'd wake up.

When I turned back around, Missy was already standing in front of the curtain. Her hand tightened around the fabric as she pulled it back, peering into the next room.

"Ella," she whispered. "Ella, come here."

I took a deep breath, steeling myself, and peered over her shoulder, ready to see the haunted eyes of a hundred ruined girls staring back at me, but the room was merely an extension of the one that we were standing in, identical in almost every way. The rows of beds continued. I squinted, trying to make out what was so different about the bodies in these beds.

A few rows down someone stirred, moaning softly.

Missy pulled the curtain back a little further and I moved past her, stepping into the room, amazed that my legs agreed to carry me. Missy followed closely behind.

"Hello?" I whispered.

"It's one of them," the girl said. "Should I call someone?"

"No, please." I crossed the distance between us in a few hurried steps. "Don't press any buttons. Please. We're only…" I stopped mid-sentence.

The girl's face… It was different, not deformed, but certainly not the face of any pet I'd ever seen before. Her eyes, which had gone wide, were set a little too close together on her face, making everything about her seem a little bit pinched. Her nose was broad and turned up on the end. Even in the pale light I could tell that her skin was pocked along her jawline.

Nothing about her looked like the streamlined perfection of a Greenwich girl, or any other pet for that matter.

She looked…normal.

"Who are you?" I asked.

Her thin lips turned down in a frown and she brought her hand to her stomach.

I wasn't sure how I'd missed it before, but now my eyes traveled down to the huge bulge beneath the blanket.

"That's… You're *pregnant*." The kennel and training center had gone out of their way to keep us from understanding what could happen to a human body, but *I* knew.

She turned to the other girl, confused. "What should we do? They said—"

"Don't look at me," the other girl said, pulling the covers up to her chin and turning away from us all so I hardly even caught a glimpse of her. "I'm not messing with no one no more. Those doctors are wack. I don't want to end up like the rest of them, all drugged out." She shut her eyes, still shaking her head back and forth.

The girl with the pocked skin turned back to us. "You know you're not supposed to be over here, right?" she asked. "You could get in serious trouble. You could get *us* in trouble, too. When I got here there was one of you that came over here a couple times. She knew about babies and stuff, even though I didn't think…oh, never mind. She kept asking all these questions about what it felt like when the baby moved. She was kind of obsessed with it, but I think they…" Her voice trailed off and she drew her finger across her neck. "But, I mean, I could be wrong."

"We know we shouldn't be here," Missy said, folding her arms over her chest as she stepped a little closer to the girl's bedside. "We shouldn't be in this horrible place at all. Nobody should. Something majorly messed up is happening. And you…you…" She pointed her finger at the girl.

She scooted back in her bed, clearly afraid.

I stepped sideways in front of Missy, trying to push her back with my body. "I'm sorry," I said. "It's just that none of this makes any sense. We just want to understand."

"Well, I'm not the one who should be telling you anything."

"Please," I said. "We don't want to get you in trouble, but it's really important." Tentatively, I lowered myself down onto the edge of her bed. "At least tell me who you are?"

She sighed and glanced at the rounded back of the girl she'd been talking to before we came in as if she wanted permission to speak to us. But the girl didn't budge. Her shoulders rose and fell ever so slightly with each breath, but that was all.

"Not here," she finally answered.

She swung her legs over the side of the bed and held her lower back as she eased herself from the bed. Her stomach had looked large before, but now that she was standing it seemed impossibly big. She wore a white jumper very similar to the one that Missy and I wore, but it was so much larger. It had to be to accommodate a stomach that huge.

She glanced down at herself and then back at us. "Well, I guess we don't need to ask who wore it best." She snorted softly, looking at me and Missy like she'd just told a joke. "Get it? Like in the magazines." When we didn't respond she rolled her eyes. "Oh never mind." She waved the comment away with a flap of her wrist and shuffled off down the aisle between the beds, waddling a little as she walked.

Missy looked just as confused as me, but we scampered after her anyway.

She surveyed the girls as she walked, stopping every few steps to make sure they were really asleep. "I'm not worried about most of them," she whispered. "But believe me, there are a couple in here you don't want watching you. Some of these bitches think they're all high and mighty. They've been in here three, four times some of 'em."

"What do you mean, three or four times?"

She shook her head and waved away my question, bringing her finger to her lips before she pointed to the door. Slowly, she cracked it open and stepped out into the hallway.

"They'd probably put me in the lockup if they knew that I left my bed like this at night, but sometimes I've just gotta get out of there," she whispered once we'd closed the door behind us. "I had an older brother growing up, but he was five years older than me, so I might as well have been an only child."

She glanced up and down the hall, deciding which way to go.

"There's a supply closet that I go sit in sometimes. Pathetic, huh?"

"I get it," Missy said, following close behind her. "Sometimes I used to hide in the laundry room because no one went in there. I'd listen to people calling for me and I'd just sit on the washing machine and sniff the dryer sheets because I liked the way they smelled."

The girl paused in front of a door and turned around to look at us like she was seeing us for the first time. "That's messed up," she said.

Missy shrugged. "Probably."

"I mean, I get that, about the dryer sheets. Those things smell good. But they're expensive. We just always had clothes that stuck together." She narrowed her eyes, studying us. "I'm Riley, by the way. It's funny, 'cause I've been here almost two full-terms and I've never actually introduced myself to one of you."

I held my hand out. "I'm Ella."

Her hand was large in mine. The palm was rough but warm and she pumped it up and down in a sturdy shake.

"I guess I just always assumed you all were too snobby and stuck up to talk to us. Like, you should be grateful to us, for this I mean," she said, pointing to her stomach. "But then again, I know we're not in the same class of people or anything."

"I'm sorry," I said, shaking my head. "But you've lost me. Can you just back up a little bit?"

She glanced nervously down the hallway before she opened the door to a small room lined with bottles of cleaning fluid and containers of paper towels and ushered us inside.

"Here, you all can sit on these," she offered, flipping some crates upside down.

"You sit," Missy said, eyeing the way she held her lower back.

Riley smiled. "Fine. You talked me into it." She lowered herself down and sighed. "This is weird. This whole *thing* is weird, you know?"

"Actually, we don't know," I said.

"But you grew up here, right?" she asked. "I mean, they

said this was where they raise the pets before they send them off to get trained."

I nodded. "I grew up here. But this is new, all of it. Before I got here today I'd never seen any of this. Those girls, the other pets." I pointed back in the direction we'd come from. "I don't know what's going on in there, but I know something isn't right. And you…" I shook my head, gesturing to her.

"But you know about the incubators?"

I shook my head.

"It's not like I agree with what they're doing to you," she said, "but I don't have a problem with being a FTS. That sort of money is more than I would make in like five years. And it's kind of for a good cause, you know?"

"No, we *don't* know," Missy snapped. "What's a FTS? What's an incubator? What are they doing to those girls?"

"Geez, chill out," Riley said, throwing up her hands. "FTS stands for Full Term Surrogate, but we just say incubator. Well, I say oven." She chuckled. "I mean, tell it like it is."

"Surrogate?"

"For the babies," she said. "You saw those pets in the other room. I've heard that they've been trying to get them to have babies ever since they started this program, however many years ago *that* was."

"What about the lab?" I asked. "The babies are made in the lab."

"If you want to call this place a lab, I guess they are," Riley said.

I slumped back against a row of mops. The handles knocked together and one toppled to the floor. We all froze, looking at the door like we expected an army of orderlies to come charging through. But nothing happened. The room stayed silent.

"I'm sorry," Riley said. "That was kind of rude of me, to just blurt that out like that. I kind of forgot that you were one of them."

"They're trying to *breed* us?" Missy said, her voice a rough whisper.

"Well, it doesn't seem that weird. This is a breeder, right? They might as well use the ones that get returned to carry the babies. It would save them a lot of money. All they'd have to do is feed them and have them pop out babies for them, if it's even possible for them to have babies, that is."

"But we can," I blurted. "I know pets can get pregnant." My face burned just thinking about the congressman's other pet. If she were sent back over a year ago, would she still be here? Had I just spent the last few hours in the same room as her without even realizing it?

"It's not the getting them pregnant part that's hard," Riley said. "Some of them come in that way, you know? That's how they got the name 'tarnished,' even though that's what they call *all* of them now. That alone is creepy as all get up, if you ask me. Like they're some piece of jewelry that got ruined or something. Maybe it makes them feel better about what they're doing to them, giving them all those shots. They fill them up with drugs thinking they're going to get a baby out of them, but they can't. They just can't have 'em. I think the longest they can carry one is three months before they both just die."

"They die?" Missy spat.

Riley swallowed, realizing what she'd just said, and nodded.

"Are you sure?" I asked. "All of them?"

Riley nodded again.

Missy plopped down on one of the crates next to Riley and rested her forehead in her hands. "I guess deep down we always knew they'd try to kill us, right? I knew. Don't tell me you didn't. If we weren't perfect enough they were always going to get rid of us. Maybe we didn't know they'd use our bodies for a science experiment first. But we always knew we were expendable."

"What if we tell people?" I asked. "We were looking for a way to expose them. Maybe this is it."

"You think people are really going to care?" Riley asked. "Not to be rude, but they won't. Maybe you'll have some of those PETA people that get all pissed off, and get their picket signs out and stuff, but most people just don't care that much. How do you think that whole law got passed? Hell, it's not like I paid any attention to it before. You hear all this crap about corporations and big money or whatever, but you think people have time to really think about that stuff? They've got jobs and car payments and rent that's too high. Besides, it's not like anyone really sees you as people. You're pets. Maybe you kind of look like us and you have most of the same genes or whatever, but so do apes, right? And nobody cares about them."

"You really think that about us?" I asked.

She looked sheepishly down at her hands. "Maybe I used to," she said. "It's easier to believe the things that people tell you to believe, you know? When all these people that are so much smarter than you and so much more important than you tell you stuff, you just assume they're right."

She stopped talking and Missy and I stood in stunned silence. This wasn't just shock or confusion or disgust. When we walked back inside this kennel it was like a piece of ourselves had snagged on the jagged corner of the doors and the further we ventured inside these walls, the more unraveled we became. I could feel myself coming undone.

Unspooling from the inside out.

Maybe Riley was right. Maybe nobody cared.

Riley glanced uncomfortably between the two of us. “It might not be any consolation, but I kind of know how you feel. Do you think anyone gives a crap about a poor girl from Camden? I know what it’s like to feel like you don’t have any choices.”

“So what do we do?” Missy asked. “We can’t stay here. They’ll kill us.”

“We can’t leave yet,” I said. “We haven’t fixed anything.”

Missy threw her hands up. “Does this look like something that can be fixed? We should just get out of here now while we still can.”

“It’s not like I can help,” Riley said. “I would if I could, really, but they’d make my life a living hell if I said anything. They’re paying us a lot of money to do this and most of that’s for promising to keep our big mouths shut. They had me sign this gazillion page legal document saying that I wouldn’t ever tell anyone about it.”

“Why?”

“Because people would freak out if they knew about this,” she said, pointing to her stomach. “I guess I kind of knew this was wrong when I signed up for it, but I needed the money, you know? Anyone would have done it if they grew up where I grew up. In my neighborhood people steal, or deal meth. This seemed like a better choice than that. At least I wasn’t hurting anyone. I didn’t think I was. And I always thought being pregnant would be nice. I’d get paid to just sit around and eat and sleep for a year. It sounded nice not to have to worry about all of the crap I grew up worrying about.”

“And you think people would be upset if they found out

that NuPet was using *you*, but they wouldn't be upset about them using *us*?" Missy asked.

Riley snorted, laughing. "No! I don't think people give a rat's ass what happens to me! They'd just be freaked out by the whole thing, you know? If these guys have spent all this time and money selling you as pets, telling people that you're different from us and that's why it's okay to own one of you, then they aren't going to want people to find out that you weren't grown in labs or bred by other pets. And I sort of get it, I mean, these rich guys are paying all this money for their perfect pets…they don't want to find out that they used poor, trashy girls like me to give birth to them. They'd rather just picture that you all popped out of a plastic tube somewhere or something."

She placed her hand on her stomach and for the first time since we'd arrived I really thought about the fact that there was a baby in there. A tiny living thing. That baby girl that grew inside her wouldn't be too different from me. Like me, she would have been engineered to have a petite body, large eyes, a rose petal mouth. She would have been made for the sole purpose of bettering someone else's life. That's what we'd been told. We existed to serve. We existed for our master's pleasure.

But was that really the truth? It wasn't what I believed. But now I wondered if it was even the truth as far as NuPet saw it. Were they really worried about creating lifetime companions for people, or did they only care about the money? Maybe no one actually believed that we had been created for any of the reasons I'd been taught. Even the people who were buying pets didn't believe it. They only cared about prestige and status and the way other people perceived them.

I wondered if Riley had really thought about what she was doing to that little baby that lived inside her, if she'd thought about the life that it would have.

She saw me staring at her stomach. "You think I'm a terrible person, don't you?"

"No."

She closed her eyes and placed both of her hands on her belly. Her brow wrinkled like she was concentrating on something.

"The thing they don't tell you is that you'll get attached to it," she said softly without opening her eyes. "I did it the first time and it nearly killed me. This time I'm trying not to think about what's going to happen to her. Sometimes I kind of wish that we didn't know that they were all girls, like it might make a difference, might make me less attached since I wouldn't know what it was. But then I just get to thinking that I don't care about any of it as long as she's not a discard, you know?"

Chapter Sixteen

"Discard?" My skin prickled at the word.

Riley nodded, her face solemn. "When I got here the first time, I thought those stupid high-and-mighties were just trying to scare us newbies. I figured the doctors gotta know what they're talking about. They've been doing this for long enough. They can't mess up a baby! But then I had one."

I looked to Missy to see if she understood what Riley was ranting about, but she looked just as confused as I was.

"I got all the way to term, too, so I thought it was safe. Not all the women here do, but I delivered without any problems. That saves 'em money, you know? And then I heard it cry, which is weird 'cause you wouldn't think that would be a sound you'd like, but with a baby it is."

She smiled for a moment, her eyes glistening, but the fleeting happiness slipped away almost immediately. "The doctors, though… Damn, those are some stone cold bastards. They took the measurements and look at me like

I did something wrong. Like I ruined her by being me, or something."

"What happened?" I asked. "To the baby?"

Riley's face sobered. "They said she was sub-par and took her away. Took her to the other side of the room and pulled a curtain across so I couldn't see her anymore. But I could still hear her. And then the crying just stopped. It stopped and it didn't start any more after that." She leaned forward. "They think we don't know what they're doing, but we're not stupid."

Dread flooded my gut. Surely she wasn't saying what I thought she was saying? Because if she was… I looked at Missy. Her face had gone white and her pale blue eyes were wide and round.

Riley lifted her chin before I could ask what, exactly, had happened to her baby. "I can't let myself think about any of that stuff anymore. I'm here to do a job and I gotta do it," she went on. "So I'll just keep on imagining how spoiled she'll be. She's going to grow up and go live with someone that'll give her the comfortable, pampered life I always wanted."

Missy still stared at her, but the color had returned to her face, and a familiar fire simmered in her eyes. I knew we were both thinking the same thing, but neither of us would tell Riley what it was really like. For just a few minutes more, maybe we *all* needed to believe her next baby's life was going to be wonderful. It hurt too much to imagine any other scenario.

Riley's eyes filled with tears as she looked between us. "Maybe I was wrong," she said. "They don't want to admit that you're just like us, but you are. They can change how you look, but they can't change the fact that you're humans.

You grew inside someone. You heard her heartbeat for *nine months*. That's gotta count for something, you know?"

My throat tightened. She didn't have to tell me we were human. I already knew.

Suddenly, she sat up straight, determination replacing the longing in her eyes. "There is one room that has something you could use, if you're serious about trying to expose things."

"Will you take us?" I asked.

She nodded. "Yes, but we have to go now. It's down a different hallway by the delivery rooms and it's kind of close to the orderly's office. He's usually sleeping this time of night, even though he's not supposed to, but he won't sleep that long."

We followed after Riley as she slipped out of the little supply closet and padded down the dark hallway. It was lined with doors, some of which stood open, leading to rooms that were almost identical to the ones that I'd seen on the other half: a dining hall, a bathing room. But other doors were closed, leaving me both curious and anxious about what lay behind them.

At the end of the hallway Riley paused, holding up her hand to stop us. "It's around the corner," she whispered, pushing her back up against the wall. "The doors on the right are all their offices and stuff," she said. "The door you want is at the very end of the hallway."

"You aren't coming?" Missy asked.

She shook her head. "I can't. I've only got a few more weeks and then I'm done here. I'm so close to getting out and getting paid. If they caught me…"

I lay my hand on her arm. "It's okay."

"I know you probably think I'm a coward. But it's the

best I can do," she said. "Now listen, the room you're going to go in is bad, but don't let it freak you out. There's a whole wall of filing cabinets on the right. That's what you need to focus on. I found my file in there, so I know they keep track of things."

Missy and I nodded. I had no idea what we were supposed to do once we got the files, but at least it was a start. "We'll try," I said. "But I'm not sure what we're looking for."

"It's all in there: contract terms, reports, everything you need," she said. "Well, I'm getting out of here. This sort of stuff makes me too nervous, like I'm going to go into labor or something."

She gave us an awkward wave and turned back down the hallway, not even bothering with a proper good-bye.

I grabbed Missy's hand. "Let's get this over with."

She nodded and we rounded the corner together. It was dark, with only one small light mounted in the middle of the hallway casting a yellowish glow down the hall, so we couldn't really see the door at the end of the hallway right away.

Missy spotted it first. A small yelp escaped her lips as she stopped, yanking my arm back with her.

Her hand tightened around mine, squeezing my fingers so tight that I might have yelled out in pain if the sight of the door hadn't sucked the air straight from my lungs. I'd known it was here. There was one in every wing of this building. But even though Riley had talked about the door, I hadn't actually expected to see it. The shape was no different from any of the others, but that color was unforgettable.

Red.

Like blood.

A shock of color that pulsed behind my eyes.

"That can't be where we're supposed to go," Missy said, shaking her head back and forth, back and forth, like a girl possessed. "She's got to be wrong. This is where they take the babies, right? Not where they'd keep cabinets full of paper."

I held tight to her hand and yanked her forward again. "Calm down."

Red.

Red.

Light shone out from under the door to our left. The orderly's room.

My heart thudded madly and the floor wobbled beneath my feet. *Think*, I told myself. *Breathe*.

"We have to do this," I whispered. "We have to go in."

Missy's eyes widened and she shook her head even more violently, planting her feet on the ground and tugging on my arm. "No. I won't do it."

Behind the orderly's door, something rustled. There was a small *thud*, followed by a *click* and the light that shone out from under the crack intensified.

"We have to go. *Now*."

Missy gritted her teeth as I dragged her toward the red door. Anger flared through my chest. Did she think she was the only one who was terrified? Did she think the red door only haunted *her*? It stained all of our nightmares. Every one of us. They'd painted it red for a reason. It was a sign. A warning.

Do something wrong and you will be punished!

I blinked and I could see afternoon light streaming down the hallway. I was just a little girl. I could feel the wood of my doorframe beneath my hand as the starched white pants of the orderly passed by, the man wearing them dragging a girl by her hair. I heard the screams. Saw the door open. This much was always the same, in every poisoned memory, but suddenly I understood. They'd made us watch. It wasn't just a coincidence that I'd been standing in my doorway. They'd forced us there, each time, to watch as someone disappeared behind that red door forever.

I blinked again, and time rushed forward.

From behind the orderly's door, the sound of a chair scraped over the tile and it was like I could see through the wood into the room beyond it. I could see the man in his white shirt and pants, rubbing his tired eyes as he scooted back from the cluttered desk.

I shoved my shoulder against the door and pulled Missy through behind me…right as the door to the orderly's room creaked open. We toppled inside and I silently swung the red door shut behind me, closing us in.

Missy and I both collapsed against the door, holding each other. The room was too dark for me to see the ghostly structure of a room we'd probably all constructed a million times within our imaginations.

"They had a room like this at the kennel where I grew up," she said. "They killed girls in here."

I squeezed her hand. "I know. And unless we see something that proves Riley wrong, they might be killing babies in here, too." I fumbled along the wall for the light switch. "That orderly was probably headed back to the dormitory. That doesn't give us very much time before he notices we're gone."

My fingers found the plastic switch plate and a moment later the ceiling light flickered to life, drowning the room in a bright fluorescent glow.

Missy and I both shielded our eyes. The room wasn't

huge, but the reflections that bounced off the metal tables and counters made it look far bigger than it actually was. The wall to my right was covered with filing cabinets exactly like Riley said it would be, but as much as I tried not to let my gaze drift, it was impossible not to see the rest of the room.

I'd only ever caught the smallest glimpse at what lay beyond the red door when I was a child, but I couldn't forget the shelves full of glass vials and syringes that covered the walls. The machines that I'd seen lining the counters had seemed like monsters with their blinking red eyes and tangled wires that hung down like tentacles ready to reach out and strangle me. I cringed, standing this close to them now. Even though I knew that these things couldn't do anything to me on their own, I still shrank away.

"Get up," I whispered, pulling Missy to her feet.

She moaned, uncovering her eyes as she took a few steps further into the room with me. "Oh God, this is bad," she said. Her gaze stopped on the cold metal table in the middle of the room. "Are those straps?" she asked, pointing to four thick white pieces of leather that hung from each corner.

Beside the straps, a tray sat at the center of the table, neatly arranged with a pair of latex gloves, a syringe and half a dozen tools.

I turned around and grabbed her hands. "We can't look at this now," I said, pulling her so close that our noses touched and she had no choice but to look at me. "We need to focus, okay?"

"I know. It's just that it feels like this place is the root of everything bad that's ever happened to me. It's the center, like everything I'm afraid of radiates out from here."

I leaned my forehead against hers. "I understand," I

said. "But we can't let it control us. That's exactly what they wanted, isn't it? One glimpse of this door and they could bring us to our knees. They could mold us into whatever they wanted."

She nodded, and a little bit of the wildness left her eyes. "Okay."

"Are you ready to do this?"

She nodded again and we both turned to the wall of filing cabinets.

"How do we even know what we're looking for?" I asked, opening a drawer toward the middle of the wall.

Dozens and dozens of tan folders packed with papers filled up the drawer. I riffled through them. Each of the folders had a bright red number drawn on the tab, and next to that, a line followed by another two numbers.

"What do you think this means?" I asked, running my finger over a folder with the numbers 5-23.

Missy looked up from the drawer she'd just opened. "These ones have them too. Check to see what's inside."

I pulled out one of the folders and flipped it open, thumbing through the stack of papers, but they were just a mad tangle of ink, a jumble of letters and numbers. "It doesn't make sense. I can't read any of this."

Missy sighed loudly and began flipping more quickly through the files. "It must all be important if they kept it," she said. "Maybe these are all the files of the girls they've put down over the years?"

I jerked my fingers back from the file I was holding. There were too many. A wall full of them.

"No." I shook my head. "That doesn't make sense. There's no way they could have killed this many girls."

Missy shrugged. "I don't know. Riley said all the girls

they've experimented on died. Who knows how long this has been going on?"

I shook my head. I couldn't think about that right now.

Missy sighed and closed her file cabinet. "It doesn't matter. If NuPet's killing babies, those are the files we need to find. People aren't going to care about the other stuff."

I glared at her. "I'm sorry, but I refuse to believe people lack that much empathy. They would care. They have to care."

"Fine, take some of those folders, too," she said, nodding toward my cabinet.

I opened a new drawer and flipped through the files, adding random ones to Missy's small pile.

"How do we know if these are the ones that Riley was talking about?" I asked, looking behind me at the door. We'd only been in here for a few minutes, but I didn't know how much more time we had. What if the orderly noticed that we weren't in our beds? What if someone had seen us leave? What if Riley told him where we were?

I pulled the drawers open faster, working my way left, while Missy worked her way to the right.

"These all look the same," Missy grumbled. She abandoned that drawer and moved all the way over to the wall, pulling one open on the farthest side. "These are different," she said excitedly. "Look!" She pulled one out and held it up. "The tab has words on it and then a number. Can you read this?" she asked, shoving the folder at me.

"I can't read the word, but look at the numbers," I said, almost jumping. "They're just like the numbers on the files I have. Some of them are even the same."

"Let me see," Missy said, snatching the folder out of my hands. "I bet they go together."

My heart pounded faster. "Should we try to match them up?" I scooted up next to her, pulling out the drawer underneath the one she was looking through. My head was spinning, all those numbers bouncing in front of my eyes. Were they the numbers they assigned us? How many girls were born? Or… "Wait, what was the highest number that you got to on the files?"

Missy shook her head. "I don't know. I didn't check the bottom drawer."

I yanked open the bottom drawer. 1-32, 2-32, 3-32. Thirty-two? They'd really been breeding pets for that long? If so, it shouldn't be too hard to find my own file.

Missy yanked on the bottom drawer of the next cabinet. "This one's locked."

I ignored her. I needed a pen and some paper. We'd learned a little bit of math at the training center, simple addition and subtraction. It wasn't much, but it was all I needed right now. I scanned the room. There were a million crazy items, but nothing that I actually needed.

"Did you hear me?" she asked. "What do you think is in this one that they don't want people to find?"

I closed my eyes, trying to imagine the numbers in my mind. If I was sixteen and the program had been creating girls for thirty-two years… I tried to line up the figures, thirty-two over sixteen.

"Grab me that knife," Missy said, jiggling the handle of the drawer.

"What?" I couldn't concentrate with her talking to me.

"That knife." Missy pointed toward the shining instruments on the table in the middle of the room. "I need it."

I picked it up. It was slender, like a pencil. The blade at the top was small, but I didn't want to think about how sharp it could be.

"Stop staring at it and give it to me," Missy snapped, snatching it out of my hand.

She jammed the knife into the keyhole, jiggling it.

I whirled back around to the cabinet I'd been searching through. My own small history was in one of these drawers. Those letters, littering those pages, dots of black against the stark white page, might tell me something about myself that I didn't know yet.

I wanted that file. Needed it.

Behind me, there was a small click and a drawer popped open. Missy started to speak, maybe to boast about being able to open locked drawers, but before she could get out any words, a deafening alarm blared out.

"The drawer!" I yelled, lifting my voice over the screeching. "There must be an alarm on it!"

"Don't yell at me!" She pulled the drawer open anyway, snatching up files, each marked on the front with an angry red stamp. "These have to be the ones. Why else would they lock them up? Hurry up and help me get these."

The noise filled up my whole head. How was I supposed to figure out what file I needed if I couldn't even hear myself think? I closed my eyes and covered my ears. Thirty-two minus sixteen. Twelve minus six was six. Two minus one was one. Sixteen. The answer was sixteen.

I pulled the drawer open, shuffling wildly through the files. Where was the one that I needed? 8-16. 8-16. 8-16.

"Ella! Are you out of your mind? *These* are the ones we need!" Missy said. Her face was red, her eyes wild, as she shoved files from the locked drawer into a plastic garbage bag she'd found.

Finally, I saw it. There wasn't time to linger over the

letters that had been printed in front of it. I grabbed the file I hoped held all my secrets.

"Ella!" Missy yelled, slapping me. "We've got to get out of here."

The alarm was so loud that we didn't hear the orderly coming until the door crashed open. His whole body filled the doorframe.

"What the hell?" he said. His groggy stare took us in, traveling down our bodies to the files we clutched in our hands. "Put those down right now."

Missy's fingers tightened around the files.

"I said drop 'em." His voice boomed as he lunged toward us.

The file I was holding fell to the ground and my hand darted to my pocket. A second later the orderly was barreling down on us, his face red with rage as his gigantic hand clamped around Missy's neck.

"No one disobeys me," he spat. His grip tightened and Missy sputtered for breath as he lifted her by the throat. "Especially not one of you bitches."

Chapter Seventeen

In one quick motion, I uncapped the syringe and threw my body against him. He was a wall. The force of my body hardly budged him and he moved his arm to flick me away, but before he could, I raised my hand, bringing the needle down into the exposed skin of his neck.

He bucked, dropping Missy and smacking me with his fist. I fell back and he turned to face me where I lay on the floor. His eyes flared with rage as he lifted his hand to his neck. A drop of blood fell from the hole where I'd stabbed him. His finger grazed it. Ever so gently, he pulled it away, peering down at the red smear on his hand.

"I'll kill you both my—"

His eyes glazed over and the next moment he was falling, landing with a thud against the side of the table before he slid to the ground.

I scrambled to my feet, backing away from him.

Missy stared up at me from where she knelt on the floor.

"Quick, close the door," she wheezed. "We don't have long before the rest of them get here."

I slammed the door shut. For a moment, our eyes met. All the terror and adrenaline that I felt were mirrored there as perfectly as if I was staring into my own eyes. As if we were connected to the same brain, our eyes moved in synchronicity toward the door.

"They're coming," Missy said, staring at it as if she could see through it toward the hallway behind.

I turned back toward the room, hoping that another exit had magically appeared.

"What's that?" Missy said, staring over my shoulder.

There was a long, metal drawer built into the wall. It was narrow, maybe two feet tall and three feet wide, almost the exact height of the table in the center of the room. At the top of it was a wide handle.

A strange look crossed Missy's face.

"We can't hide in there," I said, shaking my head.

She grabbed the handle and the drawer swung open, hinged at the bottom like a mailbox. We both paused, bending over to stare inside. I'd expected a drawer like the ones on the filing cabinets, but it wasn't a drawer at all. The inside was lined with shiny metal, like the table, and after the first foot, the metal slanted down at an angle, like a slide, disappearing into darkness. It wasn't a drawer at all. It was a garbage shoot of some sort.

"Hurry!" Missy said, shoving the bag of files through the hole.

I grabbed her arm. "Wait! We don't even know what's down there."

"You're right," she said. "But I know what's out there." She pointed toward the door. "And I'm guessing you don't have enough needles in your pocket to take them all out."

Over the scream of the alarm, I heard the pounding of footsteps. Missy took a deep breath and dove into the dark shoot. My legs trembled. Behind me, voices called out in the hallway.

I scrambled into the hole, the smooth metal icy cold against the bare skin of my legs. The ramp slanted but not too steeply that I had to fight to keep my body from slipping. I grabbed the front of the metal door and pulled it closed before I pushed off, sliding down the tube into the darkness below.

The ramp tapered off at the bottom, sending my body slipping across the cement floor and directly into Missy. The file that I'd been clutching tight flew out of my hands. The papers fanned out, some of them sliding beneath a dark crack underneath the far wall.

Next to me, Missy moaned, clutching her side where I'd just crashed into her.

"Are you okay?" I asked.

She nodded. "Where are we?"

An orange light cast the room we'd landed in with an eerie amber glow. It was a small room. There were a few metal tables, similar to the one in the room we'd just come from, but these tables were bare. No straps. No instruments. Besides the tables, the room was empty other than a few large metal cabinets that ran along one of the cement walls and a tall brick fireplace.

Slowly, I propped myself up. The faint shriek of the alarm still sounded above us, but it no longer pounded in my ears. Missy's garbage bag full of papers had stayed mostly intact in the fall and I scooped it up as I crawled past it, snatching up the scattered papers from my file.

"Just leave them," Missy said, getting to her feet. "We've got to find a way out of here."

We both knew they'd have found the orderly's body by now. They would have figured out that we'd stolen their files and guessed where we'd gone. Even if they didn't fit down the metal shoot themselves, it wouldn't take them long to get down to us.

On my hands and knees, I scrambled to reach underneath the tall metal cabinets where the papers had slid. The space beneath them was hardly big enough for my arm to fit. I lay down on the cold cement, straining to grasp them. The very tips of my fingers brushed against the edge of a sheet of paper.

Missy paced the room. "This can't be the only way out," she said, tugging the handle of the steel door. It rattled in her hand. Locked.

I pressed down with the pad of my pointer finger and pulled. The paper slid ever so slightly toward me.

"Ella!" Missy shrieked. "Help me!"

"Hold on. I almost have it!"

Missy threw her hands up and kicked the door before she spun around wildly, looking for any other way out.

The paper slid closer to me and I finally grabbed ahold of it. It was too dark to see if there were any others that I'd missed, and we were out of time.

I eyed the brick fireplace on the other side of the room. A steel door covered the front of it. I scrambled over and threw it open, leaning into the deep box.

"Is there a chimney?" Missy asked, standing beside me. "Maybe we can climb out."

I pulled my head out, wiping the black ashes that clung to my hands across the front of my jumper. "The opening is too small. It isn't more than a foot wide. We won't fit."

"Well, maybe if we go back up the shoot," she said. "They might not be up there anymore."

I looked at the rows of steel doors across the room. "What about those?" I said. "Maybe they lead somewhere."

Missy nodded hopefully, tugging open the one closest to her. "It's dark and really cold. I can't tell if there's…" She jumped back, dropping the bag of folders "*Noooo...*" she moaned. "No. No. No." She brought her hand to her mouth and turned away.

In a second I was beside her. The door to the cabinet was still wide open and as soon as I stepped in front of it, I was met with a puff of icy air. It was a gaping dark hole easily big enough for the two of us to climb inside.

"Missy, what's—" I started to ask.

My breath fogged the air in front of me. The cabinet was deep. On the bottom, there was a rolling metal shelf that my gaze followed back into the dark. And then I saw. There, more than an arm's length back, was the ghostly outline of two pale feet, still and stiff and cold. Wrapped around the big toe was a paper tag marked with black ink.

I gagged and turned away, slamming the door shut.

"You don't think all those…" Missy's voice trailed off as she stepped further away from the metal doors that lined the wall.

All those doors. All those shelves. Were they full? Full of bodies?

Above them was another row of smaller doors, too tiny for one of us to fit in, but big enough for… Oh God.

I stared down at my black hands. Ashes. It was their ashes.

"They burn them," I cried, trying to wipe away the remnants that clung to my skin. I could feel them coating my hands, my throat where I'd breathed them in. Penn was right. This was the way the kennel disposed of girls. They stuck them in an oven and they let them burn until there was nothing left.

I snatched the garbage bag off of the floor. We had to get out. I'd break that stupid door down if I had to.

Missy tugged on the handle again and looked desperately around the room. "There has to be something that we can use," she said.

Beside the door, above the light switch, was another metal box, hinged at the top. I flipped it open. Inside was a keypad.

"These are just like the ones on the doors upstairs."

"It's a security system," Missy said. "It's not going to do us any good unless we have the code."

My fingers trembled against the plastic keys.

Please, please let this work. I took a deep breath, trying to imagine the man in the white coat as he'd led us down the hallway yesterday. It seemed like an eternity ago, but if I concentrated, I could remember.

2-9-4-6. I pressed each number slowly, deliberately.

"You can't just start typing numbers," Missy said.

My finger hovered over the last one. Eight. My number. For my whole life, that number had connected me to the kennel, but maybe not anymore. Maybe, this time, it was the key out.

I pressed the button.

The lock clicked. There was a small hiss followed by the puff of air releasing from some cylinder that had kept the door tightly closed and it cracked open.

"Ella..." Missy's mouth hung open. "How did you—?"

"It was your idea. Your owner's safe, remember?" I snatched the garbage bag off the floor and pushed the door open. The hallway was dark and silent. And then, somewhere far away, I heard the echo of voices.

"Which way?" I asked.

The hall split in three different directions. It was a maze of corridors down here and I was completely turned around. Upstairs, I at least had some idea which way would lead to the outer wall of the building, but not down here.

"Go straight," Missy said, shoving me forward.

"Are you sure?"

"No," she said. "But we can't stay here. Move."

We ran down the hallway, past more doors like the one we'd just come out of. I didn't want to think about what else might be hidden down here. At the end of the corridor, it split again and without stopping to ask, we both turned right.

"There!" Missy pointed.

This hallway was shorter than the others and at the end, a small cement stairway led back up to the main level. At the top of the landing there was another door, this one even bigger than the one we'd just come through. On the front of it hung a large plastic sign with bold red lettering and a picture of a dot with three curved lines radiating off of it.

"What does it mean?" I asked.

Missy shook her head. "I don't care," she said, shoving her arm against the push handle.

The rush of fresh air startled me as we stumbled out onto the side of the building. The night was dark. Only a few small white lights shone down off of the windowless side of the building. From inside, a new alarm buzzed.

I had no idea which direction we needed to turn to get to the front of the building. In front of us, a long stretch of grass slanted down toward a row of trees. I swung the bag full of files up over my shoulder and let Missy drag me forward. The plastic slipped in my sweaty grasp, and I held on tighter, the tips of my fingernails biting into my palms. The sharp edges of the folders dug into my back as I ran, but I couldn't stop.

We reached the bottom of the hill and the sharp sound of voices cut through the night somewhere behind us. Suddenly the tops of the trees lit up in front of us and I screeched to a halt.

"Don't stop!" Missy grabbed my arm and pulled me after her.

The trees only stayed alight for a moment before the beam swept across the hill and then looped back around to the other side of the building.

"It's a searchlight. I don't think they saw us."

A few more steps and we disappeared inside the trees. The trunks were spindly and tall and we darted between them, running in as straight a line as we could away from the kennel. Through the branches above us, the wedge of moon flickered in and out of view. If we were in the open, we would have been able to see the stars. In Ruby's books there were people who could find their way using the constellations. I didn't understand how. Maybe they could read them, like words?

Someday, I'd learn to read the stars, too.

"How are we…going to find…Penn?" I panted.

Missy slowed, holding her side. "I think we should just keep going straight until we come to the road. It seems like we're almost there, right?"

I nodded, even though I wasn't so sure. The people from the kennel knew this property. Maybe they even had ways to track us. If we didn't find Penn soon, they'd find us and kill us. I was sure of it.

Our feet were raw, but we stumbled forward. One minute

we were in a dense pocket of foliage and the next…we were in the open. I blinked up at the stars, half expecting there to be a big arrow flickering in the specks of light, pointing us toward Penn.

"Which way?" Missy asked, looking in either direction down the wooded road.

I looked to the left and then to the right. This stretch of road looked the tiniest bit familiar. Had we passed this on the way to the kennel? Or was I remembering a long-ago drive from the kennel to the training center?

"We should stay in the trees," I said.

Missy nodded, following me back into the cover at the side of the road.

"Are those lights?" she asked after a minute.

We both stopped. She was right. Through the trees I thought I saw a faint glow. I held tight to the nearest trunk, trying not to move as I waited to hear the snap of sticks and the crunch of big boots, but the woods stayed silent except for the chirp of frogs and the rustle of the wind through the branches.

I focused on the light, expecting to see the beam sweep over us, but its glow was as still as the moon's in the sky. We pushed through the trees and stumbled into a small clearing.

There was a car there, all right, but it wasn't Penn's. A dark blue van sat parked on the slight slope, its front tires pointing up toward the road, as if it were ready to take off at a moment's notice. But for now, the engine sat silent.

The back doors were cracked open just enough to send a bit of light from the single bulb out onto the trampled dirt.

Missy and I backed carefully into the cover of the trees.

We held still, waiting for someone to emerge from the clearing, but it was empty. If someone had been here, they must have heard the sound of the sirens and left.

"Is it from the kennel?" I whispered.

She shook her head, pointing to the side where the remnants of an eagle's head were spray painted in red.

"Like the one from the train?" I asked.

Slowly, Missy stepped closer to the van, her arm outstretched as if she wanted to touch it.

"We have to go," I said. "Penn's waiting."

Missy took another step. "Just let me— "

She stopped and covered her mouth with both hands.

"Missy?" I crouched beside her. "What is it?"

She fell to her knees, and a low moan escaped from her lips.

"What?" I asked again, looking up at the van.

And then I saw. Peeking through the crack in the back doors was a hand, the small white palm pointing skyward.

"We have to go," I said, tugging Missy to her feet.

We stumbled back into the trees. Missy held onto me, and I pulled her against my side, moving for the two of us.

"I can't do this," Missy cried. She slipped from my grasp and crumpled onto the ground. "This is too much. Getting you back here was one thing, but all of these dead girls? I can't *do* this, Ella."

I grabbed her beneath the arms and hoisted her to her feet. "I know. But you can. You're the strongest person I know. It's just a little bit further. Come on."

I helped Missy up and supported her slumping frame as we slipped back into the trees. The foliage grew denser. Thick patches of holly caught the fabric of our thin jumpers and clawed at our calves and thighs. I wanted to stop, too. Wanted to lower myself down in the underbrush and close my eyes, but I couldn't. I'd meant what I said to Missy, but it was time for me to be the strong one.

“Who told you to look for that shape the first time?”

“It must have been a mistake,” Missy said. “We must have seen it wrong. We *had* to have.”

I didn’t need to ask again. I saw the answer streaked across her cheeks.

Seth. It was Seth.

“It doesn’t matter now,” I said, wanting to believe it as much as she did, but we both knew it was a lie. It *did* matter. We wanted so badly to believe that there were good guys, but we’d been wrong.

We walked on. Ten minutes turned into twenty and then suddenly it was there, the yellow glow of the gate’s small lamp. We stumbled into the small clearing in front of the kennel’s long driveway. Somehow, by some generous stroke of luck, we’d found it.

“He’s not here,” Missy said, her hands on her hips, as if she’d expected Penn to be sitting behind the wheel of the car with the engine revved and his hand resting on the gearshift, ready to pull out at a moment’s notice.

“Stop it,” I whispered. “He said he’d be here.”

“What if he’s not, Ella? What if they got to him already?”

I readjusted the bag over my shoulder, ignoring her.

We were standing in front of the kennel’s gate, out in the open. Of course Penn wouldn’t wait there. “He said he’d hide the car,” I reminded her. “Come on.”

The gate’s wrought iron bars sat open wide, attached on either side to two wide columns, about six feet at its tallest. From there, it sloped down on either side, curving a bit toward the road. It was only about a dozen feet long, but there was probably enough room to hide a car back there.

I tromped down the small incline behind the brick wall. The foliage was thick with bramble and bushes but it was clear that there were no cars hiding here.

"Maybe he's on the other side?" Missy whispered hopefully near my ear.

We pushed through the tangle of branches and paused at the edge of the road. The kennel wasn't visible from here, but the bright beams of the searchlights were. They looped in circles through the dark sky, illuminating the grounds in bursts of light.

We were too far away to be spotted by the beams, but still we held our breath, waiting for just the right moment to dash across the empty road. The smooth pavement soothed my aching feet, but I didn't stop to savor it. A second later we crashed through the underbrush on the other side.

My eyes darted over the scene and the bag slipped from my hand.

There it was. The car.

Chapter Eighteen

I could barely make out the car's shape behind the mound of long evergreen branches that Penn must have draped across the hood and along the roof, but it was there.

I had no idea what time of night it was or how long Penn had been waiting, but he must have been awake, because the door flung open and a second later he was in front of me.

All the fear that I'd been carrying like this heavy bag across my back dropped away as I collapsed into his arms.

"Thank God you're here." He pulled me into his chest, squeezing me so hard that it felt like I might burst. "I had the windows cracked, listening for you, and I swear I heard an alarm go off." He sounded hoarse, like his voice might break at any moment. "I didn't know what to do. I didn't know if I should stay here or come looking for you."

His warm hands closed around my shoulders and he pulled back, staring down at me. It was dark, but a bit of light reflected off the tears that had welled in his eyes.

"You did the right thing." I lingered in his embrace a moment longer before I snatched up the bag of files and began pulling evergreen boughs from off the car. "We need to go," I said. "Now."

Penn stared at me a moment longer. The need to flee pounded against my back, pushing me forward, but I understood the hesitation in his eyes, the need to remind himself that we'd found each other. Again and again. We found our way back.

The passenger side was still covered in boughs, so the three of us piled in through Penn's door and he cranked the key. The engine revved, the sound of it growing in the night, spreading out like a beacon, echoing across the kennel grounds before the car sputtered and died.

Penn hit the steering wheel. "Damn it, start!"

"Try again," I begged, leaning forward in my seat as if the crazy whirring that rushed through my veins could feed the engine.

He twisted the key again and it sputtered. Chugged. Once more and the engine caught. The car shook beneath us and Penn threw it into drive. The wheels spun, digging into the damp dirt before finally finding traction. Branches whacked the windshield as we shot forward, bouncing up onto the blacktop.

Missy's head flopped forward against the back of my seat and her hand snaked up over the backrest, settling on my shoulder. I reached up and held it as beneath us the tires purred against the asphalt. Dark trees whipped past our windows and still I held tight to her hand. We'd done it. I don't know how, but we'd done it.

The bag full of files slumped beside Missy in the backseat. They were only papers, bits of wood pulp and ink, but it felt like they were alive. It felt like we'd managed to rescue something more than just some scribbled notes and documents. More than proof. Those files breathed and something like a pulse moved through them.

Missy ripped off the kennel's white jumper as soon as the car hit the freeway. I couldn't get out of mine fast enough either. The smudge of ashes cut across the middle of it like a dark wound. I balled the fabric into a tight ball and shoved it beneath the seat.

I wiggled back into my old jeans and T-shirt. Already I felt better just being in my own clothes. The fact that they were dirty didn't bother me a bit.

Dawn was beginning to break as we pulled into Hartford. In the backseat, Missy was sprawled out with her feet propped up against the window. Her mouth had fallen open in sleep and she snored softly. Nothing about her looked refined or sophisticated and my heart swelled for her. It felt weird, this love. It reminded me a bit of the way I felt about Ruby, but it surprised me to feel this way for her. Maybe it was because I'd been taught my whole life to distance myself from the other girls at the kennel. Pets weren't meant to be friends; at least, that's what I'd been told.

We drew nearer to the city and Penn pulled into the nearly empty parking lot of a grocery store. He put the car in park and laid his head against the steering wheel, his face still blank, unreadable. During the drive I'd whispered the things we'd seen inside the kennel, letting the words spill from my mouth like a sickness that I needed to expel from my body.

His hands had clamped tighter and tighter around the wheel as I spoke, his eyes dark and stony, locked on the road.

"You look tired," I said, reaching out to lay my hand on the back of his neck.

His eyes were red and his short hair poked out at a funny angle, stuck this way from all the time he had spent running his hands through it.

"Why don't we find a place to rest?" I suggested. "It doesn't have to be for long. Only an hour or two."

Penn shook his head and rubbed his eyes. "No. I don't want to have this stuff any longer than I have to." He glanced uncomfortably back at the bag of files, which had slipped down onto the floor of the backseat. "If they find us with them… It's bad enough that I committed fraud by selling you two. This is proof."

"Good," I said. "Proof is exactly what we need."

"You're right." Penn nodded. "I guess we need to look through them first and then we can find someone to take them to."

"Who? The police?"

"No." He shook his head. "My dad and NuPet have the police wrapped around their little fingers. You said so yourself. Besides, they wouldn't care unless a crime had been committed and as far as I can tell, we're the ones who committed the crime."

"You don't think it's a crime? What they're doing to those girls?" My voice shook. "They're killing them. We saw the bodies!"

He reached out for me, cupping my face in his hand. "I'm sorry. I'm sorry. You're right. I'm not saying it isn't horrible. It is! I know that. Anyone with even an ounce of decency would know that."

I covered my face with my hands, pressing my palms into my eyes. "I don't want to see it anymore," I said, shaking my head. "They sent their bodies down a garbage shoot. That's all they were. Garbage. I can't— " I choked on the words.

"Shh. It's okay," Penn said.

I concentrated on the warmth of his hand as it stroked the back of my neck. I didn't want to think about what was happening inside the kennel. I wanted to shut it out of my mind and never think about it again, but I couldn't. I couldn't forget those girls. It wouldn't be fair.

"So who can we tell that will care?" I asked, sitting up.

Penn sighed, reaching back for the bag of folders. "You really think they're killing those babies because they aren't perfect? What if that woman you talked to has it wrong? What if they were stillbirths? What if they're dying for other reasons? Health reasons. Maybe that's what the doctors knew when the babies were born."

"We saw them."

"You saw the *cabinets*," Penn said. He pulled a file out of the bag and laid the stack of papers in his lap. "The only bodies you saw were of older girls."

I gaped at him. "Are you saying I'm lying?"

"No, not at all. I just want to be sure. That's all."

"So look at the papers, then," I snapped.

He sighed and looked back down at the paper in front of him, running his finger along a line of print. He was quiet for a moment, reading, and his brow crinkled as he studied the words.

"I don't get what a lot of this is," he said after a while. "There's a bunch of scientific terms…stuff about performance, but I don't know. What if we can't find anything to use against them?"

"But that's just one file," I said, straining to reach into the back for another one. "And it's one of the first ones we found." I shuffled through the bag until I came to one of the folders that came from the locked drawer. I handed him the file. "Try this. Some of them have something different on the outside like this one." I pointed to the red word stamped across the manila file.

Penn sat up a little straighter. "Terminated?"

A chill spread up my arms.

"It doesn't necessarily mean they killed them," he said. "It could mean something else. It could…" His voice trailed off as he thumbed through the file, stopping every once in a while to read, and I flipped back and forth between watching his face and watching the way his finger traced the shape of the sentences.

"This is messed up," he muttered.

"What? What does it say?"

He licked his lips. "I don't even know what it all means," he said. "There's a lot of these legal papers in here. I can't understand all the jargon, but I think it's saying that they'll pay these women forty thousand dollars for the use of their uterus and an extra ten thousand for a live birth. And then on top of that it says they get five thousand dollars each year just for keeping quiet about it. And then there's lots of doctors' notes and I think this is a psychiatric exam." He picked up one of the papers and shook it. "And this! God, Ella, look at this!"

"What is it?"

"Right here," he said, pointing to a spot on the paper. "It says subject unviable." He ran a hand over his face. "It says this woman had a live birth, but that the subject was found to be defective. Look at this. They list a bunch of numbers and stuff: length, weight, facial girth—whatever that means. And then it says 'sub-par: terminated.'"

In the backseat Missy sat up. "See? They killed it. It didn't die on its own."

Penn shook his head. "No, it didn't. The woman at the kennel told you the truth," he said. "All of it. The surrogates. The payments. The dead babies. All of it."

Missy leaned over the seat. "Of course she told us the truth," she said, rubbing her eyes. "So now what do we do?"

"We need to take this to someone." He held up the folder.

"Who?" Missy asked.

"There's the newspaper, but nobody reads that anymore. We need people to hear this. We can't risk all this and just end up with some little story that's going to end up at the bottom of someone's birdcage."

"Television?" I asked.

Penn nodded. "Yeah. I think it's our best bet. But…" He rubbed his eyes again.

"But what?"

He couldn't hide the worry in his eyes when he looked up at me. "What if they want to interview you and Missy? That's fine if it's in the newspaper, but what if someone recognizes you on TV? We can't risk that. If my dad finds out that we—" He stopped short and swallowed.

"Then I'll be the one they interview," Missy said. "If they need someone on camera, it can be me. I couldn't care less who finds out." Her cheeks were rosy, maybe from sleep, or maybe from the fire she must have slowly been rekindling since the kennel.

"Fine." Penn nodded. "We'll go. I just hope we can find someone that's willing to listen."

Penn held the crumpled-up page from the telephone book in his hand as he clutched the wheel and pulled into the parking lot of the Eyewitness News broadcast studio.

"I can't believe we found it," he sighed, tossing the paper down by his feet. "I just assumed it would be closer to downtown."

The news studio was actually located in a big office building just off the highway a few minutes south of the city. The building didn't look like the kennel. It was taller, with wide windows that shone like mirrors reflecting the peachy sky, but still, there was something about the size of it, the overbearing way it loomed over us, that made my palms sweat and my mouth go dry.

Across the parking lot a woman got out of her car and Penn sat up straighter in his seat.

"What is it?" I asked.

"That's Diane Westly. I recognize her from TV," he said, already grabbing the file sitting on the seat next to him.

Missy and I scrambled out after him as he jogged across the parking lot to catch up with the woman who had just started to climb the wide cement stairs that led up to the building's front door.

"Excuse me, Ms. Westly," Penn said.

He reached out to grab the starched edge of her blazer and she pulled her arm back, startled.

"I'm sorry to bother you," he said, backing up a bit. "But we have a story that we think you might be interested in."

She turned around to study the three of us and I finally got a good look at her face. From behind, I'd thought that she was younger. Her hair was very blonde and styled in a stiff bob that looked like it wouldn't move even in a gust of wind. Up this close, her makeup was caked on so thickly that it cracked as she frowned at us. Her thin lips, which were painted a bright shade of pink, tightened into a line and her nose wrinkled a bit in distaste.

"Well thank you for thinking of me," she said, plastering on a fake smile. "But I really don't have time to talk this morning."

She turned around and trotted up the rest of the steps.

Penn ran after her. "It's a big story," he said, grabbing her arm more forcefully this time.

"If you'll kindly get your hands off of me," she said, shaking him off. "May I suggest that you don't grab people like that, young man? Some might consider it assault."

Penn's face reddened.

"Please," I said, hoping she'd listen to me. "If you'll just give us five minutes."

She narrowed her eyes at me. "I'm sorry, but I can't give five minutes away to every person with a 'story.'" She rolled her eyes at the word. "My time is valuable. I know you kids want to believe that since you've seen me on TV we have some sort of connection, but I'm sorry to inform you that we don't. I don't owe you anything."

She turned, swinging open the wide door. We chased after her. The door swung shut behind us and she glanced over her shoulder, obviously irritated that we'd followed her inside.

Missy grabbed the file out of Penn's hands and thrust it at her. "Will you just look at the goddamn papers? Maybe if you stopped judging us by what you *think* you see and actually look at the evidence you'll surprise yourself. We've got documents that could uncover a scandal with the—"

"Bob!" Ms. Westly hollered, slapping Missy away and waving her arms at the big man in a security suit who sat behind a desk in the corner. "Will you please escort these people from the premises? I've been assaulted twice in the space of thirty seconds."

"Yes, ma'am." The man nodded. He scooted back from his chair and glared at us.

At the sight of his uniform, my knees went weak. If the guard got to us before we broke the story, he would turn us in to the police. And I already knew what happened once the police found me. They wouldn't care about news stories or dying pets. They would only care about returning property to its rightful owner. They would only care about returning me to the congressman.

My body moved before my mind had time to reconsider.

"We have proof that Greenwich Kennel is killing babies!" The words burst out of my mouth, so loud that they echoed off the granite floors.

The security guard paused, glancing back at Ms. Westly, but her face was unreadable. The angry slant of her brow had frozen on her forehead. Her tight lips opened ever so slightly, but whether it was the beginning of a sneer or a smile, I couldn't tell.

"Ma'am?" the security guard asked, looking between us. "You still need me to escort them out?"

"No, no, never mind, Bob. Thank you." She waved him away and he returned happily to his spot behind the desk.

She turned back to us, a rehearsed smile on her face. "It does sound like an interesting story, really, but you'll have to forgive me for saying it sounds unlikely."

She gave us a final shake of her head before she stalked toward the elevators, her heels clicking loudly against the tile floors.

"But—" Penn started.

"They're killing babies, you idiot!" Missy growled.

Ms. Westly jabbed her finger impatiently into the button.

"We have proof!" I shouted. "We have files that we stole from the kennel."

In front of her, the elevator doors binged, opening with a swoosh, but she didn't step forward.

"There are legal forms and doctor's records," Penn said. "They've been hiding it for years. Probably since the program started. There are so many things happening there. Bad things. It's all in the files."

Ms. Westly turned, studying us all more closely, as if she was finally seeing us. Her eyes widened as she focused on me and a look of recognition crossed her face. She saw it now: two pets and the son of a prominent politician. She nodded slowly.

"We aren't lying," I said. "They're killing babies. And the longer we wait, who knows how many more will die."

"You're sure?" she said, but her eyes gleamed with something that looked like hunger.

"Just let us show you the files," I said. "Please."

She gave a nod and motioned for us to follow after her. "I'm sorry," she said. "I should have listened, but I'm swamped. If you knew how many people I get in here trying to push their ideas at me… I have to be careful that—"

"It doesn't matter anymore," Missy said.

Ms. Westly's gaze traveled down to the file that Missy still held. She licked her lips. "That's it?"

Missy nodded and her fingers tightened a little around the folder.

"Look, why don't you all come with me," Ms. Westly said.

"I'll get us a boardroom and you can show me what you've got."

The security guard buzzed us through a metal gate and we followed her to a small room down the hall. She closed the door behind us and motioned for us to sit at a large table. The reflection of the sky floated across the top of the polished wood surface. The three of us sat down tentatively in a row, and she made her way to the other side of the table, pulling out a chair across from us.

"I don't want to get your hopes up," she said. "My producer is very particular about protecting the station from lawsuits. If the story seems suspicious in any way, we won't be able to air it. Especially when the accusations are as serious as these."

She glanced down at the file, which now sat on the table.

"It's legitimate," Penn said.

"How long have you been sitting on this information?" she asked.

"We came straight here," he said. "We didn't know where else to go."

"And you obtained this file yourself?"

Penn shook his head. "Ella and Missy did."

She glanced between our faces, finally settling on mine. "You got this from inside Greenwich Kennel?"

I nodded.

"How?"

"We stole them," I said, bluntly. "Is that a problem?"

She shook her head, seemingly unconcerned about

whether or not it was legal. “Well, I’m certainly not going to report you, if that’s what you’re asking. I’m more concerned about getting the public a good…” She took a deep breath, reconsidering. “An *honest* story.

“We’ve done stories on pets before,” she went on. “The public was concerned at first, but as you can imagine, their attention spans are short. People get worked up about something until the next issue comes along. I hate to say it, but I’m not sure anyone cares anymore, especially now that the legislation has officially passed. It just isn’t news.”

“But *this* is news,” Penn said, smacking his hand down on the pile of papers. “They’re killing babies! Human babies! And for what? Because they’re sub-par? Who gets to decide something like that? And paying the surrogate mothers not to talk about any of this? It’s not right and everyone needs to know it.”

Ms. Westly nodded. “I doubt people will be crazy about the fact that there are surrogate mothers involved, but honestly, it’s the babies that will sell the story.”

“Then see for yourself,” Penn said, sending the papers skidding across the wide table.

Ms. Westly grabbed them greedily. The three of us sat quietly as she opened the file. Her eyes flicked from side to side as she scanned the page before flipping to the next and then the next. She leaned forward, pulling the papers even closer, and the look on her face changed. The mask that she’d been wearing since we first saw her slipped away. She wasn’t the stiff, fake TV persona that we’d seen since we met her. Her face grew animated. Her brow furrowed and stretched. Sometimes her lips moved as she read and reread words.

“My God,” she breathed.

Chapter Nineteen

Finally she flipped the file closed and sat for a long moment, just staring down at the pale beige backside. When she looked up at us, her eyes were bright.

Penn reached under the table and squeezed my hand.

"Well, you weren't kidding," she said. "There's a story in here. A big one. And we're going to blow it out of the water. Is this all you have? Is there anything else?"

"Oh, no. There's more," Missy said. "They're killing full-grown pets, too. Probably hundreds of them. I think they're scared this is going to get out, so they've been trying to breed them instead of using these other women, but it doesn't work. They always die."

Ms. Westly's lips pursed. "Yes, that's horrible," she said. "But I don't want to spread this story too wide. We have to focus on one thing or the audience will get confused."

Missy narrowed her eyes, but she didn't argue.

Ms. Westly patted the folder. "Do you have anything else

like this?"

"We have a few more files," I said.

"And you'd let me see them?"

I nodded. There were almost a dozen files like the one in front of her and she could have them all. There was only one that I wanted to keep.

"So, you'll do it?" I asked.

"If you're willing to give this to me for an exclusive, I can promise that every news station in the country is going to wish they were the ones that broke this story. I wouldn't be at all surprised if we get picked up by national news outlets." A smile blossomed across her face. "Hell, we could go worldwide with this."

"Here's the thing," Penn said. "A lot of very important, very dangerous people are going to be pissed off if this breaks. I know because my dad is one of them."

"Congressman Kimble?" Ms. Westly asked.

Penn nodded.

"I thought I recognized you from the press conference."

"This could ruin him," Penn said. "Seriously, this kind of scandal? I don't know if he can bounce back from it."

She chuckled. "Yes, there are going to be a lot of very rich, very upset people."

"So what I want to know..." Penn said, "is can you keep Ella and Missy safe? If not, then we can't let you run the story."

"What are you talking about?" Missy snapped. "Of course we're running the story. I don't care how dangerous it is."

"She's right, Penn," I said. "It has to be done. NuPet has to be stopped. We didn't go through all the trouble to get this information to just sit on it."

"Not if you're going to get hurt," Penn said. "It was bad

enough letting you go back inside that kennel before we knew how bad things were." He shook his head. "I really don't think they'd hesitate to kill you, Ella. Maybe a part of me kind of doubted it before, but now…"

Ms. Westly's gaze tracked between the three of us, a worried look replacing the unbridled excitement she'd worn only a few minutes earlier. Maybe she was legitimately concerned about us, the way Penn was, or maybe she was scared that the biggest story of her career was slipping away.

"What if I can promise to keep them safe?" she asked.

Penn stared at her. "How?"

"We'll put all three of you up in one of the company's houses," she said. "Make sure you have everything you need while the story breaks. You won't have to worry about anything."

"What else?" he asked.

"I won't use any information related to Ella or Missy," she said. "If you supply me with the other files, I'll have plenty of material. These stories are always better with a personal element, but I'm confident I can get one of these women to talk."

"But those legal forms?" Penn said.

She waved his observation away. "Most of these women aren't going to talk, but there's always one. The lure of fame is enough to make almost anyone reconsider their prior arrangements."

Penn leaned forward, urgency tightening his eyes. His mouth. "And after the story? What happens a week from now? A month?"

"We have resources," she said. "Connections with people whose entire job is to protect whistleblowers. They can help you."

Penn continued to stare at her. It was impossible to know what was going on in his mind. Was he imagining what our life would be like if we went ahead with the story? Or was he trying to play out the other scenario? Either way was a gamble. I knew what he wanted, to see our future like a clear, bright path before us, instead of this blind darkness.

Finally, he leaned back. "Okay." He nodded. "What's next?"

Ms. Westly didn't try to hide her smile. "You get me those files, I'll take care of the rest."

After our stay in the motel, and then in the kennel, I couldn't wait to get to the house that Ms. Westly had arranged for us. For the past two hours, as she'd made calls and pored over the files in the boardroom, I'd done nothing but fantasize about a bed. I was hungry for one, hungrier for the soft white sheets and fluffy pillows of a big bed than I was for a hot meal.

It was late in the afternoon by the time we pulled up in front of the two-story townhouse. Ms. Westly had offered to drive us, but Penn had insisted on taking our own car, no matter how beat up it was.

He shook his head, coming to a stop in front of the red brick building. "This thing is in the middle of downtown," he muttered.

The street was busy. Cars rushed by and a few people strolled down the sidewalk.

Ms. Westly hopped out of her car and trotted over to Penn's window, motioning for him to roll it down.

"How is this hiding us?" Penn asked.

"It's a quiet building," she said. "I think it'll surprise you. Besides, you're safer in an urban area than in some remote location. Believe me."

Penn sighed, obviously too tired to argue.

"There's an alley around back," Ms. Westly said. "No one will see you coming or going."

She dashed back to her car and we followed her into a quiet alley that ran behind the buildings. The little backstreet was empty except for a couple cars and a row of garbage cans. We parked next to a small Dumpster and gathered up our few measly belongings.

We'd given more than half of the files to Ms. Westly, but there was still a large stack left in the garbage bag. Penn eyed them warily. I knew that he wanted to be rid of them. He wanted to shred them, to burn them, anything to separate them from us, as if they were something toxic and dangerous.

"Can't we just throw them in the Dumpster?" he asked.

"I don't think we should get rid of them yet," I told him, straightening the stack of folders. I wrapped them tightly in the plastic garbage bag and tucked them up under the backseat. I didn't want to say it aloud, but I worried we'd still need them.

"It's right this way," Ms. Westly said, interrupting us.

She swept us up the small back staircase, fiddled with the lock on the back door, and ushered us into a warm sitting room.

Without the constant pump of adrenaline through our veins, the past few days finally caught up to us and Missy, Penn, and I stared slack-jawed at our surroundings, hardly able to take it in.

Ms. Westly waited for us to speak. She looked around the room, too as if she were trying to see it from our point of view.

"Well, I'm sure it's not quite what you're used to, but it's comfortable," she finally said, presumably taking our silence for distaste.

"No, no," Penn said, shaking his head and focusing on the room. "It's perfect, really."

She paused for a moment as if she were deciding whether or not to believe him. "Good. My assistant stocked the fridge and arranged for a couple of changes of clothes for all of you. I can't guarantee that they'll fit perfectly, but…" She shrugged. From the look on her face I guessed she wanted to say that at least they would be better than what we were wearing now, but her tact stopped her.

We each thanked her, nodding numbly as we followed her from room to room as she listed everything we'd need to know about the house. Finally, we made our way back to the room we'd started out in. She sighed as though she'd even exhausted her own attention.

"So that's it," she said, making her way to the back door. "I'll be in touch. If everything goes as planned, the story will run in a few days. You just lie low. Don't go anywhere. Don't call anyone besides me. If you need to get in touch, there's a landline in most of the rooms. Here's my number." She handed us each a card. "My home number is on the back, but only call it if there's an emergency. I'm hardly there anyway."

"Thank you," I said, stepping closer to her.

We hadn't been raised to show physical affection, but it didn't seem like enough to simply say the words. I wrapped my arms around her waist and her body stiffened. She stood without moving for a moment, shocked perhaps. Finally her body loosened just a little.

"It's really no trouble," she said, raising a hand to awkwardly pat my back. "I hope the story will make a difference. I'll do my best. I promise."

For the next twenty-four hours that promise hung in the air like strong perfume that had soaked into the fibers of the couch, the rug, the drapes. Every once in a while we'd get a whiff of it and the hope that the story would actually change things would make us take a deeper breath, holding it inside our lungs for as long as we could.

As soon as Ms. Westly left, the three of us had stumbled into the bedrooms, collapsing from exhaustion. We rose only once to eat a picnic of cheese and sliced turkey on the bedroom floor before we crawled back under the covers, each falling into a deep, motionless sleep.

It was already well past three when I woke the next day. Next to me, the bed was empty, the pillow crumpled and indented with the shape of Penn's head. I rose up on one elbow and looked around the room. The curtains were drawn, but the sun illuminated the yellow fabric, making the room appear golden.

I crawled out of bed and padded down the hall. The door was cracked to the room where Missy had fallen asleep. From where I stood, I could only see a bit of the bed. Her arm was flung above her head with her hand hanging limply off the edge of the mattress. For a moment I considered waking her, but the slow rise and fall of her breathing sounded too peaceful. I didn't have the heart.

Downstairs, Penn stood at the front window with his arms folded over his chest. The curtains were only parted a few inches, wide enough for him to peer through without being seen from the street.

"You're up," he said, folding me into his side as soon as I reached him.

"Have you been awake long?" I asked.

"A couple hours," he said. "Ms. Westly called."

My pulse quickened and I stepped back from the window, remembering that there could be people out there watching us, people that wanted nothing more than to hurt us, to get rid of us.

"What did she say?"

"She just wanted to give us a heads up," Penn said. He must have sensed my discomfort because he backed away from the window, too. "I guess things are going better than she anticipated. She's talking about airing the story tonight."

"That's good, right?" I asked.

He smiled, pulling me back into his arms. "Yeah, it's good."

"So by tonight…" I couldn't finish. My throat constricted. I was almost too scared to think of what I actually wanted to say.

"…things could finally change for us," Penn said. He traced a finger along the side of my face. "We could really be together. Not just in secret. Can you imagine how awesome that would be?"

He leaned in, his lips hot and sweet against mine, the taste of him like a memory that left me tipsy, and all at once that familiar ache broke open inside me.

My head tipped back and his lips moved down my neck, each kiss a tiny golden coin pressed against my skin. So soft. So delicate. A small moan broke free from my lips like a sob.

Pain and pleasure existed on the same plane.

Penn eased me back across the couch and his hands found my hips. His fingers wound around the belt loops of my jeans and he pulled me against him, his own hips pressing into mine. Softly, slowly, his fingers lifted the edges of my shirt, grazing the strip of skin above my pants. It was just the smallest touch, but my skin burned from it.

My lips found his again and I drank him in. I felt like a girl who had been stranded in the desert. Parched. Thirsting for this. I grabbed his shirt, then mine, peeling back the layers that separated us. I wanted to feel him against me, on top of me, inside me, the heat of his skin, the weight of his body.

"I love you, Ella," he breathed, the words hot in my ear.

My body pressed against him, wanting to tell him how much I loved him without words. It was there, all over me. I wrapped it in my arms, pressed it against my chest.

I closed my eyes and let the fire consume me.

Finally, we collapsed against the pillows, breathing hard. I lay my head against Penn's chest, resting my cheek over his thundering heart.

"I don't want to get my hopes up, but I can't help it," he whispered. "We're so close."

He was right, but I was afraid to hope. It was there, in front of us. I could almost see the shape of it, solid and whole like a figure emerging from the fog.

"All I want is to be a normal person," I said.

Penn tucked a lock of hair behind my ear, staring down at me. "You'll never be just a normal person."

I frowned. "But you said—"

"I don't care what happens with the kennel, or my dad, or this law. You'll always be extraordinary," Penn said. "And I'm not talking about how you look. I'm talking about who you are."

My cheeks warmed.

"You're biased," I said.

"No." He shook his head. "It isn't just me. Look what you've done. Without you, this story would still be hidden inside those drawers back at the kennel."

"Don't forget Missy," I said, nudging him in the ribs.

"Sometimes I'd like to." He laughed. "But seriously, if they really do blow the top off of this story there's probably going to be an investigation. There's no way the kennel can hide what it's been doing. My dad can't pay enough people to keep this quiet."

"And then what? What will happen to all those pets?"

"I don't know," Penn said.

I looked up at him. "Do you think they'll be set free?"

"I hope so."

I snuggled back down into the crook of his arm and pulled down a thin afghan that had been folded across the back of the couch, spreading it over us. This was what I was fighting for, wasn't it? Moments just like this one. It was so simple, the drape of an arm, the curve of a spine, the sweet press of skin against skin.

I wasn't asking for much.

Chapter Twenty

At 5:59 Penn and Missy and I finally switched on the TV. The house had been quiet for most of the day, maybe because we'd still been moving in a bit of a daze, or maybe because we were afraid to make too much noise for fear that someone next door would hear us. Now, as Penn flipped to channel three, we all cringed at the overly animated sound of a car commercial.

Penn thumbed the volume button on the remote until the sound was almost all the way down. We all leaned forward a little in our seats.

"Did she say what time it would be on?" Missy asked.

"I don't know," Penn said. "She said it was a top story, but that's all I know."

The car commercial ended and the TV went black for just a moment before the Eyewitness News logo appeared on the screen. The music swelled and the deep voice of the announcer cut in. "Live from studio three in Hartford, this is

Eyewitness News at six."

The image changed. Two news anchors sat perched behind a shiny desk, their faces set in almost identical looks of thoughtful focus. It looked like an expression they each must have practiced in front of the mirror every morning until it became second nature. The woman didn't look like Ms. Westly. Her individual features were different—dark hair, fuller lips, rounder eyes—but the overall package felt oddly similar. There was a stiff, almost plastic quality to them, as if someone had found a way to clone these newswomen so that no matter who was talking, the viewer always felt as if the person speaking to them was familiar.

Behind them, the news logo swirled on a giant television screen, finally coming to a stop as the music faded out.

"Good evening," the newsman said. "I'm Grant Peterson."

"And I'm Kimberly Brenan. Tonight, fire officials say early clues point to arson in the blaze that ravaged part of the City and County building Thursday."

"Two high school students are facing homicide charges in connection with a fatal crash in Stamford."

"Plus, a Newark girl is in critical condition after—"

"Why haven't they gotten to it?" Missy said impatiently, shaking her head. "She said it was a top story. If they wait until—"

"Shh," Penn and I both hushed.

On the television, Kimberly Brenan finished talking and tapped the stack of papers in front of her. "But first, we go live to Diane Westly with an Eyewitness News exclusive report. Diane?"

"Thank you, Kimberly." The screen flashed to a shot of Ms. Westly standing in front of Greenwich Kennel's main entrance. "Reporting live from the NuPet breeding facility in Greenwich, I'm Diane Westly with breaking coverage on a scandal that could rock new legislation allowing the breeding of genetically modified human pets."

The camera panned out just a bit showing Ms. Westly holding a stack of official-looking documents. It was dark, but a bright light from the camera illuminated the backdrop of the wrought iron gate, now securely locked.

I could hardly believe that only two nights earlier we'd found Penn's car hidden there, not even a dozen feet from where she stood.

"They were bred to be a new form of companion," Ms. Westly said as the image on the screen changed from the dark surroundings of the NuPet compound to the immaculate waiting room of the training center. Sitting on the tufted divans were half a dozen pets dressed in gowns. The images switched to the girls performing their different talents. Ms. Westly kept talking, pointing out how difficult it had been to pass the legislation, which allowed these pets to be sold.

"NuPet finally gained ground with the bill after convincing the public that the girls bred in these facilities weren't fully human. This new definition of personhood hinged on the idea that any individual grown entirely in the lab could never be considered human."

I cringed. Personhood? How was it even possible that a person's worth could be defined and legislated by someone else? Men like the congressman got to sit in big important rooms arguing with one another about who was human and who wasn't. As if their words were the things that made it true.

The camera switched again to Ms. Westly. "But our sources have uncovered official documents proving that NuPet executives not only hired poor and underprivileged women to give birth to pets, but knowingly and purposefully murdered healthy babies they deemed inferior. Earlier today, I had a chance to sit down and speak with one of the women formerly used as a surrogate mother to these pets. This is what she had to say."

Once again the image on the screen changed. This time a woman sat across from Ms. Westly in what I guessed must have been the woman's living room. Even though the woman's body and surroundings were clear, her face had been blurred out.

"You were hired by NuPet to be a surrogate in their breeding program, can you tell us when this was and what you experienced?"

"I was nineteen," the woman said. Her voice sounded funny, distorted and low.

"They changed her voice," Penn said, seeing the confusion on my face.

The woman went on. "They recruited me from the homeless shelter. They said they'd get me off the street, get me money."

"And did they?" Ms. Westly asked.

"Yeah, but things weren't better there. I spent ten months locked in their building. They stuck me in a bed growing a baby for them. And then when it was born they killed it."

"And how do you know they killed it?"

"'Cause I saw it," the woman said. A bit of her dark, curly hair escaped the blurred out blob on the screen. "It was a healthy baby. It cried right away. But they kept calling it 'sub-par.' They did all these measurements. Said her eyes were too small and her head wasn't symmetrical enough. They didn't even try to hide any of it from me. And they were angry at me. They didn't even let me hold her. I could have kept her if they weren't going to. I would have," she said, her voice cracking. "But they didn't even let her live for ten minutes. I saw the needle. They tried to hide it from me, but I saw. I saw her limp body when they put her on that cart and wheeled her away."

"But you never came forward before now?" Ms. Westly asked.

The woman snorted. "You think anyone would believe me? I'd just sound crazy. Plus, I didn't have no proof or nothing. We signed stuff that said we wouldn't tell, but they didn't give us papers."

"And are you worried now, to come forward publically this way?"

The woman's fingers fluttered in her lap. "I mean, I guess I'm scared, but it's time, you know. People got to know."

"And what is it that you want people to know?" Ms. Westly asked.

"You can't just kill little babies like they're rats or something," she said. "People got a right to know what's going on in there. Somebody is making lots of money using women's bodies to make the 'perfect' baby, blaming them when they don't, not paying them everything they promised if the baby doesn't come out exactly right. It's wrong."

One last time, the camera switched to Ms. Westly standing outside of the NuPet compound. Her face was serious. "As a result of our investigation, both local police and federal authorities have begun their own inquiry into these allegations. The Eyewitness News team will continue to provide up-to-date coverage on these breaking events. Back to you Kimberly and Grant."

On the couch, the three of us took a collective breath, as if all at once we had remembered the need for air. Penn's hand drifted over to mine, his fingers tightened around my hand, squeezing tight. On the other side of me, Missy laid her head against my shoulder.

The newscasters continued to speak, but their voices hardly mattered anymore. We'd done it. We'd given Ms. Westly the files and just as she'd promised, she'd given the story to the world.

Now all we had to do was wait.

Missy sighed. "Is it weird that I can't wait to live alone after all this is over and done with?"

"You wouldn't be lonely?" I asked.

She shook her head. "Maybe I'll get a cat."

And just like that, the tension in the room broke. "A cat?" I sputtered, laughing. "Doesn't that seem kind of ironic?"

"Yeah. It does." Missy snorted. "A pet for a pet."

"It's like the circle of life," Penn said.

"Well, I don't care if it's weird," Missy said. "It'll be my life, and I can have a cat if I want to. He's going to be a big, fat spoiled cat named Mr. Lickens and I'll give him cans of tuna fish and leave the kitchen window open so he can come and go how he pleases."

She'd closed her eyes and her voice got quiet, almost as if she were whispering a story that she'd told herself a hundred times.

"But mostly he'll curl up in my lap while I sit in the big chair in my living room. And there will be geraniums on the windowsill and a little radio to play music while I read books about powerful women who fly planes and cure the sick. And when I feel like taking a trip to Spain, I'll go. And when I feel like eating cake… Well, I guess I'll just have to learn to bake."

She stopped talking, but she didn't open her eyes and I was pretty sure that she could see it, her future home. I could see it too: the red flowers and the big orange cat.

"What about you, Ella?" Penn said.

"Oh, I don't want a cat," I joked.

"No, you'll be too busy flying planes and curing the sick," he said.

"Is that what you want?" Missy asked. "A big life?"

"I don't know," I said. "The only thing I've ever really wanted was to be able to make my own choices. If I can do that, then I guess anything feels like a big life. I know I want to make music and I know I want to be with Penn. Those things feel huge."

That night, the distant call of sirens drifted through the thin windows, but I hardly noticed. I slept more soundly than I had in ages, tucked securely against the warm curve of Penn's body. It seemed impossible that I'd ever been able to sleep without his chest pressed against my back or the rhythmic rise and fall of his breath lulling me.

In the morning, I woke to the sound of Missy padding down the hallway. The stairs squealed softly beneath her weight and I shifted in bed, running my fingers through Penn's hair where his head rested against my chest.

"Let's stay here all day," he said, drowsily rubbing his cheek against my skin.

The blankets were warm, a perfect nest, and I closed my eyes, feeling the way my body had already started to drift back into sleep.

"Ella! Penn!" Missy called from downstairs. Her voice was shrill, upset, and we both jumped, throwing back the covers.

We rushed down the stairs, Penn pulling his T-shirt over his head as we stepped into the family room. She stood in front of the television. On the floor at her feet a cup held the last few drops of cranberry juice. The rest bled into the pale carpet, but she didn't notice. Her eyes were trained on the screen.

"They said it's because of the story," she said, pointing to the TV with a shaking hand.

"They said what?" Penn asked, stooping to pick up the glass she'd dropped.

"The fires!" she said. She looked away from the TV for just a moment and her eyes traveled to the floor where the red drink had puddled, a look of confusion on her face.

"Fires?" I asked.

On the TV, a man with a microphone stood in front of the burned-out shell of a building. "…are baffled by the rioting and looting that has swept at least half a dozen major cities."

The image switched to a group of police officers trying to hold back a mob of angry people in the street. They were standing in front of a tall white building with a domed roof.

"That's the capital," Penn said, lowering himself down on the edge of one of the chairs.

A few of the people held signs, but the majority of them were screaming something. The camera swept over the group of them as their mouths opened and closed in a chant that I couldn't quite make out.

"What are they saying?" I asked.

"I can't tell." Penn shook his head. "There's some signs that say 'Murder Big Money.' And it says 'Protesters Storm

Capital' at the bottom."

"It doesn't matter what they're saying!" Missy yelled. "It's because of the story. It's because of us."

"I don't think so," Penn said, shaking his head. "It was only on the local news. They can't have picked the story up this fast."

Across the room, the phone rang. We jumped and stared at it, as if it was confirming everything that Missy was saying.

It rang again.

I dashed over to pick up the receiver. "Hello?" My voice shook.

"It's Diane, are you all safe?"

My hand trembled. "What? Yes, we just came downstairs and turned on the television and—"

"Good. Okay, so you know," she interrupted.

Missy moved up so close to me that her ear was practically even with mine.

"Let me put it on speaker," Penn said, pushing a button on the phone and all of a sudden Ms. Westly's voice filled the room.

"…surprised everyone, even the executives. We've never had a story go viral like this. We'd planned to be picked up by our affiliates, but we hadn't planned on this sort of coverage. It's everywhere. Can you believe it?" Ms. Westly's voice didn't hold the same terror that we felt. She sounded…excited. Elated even. "It's more than I dreamed of. Give people a dead baby story and they get pissed off."

"But it's not good, is it?" I asked. "Those fires. People might be getting hurt."

"Well the looting is never good," she said, "but you can't control it. And I promise you—it's helping your cause. You might not realize it, but these people have made it impossible to ignore."

"So now what?" I asked.

"We'll be airing coverage all day," she said. "I'd come by to check on you, but I'm swamped. I've got an interview with the police chief and Senator Hunt later today. I just wanted to call and tell you not to contact anyone. Stay away from the windows, don't answer the door. Obvious things. You should be set there for a few days and I'm confident that you'll be safe."

The three of us had been staring down at the phone that I still clasped in my hand, but now we stared at one another. How could she be so confident? We saw what had happened overnight. All it had taken was one story and the world was on fire.

"Just lie low and celebrate," she said. "I'll be in touch soon."

The phone went silent and I laid it back on the table. On the television screen, the news was showing footage that must have been shot from the night before. Throngs of people had taken to the street, dark except for the fires that raged in the buildings behind them. An angry-looking woman waved a flaming flag above her head. The camera zoomed in and it became clear that the fabric she was burning wasn't a flag. It was a ball gown.

Heat traveled up my neck, engulfing my cheeks until it felt like I was the one being burned alive. It wasn't right. They should be burning suits and ties. They should be burning fat wads of money and big fancy cars.

We weren't the ones to blame, but I worried that didn't matter.

We didn't move from the couch. After a while I lost track of time. My eyes grew tired from staring at the same terrible images of rioting and fires and angry mobs of people. The news broadcast them in a continuous stream as if a cut had been opened and these ugly pictures had spilled out. Sometimes I wondered if they were actually just showing me the same three scenes over and over again or if the events were actually changing, the way they said they were.

Each hour or so, someone would interrupt with a new bit of information: five more women had come forward claiming to have seen the babies they carried killed by NuPet; the breeding facility in California had been overrun by protestors; a retired senator from Texas admitted to taking bribes from NuPet to help speed up the legislation in his state.

Each new bit of information spurred another almost identical story, a mad avalanche of evidence crashing down around us.

A little before five o'clock the urgent drumbeat of a special report interrupted a channel three newscaster interviewing a man who claimed to be a former NuPet worker in charge of recruiting.

The music swelled and the bold red words that I'd come to recognize as "Breaking News" scrolled across the screen, and then the camera flashed to a newscaster sitting behind his polished desk. I'd seen him before, but something about him was different this time, his hair not quite as tidy as it had been before, his shirt not as crisp.

"This is Grant Peterson, Eyewitness News, coming to you with breaking news. NuPet has announced that it will be holding a press conference addressing the allegations that have surfaced over the past twenty-four hours. In a little less than five minutes the CEO of NuPet is scheduled to give a statement outside the company's headquarters in Florida. It's unclear at the moment whether he'll be accepting questions from the media."

Missy scooted closer to my side, pulling a blanket up over the two of us. Over the past few hours she'd amassed almost every blanket and pillow in the house, tucking them around us on the couch like she was building some sort of fortress.

"What could they possibly say to fix this?" Penn asked.

A huge crowd of reporters had gathered outside of the NuPet headquarters. There were hundreds of people, all of them holding cameras and microphones and notebooks. They stood shoulder to shoulder, packed around the base of the wide granite steps that led up to the giant block of a building that housed NuPet's corporate offices.

At exactly five o'clock, the front doors opened and a group of men in dark suits descended the stairs, fanning out at the bottom of the steps while a tall man stepped forward to the tangle of microphones. He was an older man with thinning hair and a jowly neck that hid what had probably once been a strong jaw. He looked out over the crowd with calm indifference that reminded me of the men that Congressman Kimble had brought to the house.

The kind of men who acted as if the world belonged to them.

"Thank you for coming out today," he said. "Here at NuPet, our mission for over thirty years has been to find a way to strengthen the connection between people and the companions with whom they share their homes. For years, people turned to domesticated animals as companions and faithful friends, but the lifespan of these sweet animals could never be extended beyond a decade or two. The loss of what could be considered members of the family left great holes in the lives of their owners, and led us here at NuPet to create a companion that could stay with a family for a lifetime. We wanted these companions to be as interactive as possible, someone to enrich the lives of the families that they lived with. In creating the Humana Karaspa, we believed our genetically modified girls would be the perfect answer to this need."

"God," Penn said, shaking his head. "It's like he's still trying to sell them."

It was true. Nothing that the man had said so far even addressed the swell of anger that was surging through the country. If anything, it sounded like an advertisement.

"But over the past twenty-four hours, it has been brought to our attention that many people are upset to learn how our facilities operate. While I do want to assure the public that the practices we've used have been approved and practiced in the scientific community, we also want to promise the American people that we've heard your concerns and we're going to do everything we can to rectify the problem."

"How could they possibly—" Missy started to say.

"This is why, effective immediately, we are complying with the government's demands for a national recall of all pets that have been bred and sold under our current program."

"A recall?" Missy asked. "What does that mean?"

"Shh," Penn hushed, not taking his eyes from the television.

"We ask that these pets be returned to our facilities immediately," the man went on. "Our clients will be issued a full refund and will be the first to receive our new product once we can guarantee that no surrogates have been used in their creation."

I cringed. Products? Did he really think that's all that these girls were?

"Our teams are currently formulating a plan to recondition existing pets once they've been returned to our facilities. We will comply with government mandates so that they'll be able to live free and fulfilling lives."

Free?

"Free!" Missy yelled, jumping to her feet. "Oh my God! Are they serious? Penn! Are they serious?"

I turned to Penn, who sat still, staring at the TV as an explosion of questions erupted in the crowd. "I…I don't know," he said, flustered. "Something feels…off."

He turned to face me and my throat tightened around the word…

Free.

I wanted to say it out loud. I wanted to scream it. But it had lodged itself too deeply inside of me. I wanted so desperately to believe it was true, but Penn was right. *Reconditioned.* That's what they'd said. Pets were to be sent back to the kennel for reconditioning.

"Penn?" I whispered. His name contained the world. Everything I wanted to say but couldn't. Every word. Every thought. Every hope. Every dream.

Every fear.

His eyes met mine and he gave his head one small shake.

"Missy," I said carefully. "Maybe we shouldn't get our hopes up yet."

"Are you kidding? Did you hear what they said?" Missy asked, collapsing back onto the couch. She sighed, staring up at the ceiling. "This is it! I can feel it."

"When have you ever been able to trust anything the

kennel says?" Penn asked.

Missy glared at him. "Why are you trying to ruin this?"

"I'm not! I'm just...cautiously optimistic."

On the television, reporters had begun barraging the executive with questions. What about the babies? Could they guarantee that no more infants would be harmed? Would the girls really be able to be assimilated into society? Did the government mandate mean that the law would be overturned? What would the repercussions be for families that didn't want to give up their pets?

Missy hopped up and switched off the TV.

"Let's get out of here," she said. "We can't just sit here when there's something like this to celebrate!"

She pulled me to my feet.

"What if someone sees us?" I asked.

"No one is going to notice," she said. "Not with all that's going on. Come on. I'm sick of being trapped in here. How can we sit inside one more cage when the world is calling to let us out?"

Chapter Twenty-One

Missy was still wearing the pajama pants that she'd found in the closet upstairs, but she didn't seem to care. Already she was slipping on her shoes.

"Ms. Westly said to stay here," Penn said.

"But that was before the press conference," Missy said. "Everything has changed."

She grabbed a wad of cash out of her backpack and headed for the door. "I can't believe you two. You've been fighting for freedom and when someone gives it to you, you're too afraid to enjoy it." She shook her head, slamming the door behind her.

I slipped on my shoes, rising to follow her.

Penn grabbed my arm. "No, Ella. Something's not right. I know you feel it, too."

I did. I didn't care what the kennel promised about freedom, about reconditioning, about giving pets a real life like any other human. There was no way I was ever going back there again. Never. “We can’t let her get too far,” I said. “Someone will see her. She’ll get caught.”

A minute later we were out the door. On the street, a car drove by, startling a flock of pigeons that had been pecking at the sidewalk at the bottom of the steps. The birds started, all taking flight at once. Their wings beat, filling the air around us with sound as they filled the sky. The pale underside of their wings caught the light, glinting as they all turned together.

We glanced down the street. At the end of the block, Missy was disappearing around the corner.

“Where is she going?” Penn asked as we raced after her.

“Who knows? She’s probably going to spend that whole pile of money on chocolate cake and filet mignon.” I kept my tone light, but all I could think about was the number of people she’d pass on the street. How many we were passing trying to catch up to her. They were less likely to notice a boy and a girl holding hands, but Missy would stand out on her own.

We neared the corner and Penn stopped abruptly. His face grew serious.

“Listen,” he said.

I paused. The sound of voices rose over the noise of traffic and car horns. We turned the corner and froze. At the end of the next block, a large crowd surged against the side of the building. They were yelling something, but I couldn’t make out the words. *Tu-Nu-Rin. Tu-Nu-Rin.* It sounded like a guttural chant.

Penn shifted uneasily on his feet. “Maybe we better go back.”

“What? No! We can’t leave Missy!”

Penn stayed rooted in place, shaking his head. Ahead of us, Missy made her way toward the crowd.

"Come on," I said. "I'm going after her."

We crept closer to the crowd. There was an energy in the air that I hadn't noticed before, but I felt it now, like the chanting and shouting of all those people had charged it with an electric current that made the hairs on my arms stand on end. This wasn't something good. This was something animal. Something dangerous.

"This is a bad idea," he said. "We need to get back to the house. Now."

"I'm not leaving her!" I broke free from his grasp, moving briskly toward the crowd.

The swarm of people spilled down the steps of the nicest house on the block. There must have been close to a hundred of them, most dressed in worn sweaters and jeans. You could tell at a glance that they weren't the sorts of people that belonged at a house like this. It was a polished-looking stone building with intricately carved details around the windows and two tall, trimmed topiaries standing on either side of the door.

I raced forward. Missy had already reached the edge of the crowd and wormed her way inside it, disappearing in a mass of angry red faces.

Penn grabbed my hand. "I'm serious, Ella. This doesn't look good."

He was right. There was no denying the reek of anger and rage that billowed off of the mob.

"Burn in hell you rich bastards!" someone next to me yelled.

"Turn her in! Turn her in!" another person yelled, and I realized that this must have been the phrase that I'd been hearing since we turned the corner.

"What's going on?" Penn asked a short, wild-haired

woman in a knobby sweater that stood at the edges of the group near us.

"Some bigwig asshole lives here with one of those pets," she said, raising her voice over the noise.

"What are they doing?" I asked. Could she tell from looking at me that I was a pet, or was she too distracted?

"They're going to get her and turn her back in. There's a huge government recall," she said. "Didn't you hear about it? They're baby killers, you know?"

Before I could protest that we weren't the ones killing babies, a group of men tipped over one of the home's large topiaries. They grasped the huge cement pot and bashed it against the front door. Again. And again. And again. With each thud, the chanting reached a fevered pitch.

"Missy!" I screamed, knowing she couldn't hear me.

Behind us, more people pressed in, shoving us forward, and I lost sight of Penn.

There was another loud crash as a stone hit the large bay window, shattering it. Glass sprayed down the steps and onto the sidewalk. Far away, I thought I heard the high-pitched squeal of a child screaming.

"Get it!"

"Burn the place!"

"Turn her in!"

The words rose together, tangling and knotting into a furious growl. There was another large bang and through the mass of heads in front of me, I saw the front door finally crash open.

I turned around, struggling through the throng, pushing against the arms and chests that fought to drive me closer to the door. I broke free just as a cheer went up through the crowd, and I turned around in time to see a small black-haired pet being pulled from the arms of her family.

In the doorway a man in a ripped dress shirt cradled his arm as he shouted into the crowd. A thin woman and a little boy crumpled against him, sobbing.

The pet struggled, too, clawing and kicking at the man who dragged her away. He picked her up, throwing her over his shoulder as he stomped toward a car idling on the curb.

My stomach lurched. "Stop!" I yelled. "Leave her alone! Can't you see you're hurting her?" I screamed, but my voice was lost in the madness.

I slumped down onto a set of steps a few doors down, biting back the anger that boiled up inside me too. It felt contagious, this rage. I'd breathed it into my lungs and now it burned in my gut, filling my chest with heat.

And then Penn was beside me.

He knelt down in front of me. "Are you okay? I lost you."

"They can't just take her like this," I said, clenching and unclenching my fists in my lap.

"They're trying to help her."

"Like that?" I yelled, pointing to the open car door where the girl still struggled against the people. She was just a tiny thing, like Missy, like me, but she was fierce. Blood oozed from the nose of the man carrying her.

Maybe we were all a lot stronger than anyone realized.

"I'm sorry, but we can't worry about that now," Penn said. "We've got to get out of here."

Down the street, Missy pushed her way through the crowd. She paused at the edge of the group, her face stunned. When she saw me, the strong mask she wore fell away and her face crumpled as she raced toward us.

"We have to do something, Ella," she said. Up close I saw that her face was smudged with dirt along her cheek.

My knees shook with fear and adrenaline. "What? What exactly do you think we can do? We can't even stay in a house when we're told to."

The group of people surged around us, a noisy, pulsing monster. I couldn't push my way back through that crowd. Not even if I wanted to.

"I don't know." Missy shook her head, not bothering to wipe the tears that fell down her cheeks, streaking the dirt. "I don't know."

And I didn't know either. I didn't know how to help or how to feel. I didn't know anything anymore. I wanted some sort of truth that I could grab onto, something real and right, but I couldn't find it here. All these choices only felt like mist, foggy and intangible.

"I want to go back," Missy finally said. "I don't want to see any more of this."

"Stay by me," Penn said, as he turned to usher us back toward the house.

His face was pained. It wasn't hard to guess why. He'd just watched our dreams for the future dragged from the safety of loving arms by the very people we'd expected to set me free.

There was no hope of that now.

It didn't take long to make our way back. But in the short time that we'd been gone, the street felt different. Dark. Dangerous. The birds were gone and with them, the feeling of hope, fleeting as it was. Something gloomy had taken its place and I moved closer to Penn, as if the solidness of his body could protect me from this feeling.

"Let's go around the back," Missy said as we neared the building. Maybe she felt it too, the uneasy sense that we were being watched.

The back alley was hidden in shadows. The evening light that had spilled down the street out front was now blocked by the tall brick buildings. The three of us dashed up the back steps and crashed through the door, slamming it behind us.

We took a collective breath, silently staring at one another. Even in the dim light of the kitchen I could see the dark smudge on Missy's cheek. I knew that it wasn't a wound, only dirt, but still it frightened me.

Penn crowded Missy, cornering her in the entryway. "What were you thinking?" he demanded. "You could have gotten hurt. You could have gotten *Ella* hurt. Do you think stuff like that is—"

"Shh," I interrupted, holding up my hand to silence him. The hairs on the back of my neck bristled.

"Ella, what—"

I shook my head and he closed his mouth.

"There's someone..." My voice trailed off. *Someone here*, I wanted to say. I could feel them. A presence. My legs went weak. What if it was the congressman? What if he'd found us? We needed to go. We needed to run. To get out of here. To get away. But where?

"Ella?" Penn started to ask again, worried, when from the other room we heard the groan of a loose board on the stairs, followed by the undeniable thud of footsteps against the hardwood floors.

My mouth went dry and I clutched the counter. I tried to form the word *run*, but it felt shriveled and small on my tongue.

"Thank God!" Ms. Westly said, appearing in the doorway. "Where were you? No one answered when I rang the bell so I let myself in. I thought maybe—"

"We just stepped outside for a little fresh air," Penn lied.

Missy's brow furrowed, and I could see the question in her eyes. Why lie for her after everything that had just happened?

"Thank goodness you didn't go far," she said. "I… It's just that…damn, I never imagined that things would happen like this. It was a big story, but it wasn't *this* big. I don't even know what this is. It's like our country has been leaking some sort of toxic gas for too long and we made the mistake of striking a match. Now the whole thing has exploded."

"I'm sorry," I said. "We didn't mean for this to happen."

"No, I'm the sorry one," she said, shaking her head. "It's so much worse than I could have guessed. NuPet is a deceitful, greedy company."

"But maybe they're changing," Missy said. "They can't keep doing the same horrible things anymore without any consequences."

"No, now they're just finding new ways of lying," Ms. Westly said. She looked at our hopeful faces and the angry scowl on her face dissipated into a look of pity. "It isn't true," she said.

"What?" I asked.

"The story they're telling the public. It's just a story."

"They aren't taking pets back?" Penn asked.

"They *are* taking them back. But it's just to divert the public's attention from the real allegations. These men aren't fools. It's a pretty story they're telling until people forget and things die down."

"But they can't say it if it isn't true, can they?" Missy asked.

Ms. Westly frowned. "Why not? It's all they've done so far." She paused. "Did you hear about the news conference?"

We nodded.

"We watched it before we left." How else would we have heard the news about NuPet?

She looked at her watch, confused. "The one with your father?" she asked Penn.

"My father?"

"He scheduled a press conference. A local one, but he must have known he'd get national press." She walked into the family room, her heels clicking across the floor as she headed for the television.

I stood rooted in the doorway.

Ms. Westly switched on the TV and there he was, the congressman. The camera was zoomed in on his freshly shaven face as he adjusted the microphones in front of him, getting ready to speak. Even with the warning that I was going to see him, I wasn't prepared for the sick lurch in my stomach or the cold fear that trickled down my limbs. To anyone else, he must have looked like a handsome, responsible civil servant: clean-pressed, calm, composed, just the sort of person you'd want to represent you. But that's not what I saw. I saw a man who had sculpted the most beautiful mask he could wear for the sole purpose of getting what he wanted.

Penn stared down at the television. His face was stiff, unreadable, as he watched his father, but when the camera panned out, Penn's fist slammed down on the end table. "He brought them to our house? Is he insane? I swear to God, if Ruby's still there— "

Behind the congressman, the front door of Penn's house looked out of place. Familiar, but no longer home.

"Oh, you can be sure he thought that one through," Ms.

Westly said. "The last thing your father needs right now is to seem any more distanced from the public than he already is. The thing he needs right now is to look like a family man. I'm surprised that he isn't sitting at the kitchen table with a mug of hot chocolate and a plate of cherry pie."

Penn couldn't seem to see past the fact that his father had brought the press to his house, but I hardly noticed the whitewashed brick or the gravel driveway that the crowd of reporters stood on. The thing that caught my eye was small and shiny, glinting in the congressman's tightly clenched fist: my pendant.

So he'd found it.

The congressman cleared his throat. "Thanks for coming out to our home," he said. "When this story exploded yesterday, I was shocked. Believe me, my family and I were just as glued to our television as the rest of you."

Penn shook his head. "The man of a thousand faces, ladies and gentlemen."

"My wife and I have spent the past day doing some soul searching," he said in a voice that would have sounded wholly sincere if I didn't know the man it was coming from. "I'm heartbroken to learn that a company I not only supported but *championed* would let down its customers and the country this way."

His voice cracked ever so slightly and he paused to compose himself.

"He's good, isn't he?" Ms. Westly said.

"Well, he's had a lot of practice," Penn muttered.

"As you know," the congressman went on, "we were one of the first families here in Connecticut to adopt a pet from one of NuPet's kennels. We tried unsuccessfully to bring not one, but *two* pets into our family, and had nothing but problems with both of them, which I now realize must have been because neither of them were the type of genetically engineered family companion that NuPet had promised us. These girls are far more human than any of us could have imagined. Dangerously human. And now that I know that they spent nine months in a mother's womb, I'm not at all surprised that these very human qualities are surfacing. This is why I'm very much on board with the government's commitment to recall all of these pets."

"Asshole," Penn hissed.

"To ensure that these pets—these *girls*," he corrected, "get the support that they need and deserve, I want to be the first to comply with the government recall and turn over our family companion for reconditioning. The very qualified staff at the NuPet Kennel in Greenwich will begin the process on our family pet, Ella, immediately."

"What? He can't, even if he wanted to," I said. "He doesn't know where—"

The image on the television changed. No longer was the news station showing the congressman's press conference, although the words that he spoke still carried over the new picture on the screen. Two of the kennel's black SUVs were parked outside of a familiar building.

"We hope that our family's sacrifice will spur other families to turn in their pets as well," the congressman said. "This outrage can't continue. It's time for healing, not violence."

Everything slowed, the world shriveling into a dark tunnel as I strained toward the window, knowing without looking that the two unmarked cars were parked only a few hundred yards away.

"Damn them!" Ms. Westly cursed.

"This can't be happening," Missy said, shaking her head.

"How did they find us?"

"The executives at the station must have sold you out," she said. "Greedy sons of bitches! Like they don't have enough power as it is." She looked around the room frantically as if she were searching for a weapon that she could use. "They knew he'd pay a lot of money to find her. He has an image problem and she's his ticket to fixing it. They knew it. He knew it. Damn! They've probably been planning something like this the whole time."

I hadn't realized that I'd been moving away from her as she spoke, until the doorknob bit into my back.

"I promise, I had nothing to do with this," Ms. Westly said, stepping closer to me. "You have to believe me. I have ethics. I never would have..."

"It doesn't matter," I said. "We have to leave."

My hand fumbled for the door.

"They'll find you," Ms. Westly said.

"We've got a couple minutes," Penn said. "It's a start."

"They'll know what car you're driving," Ms. Westly said. "If they planned this far, they would have made sure to know that much. You won't have more than a five-minute head start before they realize that you've run. They'll find you before you make it to the edge of town."

We all stared out the window.

"We don't have time," she said. "I can try to distract them, but it won't be for long. I can only buy you a few minutes."

"No!" Missy said, stepping forward. "A few minutes won't do any good. You know it as well as we do. They need the congressman's pet. It's what they came for and they won't be satisfied until it's what they have."

Ms. Westly's normally overly tanned face blanched. "Did you hear me?" she said. "They'll kill her."

"I heard," Missy said, straight-faced.

"Who the hell do you think you are?" Penn yelled, shoving past me to stand face to face with her. "Was this your plan the whole time? To use Ella as a shield? Your own sure proof protection?"

Missy rolled her eyes. "You're not understanding me."

"Oh, I think it's perfectly clear," Penn said. "Fine, if you're too much of a coward, you go. Get out of here. Run for it!"

"Stop!" I yelled. "She's right. You know it. The only way you can get away is if I go with them. It'll give you a chance. They don't know the rest of you are here. The congressman only mentioned me."

"She's smart," Missy said, smiling sadly at me. "I didn't know how smart, but I hoped."

"You're sick," Penn spat.

Missy didn't bother to look at him. "Ella, you're right. The congressman is powerful and that makes you powerful. You might not realize how much, but that's okay. I know you'll figure it out."

Outside the sharp clap of car doors slammed shut, as frightening as the sound of gunshots. I closed my eyes. I couldn't bear to see them leave. "Go," I said. "I'll wait until the last minute."

"No way. Not a chance, damn it." Penn pulled on my arm. "I'm not leaving without you!"

I squeezed my eyes tighter. I couldn't look at him now. If I did I'd break. If I looked at him I'd lose my nerve. If I looked at him I would go with him, and then none of us would have a chance.

"Oh, stop blubbering," Missy said, pulling him away from me. "She's not leaving you. I am."

Chapter Twenty-Two

I opened my eyes.

Missy folded her arms across her chest, calm settling over her face. "They need a pet. *One* pet. That's what they came for, and that's what we'll give them."

Ms. Westly blinked. "The pictures I've seen of Ella all show her with light hair..."

"Like mine," Missy said.

"It could work," Ms. Westly said. "But we have to act fast."

"No!" I shook my head. "I can't let you do that. I *won't*."

Missy smiled. "When have I ever listened to you? They want one of us, and I'm choosing that it should be me. And it's not because I'm being romantic. It's not because I believe in true love or any of that. It's not because you're younger and have your whole life ahead of you. It's because I believe in you. If anyone can fix this thing, it's you, Ella! You have the power to—"

A pounding at the front door interrupted her.

"They're here," Ms. Westly said.

"*Go*," Missy said to me. "Go!"

"I can't let you—" I started.

"You aren't *letting* me," she said. "This is a choice. *My* choice!"

The heavy pounding of a fist banged against the wooden door again. *Bang. Bang. Bang*. It echoed into the kitchen.

"Let her do it," Ms. Westly said. Turning to Missy, she said, "Wait as long as you can. Make them break down the door if you have to."

Missy nodded.

I threw myself at her, wrapping my arms around her neck. How could I let her do this for me? She was the strong one. If anyone could make a difference it was her, not me. But I also knew that there was no arguing with her. If this was the choice she'd made, we weren't going to change her mind. And I loved her for it! I loved her. Truly. As much as I loved Penn. It was a pure and unconditional love, the same love that makes people fight to stay alive.

"I'll remember you," I whispered into her ear and she nodded.

The pounding grew louder. "Open up. We know you're inside. There's no use pretending."

Missy gave us one more long glance before she nodded and turned toward the front door.

"Who is it?" she called.

"Congressman Kimble has given us your location. The U.S. government has ordered you to be turned over to the Greenwich Kennel. If you come now, there won't be any trouble."

"Take my car. It's at the end of the alleyway," Ms. Westly said in a hushed voice, slipping her keys into Penn's hands.

"They'll figure it out eventually, but it'll give you a good head start. Ditch it as soon as you can."

"Are you sure?"

"Get to New York," she said. "I've heard about an organization there that can help you. The Liberationists. You need to find them."

The same Liberationists that had tried to set me free the first time? What could they possibly do to help? "But—"

"They'll help you," she said, glancing back over her shoulder toward the door where Missy continued to try to hold off the people from the kennel.

Three earsplitting thuds reverberated through the room and the door finally gave, splintering at the lock. It crashed in, smashing against the wall, and Missy stumbled backward into the room.

Penn reached out, grabbing me around the waist while Ms. Westly moved forward, creating a shield between me and the men who'd burst through the door.

Penn's hands held tight, but I fought against him. I couldn't go through with this. I couldn't let Missy die for me.

"Stop right there," Ms. Westly yelled. "You can't just barge in here. This is trespassing!"

Ms. Westly continued screaming, but the men didn't listen. They plowed forward, eyes locked on their target—Missy. A hulking man in a black suit grabbed her by the arm and she went limp, folding into him like a rag doll.

She was going to do it. She was going to let them take her.

One last time, she turned to face me and I strained to meet her eye.

Go, she mouthed.

Ms. Westly moved again, blocking the men's view of me and blocking my last chance to see my friend as she was dragged from the house.

"Please, don't let them take her," I begged as Penn dragged me through the back door into the empty alley.

The alley was quiet except for the meowing of a mangy-looking cat that hopped off the window ledge, trying to wind around our ankles.

Penn grabbed my hand, leading me down the steps.

"We can't just let them take her like that!" I cried. "You heard what Ms. Westly said. They're going to kill her!"

He spun me around and grasped my face between his hands. "Ella, we have to go. Now."

I nodded. I knew. We didn't have long. If we didn't go now, Missy would have given herself up for nothing.

"I just have to get one thing out of your car," I said, dragging the back of my hand over my wet cheeks. We didn't have time to go back inside for Missy's backpack, but there was something that I could still get.

"We don't have time," Penn said, tugging on my arm.

I slapped at his hand, clasped tight around my own. "Let go, Penn. I need this!"

"Ella! You can't—"

I broke free from his grasp and sprinted toward the car, which sat tucked up next to the Dumpster. The door was unlocked and I dove into the back, fumbling for the garbage bag that was tucked underneath the seat. I only needed one file, but I didn't have time to look for it now. I'd have to bring all of them.

"Ella—"

My back was still turned toward the open door, so I didn't see the person sneak up behind Penn, but I heard him say my name.

I also heard the *thud* of something hitting flesh. And bone.

The world slowed as I turned around in time to see Penn collapsing to the ground. Behind him, a dark blue van poked out from the other side of the Dumpster. How had I missed it? I would recognize that van anywhere with its faded red eagle.

I scrambled toward the other door. Had those other cars just been a diversion? The van was the kennel's *real* killing machine.

A pair of hands tightened around my ankles, pulling me backward. I crashed to the ground and the world went dark as a bag slipped over my head, suffocating me. I took a breath to scream, but something hard struck me across the back, knocking the wind from my lungs.

"*Penn…*" His name made no sound as it left my lips.

The same object struck the back of my head.

The world spun. Stars danced before my eyes. And then there was only darkness.

Chapter Twenty-Three

Darkness. Black. Consuming.

A steady aching in my ribs.

The pressure of wide hands lifting me.

The revving of an engine.

Tires squealing.

The shuffle of someone shifting beside me.

The squeak of leather.

The sigh of irritation.

And then a moan.

It didn't come from my lips, although it felt as if it could have.

"Ella?"

Oh God, Penn. He was here. At least Penn was here.

Our bodies slid across the seats as we rounded a corner. We were moving. Driving. Fast.

I struggled, kicking and squirming. My hands were tied behind my back, but my feet were still free. I wouldn't let them kill me without putting up a fight. I wouldn't let them dump my body in another field or river, just to end up a photograph in Seth's desk.

"Stop fighting," a man said from the front of the car. "You'll be better off if you just rest for a minute."

"Don't hurt her. Don't you *dare* lay a hand on her." Penn's voice came out winded, as if he were straining for breath.

"You two really won't stop, will you?" someone else said from the front of the car. "There's no reason to keep their heads covered anymore, Ken. You can take the bags off."

The rough fabric scraped across my face and a moment later there were lights. Red and green and white and yellow. They zoomed past the car as we sped along. The sky out the window was growing dark, but the lights flew past. I blinked. Next to me, a bald man with a neck as thick as my waist reached back and pulled a hood off of Penn's head too.

"Are you hurt?" Penn asked me, as if the other men in the car didn't exist.

"I'm okay." I nodded.

"You'll both be fine," the man in the passenger seat said, turning to face us. "Ken was a little too enthusiastic grabbing you. I only asked him to restrain you, not to knock you out, but he's not so good with finesse."

I stared at the man's familiar face. Almond-shaped eyes. Pronounced cheekbones. Dark, curly hair. "You're the man from Bernard's market."

He smiled. "Yes. I'm Markus. Sorry we didn't formally meet before."

"*This* is how you formally meet someone?" Penn grumbled.

"You work for the kennel?" I asked. My head felt fuzzy. Too many fine tendrils of information tangling and overlapping.

"No," he said, matter-of-factly.

"Don't lie to me," I said, anger splitting through the middle of me like a lightning bolt. "I know this van. I saw it parked outside of Greenwich the other night and I know what was inside it."

Penn glanced between us, confused. "You didn't tell me about a van. And how do you know this guy?"

I glared at Markus. "They're the ones killing girls. Mutilating them and dumping their bodies."

Penn bucked against the seat, the tendons in his neck pulled as taut as the straps around his wrists. "You touch her and I swear to God I'll kill you."

"Will you two calm down? No one's getting killed," Markus said. "We're the good guys."

If my hands were free I'd claw out his eyes, I'd rip out his lying tongue. "Good guys don't murder innocent girls."

"You're right. The kennel did that all by themselves," he said, a bit of anger welling up in his voice. "Listen, I'm happy to explain it, but I need you to pay attention and calm down. First thing you need to know is that *we* haven't killed anyone. I want freedom for the pets as much as you do, maybe more."

I shook my head, disbelieving.

"Why should we believe anything you say?" Penn asked.

"Ken," Markus said, addressing the bald man sitting next to me. "Cut them free. Ella knows I'm not going to hurt her. Right, Ella? I mean we're practically brother and sister, you and me. We're cut from the same mold."

"I don't— " I started, but the words fell away as I looked at him more closely. How hadn't I seen it before? It was so obvious. Even with long, disheveled hair and the scruff of a beard coming on, he couldn't truly hide. "You're a— "

"Pet," he said. "Yes. And I promise I'll never hurt you."

I stared at him. Ken loosened the tie around my wrists before he moved back to unfasten Penn's hands. In a second Penn was beside me.

"Are you okay?" he asked.

I nodded, still staring at Markus. "I don't understand," I said. "They don't breed boys."

"They don't now. But twenty years ago, when the program was still young, they actually contemplated having male and female pets. They were going to give the customers a choice. But the trial program was a bust. People were freaked out about bringing a young man into their homes. In the end, we didn't 'represent the image they were trying to sell.'"

"If you're telling the truth," Penn said, "then where are the others? I've never seen a male pet before."

Markus's jaw clenched. "When I was twelve they rounded us up, a mass eradication. If it wasn't for Drew"—he pointed to the man driving—"I would have died, too. He managed to sneak me out."

For the first time, I looked at the man driving. He didn't look special, a middle-aged man in a dark hoodie. I leaned forward, trying to get a better look at him, and his pants came into view. White pants, exactly like the ones they wore at the kennel.

I scooted back in my seat. "You lied," I said. "He *is* from the kennel. This *is* the van I saw the other night."

Markus rolled his eyes at my outburst. "Yes, he works at the kennel, but I can assure you he's with us."

"What about this van? I saw a dead girl in it. I don't care what you say. I know what I saw."

"I didn't kill her," Drew said, glancing at me in the rearview mirror. "She was one of the girls that died in the kennel's breeding program, just like the others."

"The others?" Penn asked.

"For the past two weeks we've been sneaking them out of the kennel. Instead of cremating them, we've been planting them all over the state. We needed a story, something big to scare the public, to wake them up and make them start asking questions. The media is a fickle beast. There are atrocities happening in front of our eyes all the time, but unless the story strikes just the right chord, people will ignore it."

"And it certainly doesn't help when the police are getting paid to cover it up," Markus said, raising his eyebrow at Penn.

"If this is all true, how did you even know where Ella was?" Penn asked.

"The kennel has been in pretty close communication with Congressman Kimble," Drew said. "The moment I knew they were headed to pick up Ella, we followed them. We were just lucky we got to you first."

"And what do you want from me now?" I asked, rubbing the sore place on my wrists.

"Why do you think we want something?" Markus asked.

"I don't think people normally knock you out and put a sack over your head when they're just being friendly," Penn said.

Markus frowned. "We didn't have time for explanations. Those bastards from the kennel were moving in quick. They could have figured out at any minute that they took the wrong girl. I wasn't about to take my chances."

He studied us for a minute. "The truth is, we owe you. We've been trying to figure out how to get people to care for so long and somehow in a day and a half, you've unleashed this giant. There have been whistleblowers over the years, but their story was always buried or killed before it could do any damage. This succeeded in ways we'd only dreamed. We owe you, Ella. Truly. This cause could use someone like you, someone smart and brave."

An odd sense of pride swelled up in my chest, knowing what Missy and I had accomplished. But just as quick, I thought of all the girls who were about to die. All the surrogates who might be punished for stepping forward. The babies that might continue to be killed. "What can I do?"

"Finish what you've started," he said. "It isn't enough to hope that we can sneak a few girls to freedom. We need to save them all. We need to end it for good."

"I'm sorry," Penn interrupted, squeezing my hand, "but I think you're asking too much from her. These people want to kill her."

"I know," Markus said seriously.

"It's not that I don't want to help," I said. "I do. Believe me. But I don't know what good I can do."

"Just be you," Markus said. "You have it in you. You couldn't have done all this if you didn't. Up until now, NuPet has done an excellent job keeping pets a nameless and faceless commodity. But you've given pets an identity. Congressman Kimble has flashed your pretty face all over the world. The American people now know pets are people. We weren't grown in a tube. Every perfectly flawed piece of humanity runs through our veins exactly the same way it runs through theirs. Now we just have to show them that we're worth fighting for."

Not grown in a tube.

"My papers!" I yelled. "I had papers, in the car. I was getting them when you took us. We have to go back for them."

"Calm down," Markus said. "We've got them. Right here."

He reached down in front of him and held up the garbage bag.

"Give them to me," I demanded, snatching them out of his hands.

I tore open the bag and shuffled through the stacks of folders until I found the one I was looking for. I took it tenderly in my hands, setting the rest of the bag down on the floor.

"What is it?" Penn asked.

I swallowed, running my finger over the loopy letters on the tab. What did she look like, the woman this name belonged to? Had she given birth to more than one baby inside that kennel? Had she suffered inside those walls, too?

I didn't need the words on this page to assure me that I was human. I knew that already, even if the rest of the world wasn't ready to admit it.

I was human. Imperfect. Flawed in the same invisible ways as everyone else. Across the globe there were billions of us, all different, all suffering in the same ways. Not one was a clone, or a repeat, or a perfect duplicate, but those differences were all people looked for. It's what they were good at. Categorizing. Separating. Maybe it was easier to ignore someone if they weren't like you. Maybe it was easier to mistreat them, to enslave them, to treat them as "other" if they weren't the same.

Maybe it would take an "other" like me to fix it.

"I'll do it," I said.

"You will?" He smiled, the devilish spark in his eyes reminding me of Missy.

I nodded. "I'll do it on two conditions. First: we have to get Missy back. You owe her every bit as much as you owe me. I couldn't have done any of this without her."

"And what's the second condition?" he asked, not promising anything.

I held up the file. "I want to find this woman."

Penn's gaze traveled over the writing. In his mind those letters were already forming into a name. Her name.

"Emily Manzenares," he said quietly.

I moved my mouth around the letters, repeating it in my mind. It was a beautiful name. Round and warm. Emily Manzenares.

"Who is she?" he asked.

Emily Manzenares. She was out there somewhere. As I sped down the dark road past neon signs and a thousand taillights, she was out there, too. Maybe she was sitting down to a small round table to eat dinner. Maybe she was watering the sad-looking plants growing brown in her windowsill, or watching television, or laying her head down on a pillow to rest. She could be doing anything, living a life that I'd never even bothered to imagine before.

"She's my mother," I finally said.

The word tasted foreign in my mouth. *Mother.*

Mother. Mother. Mother.

Behind us, Missy was giving herself over to the enemy. I closed my eyes. I didn't want to imagine it, but it felt unfair not to. Right now she was probably climbing into the backseat of a dark car that would take her back to the kennel, back to the red door. In front of us, Emily Manzenares waited, even though she didn't know it yet. We were coming. We would find her. We'd find the others like her, too, and we'd make them help us. And next to me…next to me sat Penn. His hand filled mine, warm and solid and present. We would do this together.

I wasn't alone.

Acknowledgments

If coffee were a sentient being it would be the first on my list of thanks, but since I've yet to meet a cup that could carry on a conversation, I'll have to make do by thanking all the cheerful baristas at Sugarhouse Coffee for keeping me fully equipped with soy vanilla lattes and cinnamon rolls.

Thank you to Dan Beecher, the most wonderful writing partner a girl could ask for. For always making me laugh, for making me feel energized instead of overwhelmed, for brainstorming with me on sunny days, and rainy days, and windy days, THANK YOU. Your brain is my favorite resource.

Thank you to my agent, Kerry Sparks, for your continued support and dedication.

To all the people at Entangled: Kari Olson, Meredith Johnson, Jessica Turner, and Melissa Montovani, thank you for helping to make this book a reality. To Kelley York, thank you for making the most hauntingly beautiful red dress I've ever seen. And, of course, the fabulous Liz

Pelletier for giving me a home at Entangled!

To Heather Howland, editor extraordinaire, thank you for your vision, your patience, your friendship, and your insight. Thank you for loving this story even more than I do. Your enthusiasm and confidence are only outmatched by your amazing and brilliant brain.

Thank you to my mom for allowing me to create, even when it got messy. Thank you for pencils and crayons and clay. Thank you for giving me a love for words and for letting me believe that anything is possible.

Most of all, thank you to my family. Thank you to Morgan, Noah, and Rebecca for making me laugh until water comes out my nose, for learning how to do your own laundry, for loving all of my quirks (you love them right?), and for being three of the best dreams I've ever followed. And finally, thank you to my Bry Guy. You are where it begins and ends. Thank you for rubbing my feet, for feeding me, and for making sure things don't fall apart. Thank you for loving me. Thank you for believing in me. Thank you for seeing beauty and strength and brilliance inside of me. Thank you for being home.

Join the revolution...from the beginning.

PERFECTED by Kate Jarvik Birch

Ever since the government passed legislation allowing people to be genetically engineered and raised as pets, the rich and powerful can own beautiful girls like sixteen-year-old Ella as companions. But when Ella moves in with her new masters and discovers the glamorous life she's been promised isn't at all what it seems, she's forced to choose between a pampered existence full of gorgeous gowns and veiled threats, or seizing her chance at freedom with the boy she's come to love, risking both of their lives in a daring escape no one will ever forget.

Check out these exciting reads from Entangled Teen!

FORGET TOMORROW

by Pintip Dunn

It's Callie's seventeenth birthday and she's awaiting her vision—a memory sent back in time to sculpt each citizen into the person they're meant to be. In her vision, she sees herself murdering her gifted younger sister. Before she can process what it means, Callie is arrested and imprisoned, where she tries to escape with the help of her childhood friend, Logan. Now she must find a way to change her fate...before she becomes the most dangerous threat of all.

AWAKENING

by Shannon Duffy

The Protectorate supplies its citizens with everything they need for a contented life: career, love, and even death. Then Desiree receives an unexpected visit from her childhood friend, Darian, a Non-Compliant murderer and an escaped convict. Darian insists that the enemy is the very institution Desiree depends on. That she believed in. The government doesn't just protect her life—it controls it. And The Protectorate doesn't doesn't take kindly to those who are Non-Compliant...especially those who would destroy its sole means of control.

ATLANTIS RISING

by Gloria Craw

Alison McKye isn't exactly human. She's a Child of Atlantis, an ancient race of beings with strange and powerful gifts.She has the ability to "push" thoughts into the minds of others, but her gift also makes her a target. There's a war brewing between the Children of Atlantis, and humans are caught in the middle. If Alison's gift falls into the wrong hands, there's no telling what might happen. But when it comes to protecting those she loves, there's nothing she won't do...

THE BOOK OF IVY

by Amy Engel

What would you kill for?

After a brutal nuclear war, the United States was left decimated. A small group of survivors eventually banded together. My name is Ivy Westfall, and my mission is simple: to kill the president's son—my soon-to-be husband—and return the Westfall family to power. But Bishop Lattimer isn't the cruel, heartless boy my family warned me to expect. But there is no escape from my fate. Bishop must die. And I must be the one to kill him…